D0729871

ERROR
OF
JUDGMENT

A gripping crime mystery full of twists

ROY LEWIS

JOFFE
BOOKS

Revised edition 2018 by Joffe Books, London.

First published by William Collins in 1971

www.joffebooks.com

ISBN-13: 978-1-78931-043-6

To Yvette, Mark and Sarah Jane

Please note this book is set in the late 1960s in England, a time before mobile phones and DNA testing, when social attitudes were very different.

Chapter 1

It was one of those velvet, early summer mornings when a low white mist lay grass-high, curling long fingers to the lower branches of the trees in Robert Fanshaw's orchard, spreading soft tenuous tendrils upwards to caress the lead-paned windows through which he peered, sniffing with delight. He knew it would be like this right across the Down, until the road dipped through Arnleigh village and into Sedleigh. He snorted. Village! It *had* been a village when he was a boy, but though he still thought of it in those terms Arnleigh was a village no longer; the tentacles of Sedleigh, administrative and residential, had seen to that. He had always hoped he would be able to get Sedleigh as a retirement post, for the pleasure of living again in the village, but when the post had come the village was no longer there and it had been the long, splendid roll of the Down for Robert Fanshaw.

The village as a retirement situation had been just a sentimental dream, he told himself as he twitched his tie into place in front of the hall mirror. He was far more comfortable in this bungalow; the area was far more 'desirable' in estate agent terminology; the sky was

Sedleigh-golden and deep blue on the fine summer evenings when he took his walks. And, he thought, patting his flat stomach, those walks were not only pleasurable but they helped keep his fifty-nine-year-old figure in trim.

Fifty-nine. One year to go.

He wondered whether they'd ask him to stay on. He wasn't bothered really, though it was possible that when the time came the days would be long and the evenings longer, so that he'd wish for the travelling and the files and the eternal crises that resolved themselves if you only locked them in drawers and forgot about them for a few days. The department might ask him to stay; good men were difficult to get these days. And men with his presence, even more difficult. It was the one luxury he allowed himself: vanity. He knew his figure was imposing: five feet eleven in his stockinged feet, upright, slender and elegant. Rimless glasses hardened his bright blue eyes and the teeth that he had managed both to retain and keep in good condition could flash whitely in contrast to his summer tan. He looked tough, resilient, imposing and suave. He knew it and saw no reason why he should not acknowledge it to himself.

He flicked a piece of fluff from the well-cut dark suit he wore almost as a uniform, smoothed again with one hand the long, flowing white hair that he always trimmed himself with a patent comb-cutter — hairdressers were so damned expensive, and there was no reason why he should spend any of his four-thousand-a-year on such fellers — and picked up his black regulation briefcase with the small gold embossing. He opened the front door and walked out into the swirling mist.

Pale blue and gold, the sky about Sedleigh hurt his eyes as he drove in his unpretentious family saloon down through the village, but to pull down the sun visor would be an admission of weakness. He drew the car in at the kerb outside Charley Nixon's cottage and the old man was already there, hobbling out through the gate, grinning his apple-cheeked grin, eighty-three-years proud and holding out his nurtured gift.

'Carnation today, Mr Fanshaw.'

'And a splendid one at that, Charley.'

'Goin' far today, sir?'

'Not today. Just as far as Burton. There'll be time for a quiet half this evening at the Blackbird. About eight, Charley?'

'I look forward to it, sir!'

Fanshaw smiled, inserted the carnation into his button-hole, engaged first gear and drove off. In the driving-mirror he could see old Charley watch him go until he turned the bend on to the Sedleigh road.

As he guessed, the mist had gone. The sun now struck through and the trees were black against the sky in spite of the green of their spreading foliage. Fanshaw glanced at his watch and eased off the accelerator; he would be able to enjoy the summer morning for Burton was a forty-minute drive and it was just eight o'clock. He didn't want to arrive too early. Peters would want a few minutes at least to deal with his mail before Fanshaw appeared. Though that admirable Rosemary girl, Peters's secretary, would no doubt undertake her usual sifting of mail to ensure that Peters was bothered with nothing that was inessential. Fanshaw hummed to himself as he drove into the thickening traffic on the outskirts of Sedleigh. Across to the ring road, out on the North Bypass and then it was but fifteen minutes to his destination. A splendid morning, splendid.

The first signs of trouble appeared on the bypass.

Fanshaw didn't recognize it as trouble at first. He paid little attention to the van ahead of him; it was moving at about forty miles an hour and Fanshaw picked up speed to pass it. No sooner was he safely past, and tucking himself in to the left again, than the grinning van driver shot past him with an emasculated toot of his horn.

That was one of the irritating things about modern cars, they never seemed to possess a horn that a man could use with dignity. With that thought in mind Robert Fanshaw noticed that the lettering on the side of the van proclaimed in startling electric blue that it was the property of the television company based in Sedleigh.

Even then, no warning bells ran in Fanshaw's mind; he still had ten minutes' driving ahead of him. The van had pulled across in front of him and they proceeded for some two miles in that fashion until Fanshaw noticed in his driving-mirror that he seemed to have become involved in a flurry of vans. There were three such vehicles strung out behind him; he was bowling along with four television vans like a funeral cortege late for the gravediggers.

Robert Fanshaw had never admitted to being status-conscious but this situation was hardly conducive to the retention of his image. With deliberation he slowed down, and there were three derisive and similarly emasculated toots as the three vans roared past him to take up post behind their brother.

And still Fanshaw saw no cause for concern. Not even when the vans swung right at the Sedleigh roundabout, and left into Grangeway Road, not even when they passed under the railway bridge and plunged towards the motorway roundabout, not even when they took without wavering the highway into Burton, did he experience any qualms. But when they turned into Simmington Lane he felt in his stomach the little quiver that had used to come when a Minister's file landed on his desk. It had been years since he had experienced such a quiver — not because Ministers' files were few and far between but because a surfeit of anything toughens the entrails — but he experienced one now.

It was not a pleasant experience.

When the vans proceeded into Carlton Drive his worst fears were confirmed. Their destination was his. They bumped across the road running beyond the trees that Alderman Platt had planted with aplomb at the ceremony last year and once past the main gate one of them struck out across the lawn, scarring its green beauty with slashing black tyre-marks. It shuddered to a halt and as Fanshaw drove past the technicians were already bundling out of the van, unloading tripods and other mysterious television equipment. Outside broadcasters.

Within two minutes he understood.

At first there was the straggle of hoydenish females and hirsute males that he had come to expect, lurching in to their lectures after over-indulged evenings, but as he drove nearer to the looming glass and concrete of Burton Polytechnic their number became alarmingly greater until they were thronging the pavement, arguing under the trees, lounging against the white steps leading to the huge glass swing doors, draping themselves over the statue of Truth, a stone monstrosity which Fanshaw had always regarded as aesthetically disastrous, and talking, cursing, shouting, rumbling and generally converging upon the Administration building.

'Oh, my God,' Fanshaw groaned without the slightest belief that there would be any succour from that direction. He drove with circumspection, avoiding his natural inclination to remove one particularly unwashed specimen of humanity from the Burton Polytechnic student hours statistics, and took up a vacant parking spot marked VISITORS in front of the administrative block.

As he locked the car with care and turned to walk towards the steps he noticed that Peters's red Jaguar was already installed. The rector, at least, had arrived.

At the foot of the steps a small clotting of students was already engaged in eager conversation with three men who had debouched from the nearest television van. Backed by two technicians trailing wires, the clean-looking young man with the microphone was asking a grinning girl,

'And would you tell me, just what do you expect to achieve by this demonstration?'

'Well, we got *you* bastards out of bed at least, didn't we?'

Robert Fanshaw winced at the innocence in her eyes and hastened up the steps, through the tall glass doors and across the echoing hall, and without a backward glance made his way quickly towards the enquiries desk, his stride purposeful and long, his briefcase swinging. There was no one on duty, so he turned, walked up the flight of stairs to the first floor, pushed open the African cedar-panelled door facing him and proceeded in the direction of the office of the rector's secretary. He tapped the door with elegant knuckles, opened it and looked in.

The girl staring at him had a surprised, unfamiliar face, as lacking in character as processed cheese.

'Good morning,' Fanshaw murmured. 'Dr Peters, please.'

'Er . . . I'm not sure . . . er . . . who shall I say it is?'

'HMI. Mr Fanshaw.'

'HM . . . er . . . I'm sorry, what did you say?' Fanshaw frowned slightly and the girl became extremely nervous.

'Will you tell Dr Peters that Her Majesty's Inspector, Mr Fanshaw, has arrived and would like to see him for a few minutes.' She was gone with a whisk of a mini-skirt and a discreet tap on the adjoining door. Within fifteen seconds the door opened again and she was back.

'Dr Peters would like you to go in,' she said breathlessly. Fanshaw gave her a brief smile to show her that he quite appreciated what a trial it must be for her on her first morning to have an HMI descend upon the college, and walked into Peters's office.

The carpet was deep, lush and red, the walls a delicate shade of green, the furniture black imitation-leathered and executive suite-designed and the man rising from behind the broad curving sweep of the desk was worried. Dr Antony Peters came forward with one hand outstretched. There was a frown on his handsome, regular features and a pinched look about his nostrils. His wide, rather sensuous mouth was set in a grim line.

'Hello, Mr Fanshaw, I'm glad to see you. But you haven't picked the best of days, it would seem.'

Peters's grip was firm but that was symptomatic of the man. Fanshaw had seen the short-list for the Burton Polytechnic when it was first drawn up and he'd remembered Peters as soon as he saw the name, even though it had been at least five years since he'd met him for the first and only time. As soon as he'd seen that short-list Fanshaw had guessed Peters would get the six-thousand-a-year post, for Peters had a large number of assets. He had a good educational background, both as a teacher and as an administrator, he had industrial experience of some quality, he had presence, good looks, charm, a persuasive tongue and a handsome and influential wife. He was a man's man and women adored him. He'd got the job and as far as Fanshaw could make out from his infrequent visits to Burton he was making a good fist of it.

He had established close relations with industry and made this the keynote of his planning for the polytechnic; by using contacts he had made in his previous activity, he had obtained considerable financial support from large national as well as local firms. Fanshaw was personally of the opinion that such endowments could well lead to academic distortion within the college, and there was some evidence that this was happening; nevertheless, there was no doubt that Peters had been extremely successful in his fundraising.

But now his grey, wide-spaced eyes were flecked with red, and there was an angry set to his shoulders. He waved Fanshaw to a seat and took one himself, immediately next to him. Good personnel technique; don't face a man across a desk, put him at ease by sitting next to him. Peters knew how to handle HMI as he'd know how to handle most men.

A rumbling noise from outside the grand windows of the office reminded Fanshaw that it remained to be seen whether Peters could handle students.

'What are they up to this fine morning?'

'Student demonstrations, as always, are rather slow in communicating their precise desires to the administration. They are still, at the moment, indulging in mindless chanting about a number of things. Student representation on the academic body is one—'

'But this will already have been covered by your articles of government, adopted when you were established!'

'That's no reason why they should stop chanting. I told you it was all somewhat mindless. There's the representation thing, and there's an expulsion which became necessary as a disciplinary measure last week, and it would seem that they're somewhat unhappy about the content of one of our courses in the Humanities—'

'As opposed to your more vocational degrees, no doubt.'

'As you say.' Peters's voice soured into petulance. 'We don't seem to get much trouble from the accountants, or the architects, or the lawyers, or economists among our students. On the other hand, the less vocationally oriented among the student population seem to have a voice somewhat louder than their numbers would justify. I doubt whether they really seek to persuade, at all. These student demonstrations are nothing more than a self-indulgence and a desire for recognition. Any cause will do.'

'It usually seems to be a Communist or anarchic minority that starts the trouble.'

'Yes, and there are enough gulls, fools and addlepates in the student body to make such movements stronger than they actually are. You know, Mr Fanshaw, the whole thing is beginning to smack of a television soap opera — student militancy, an infinite variation upon a telegenic theme!'

'I saw some television cameras being unloaded as I came along,' Fanshaw said mildly.

'Hell! I was afraid that would happen! It's always the same; the cameras arrive whenever there's something entirely disreputable about to happen. Well, there's one person at least who won't be appearing before them today!'

Fanshaw smiled. 'The Establishment will not be taking part, then?'

'It certainly will not. The rabble can get on with it, and do all the shouting they need. I'll only get over-excited if they start to invade the administration building. That's hardly likely, however — the examination system would break down then and that they won't want. There would seem to be,' he added grimly, 'a sufficiently large number even of the rabble outside who would still like to discover whether they're likely to get through their examinations before they go down this term.'

Fanshaw stirred unhappily in his chair. He wondered whether Peters was adopting the right attitude towards student activity. There was a certain contemptuous dismissal in the rector's tone that led Fanshaw to believe the trouble might yet erupt surprisingly right under the rector's nose. Still, it was hardly Fanshaw's place to tell him how to handle his own college.

'Ah, well, we'll have to see how things go. I really only stuck my head in here, Dr Peters, to pay my respects, you know. I've come in to see Mr West, really. I'm not sure that he's properly appreciated the part that his department could play in the development of the polytechnic as a whole. I've just received from the Office a copy of his Diploma scheme and I'm somewhat disturbed that he's included no reference to any systems analysis work for the students. I mean, with the computer installation you have here it seems to me inconceivable—'

He paused. Peters was leaning forward with the kind of look on his face that presaged bad news. It lacked

9

sincerity; it was an assumed expression but it passed the necessary message on, and it added emphasis to the words.

'I'm afraid you won't see West today, Mr Fanshaw. He wasn't feeling well yesterday, and went home after lunch. When he didn't appear this morning — and you know for yourself that he always appears on the premises at eight forty-five — his secretary rang through to his home. She was just in time to speak to an ambulance orderly—'

'Ambulance orderly!'

'That's right. They'd just got there, it seems. West had a heart attack yesterday afternoon and must have been lying in the house all afternoon and last night, alone, unable to help himself, until, about eight this morning when he came to sufficiently to contact the hospital. That's where he'll be, now.'

'Dear me, dear me.' Fanshaw was genuinely distressed. He liked West; a strange man in some ways, somewhat reticent, introverted, but a man of quality. 'I must get out to see him when I can.'

'Perhaps one of his principal lecturers can helpfully discuss things with you? I think Stanley will be looking after things in West's absence.' Peters was rising to his feet, obviously regarding his discussion with Fanshaw as nearing termination. 'I'll get the girl to ring through for you, to warn Stanley you're coming down.'

'Yes, that will be fine. I've got to see Stevens in the Economics Department too, but perhaps that'll be later today. Er . . . the girl . . . you mean the youngster in your secretary's office? What's happened to Rosemary?'

'That's another thing,' Peters said with an explosive grunt. 'She hasn't turned up for work this morning either, and with those blasted students kicking up outside and my secretary away life is not going to be easy for me today.' He grinned suddenly; it was part of his charm. 'But that's what I'm getting paid for, isn't it?'

It was indeed, thought Fanshaw. He took his leave of the rector and walked out with his black, gold-embossed briefcase into the corridor. Up the broad stairs facing him, along the corridor on the second floor, and he could see across the open campus of Burton Polytechnic to the spire of the church at Sedleigh, and beyond to the faint line of the Down, distant and blue in the sunshine. But he glanced only briefly towards Sedleigh; his attention was directed to the immediate vicinity for the number of students in front of the Administration building had increased. There were now well over a hundred young people there but they still seemed disorganized, milling around with a curious lack of definition and purpose like a disturbed flock of sheep in a paddock. They seemed to be lacking a leader. Fanshaw shrugged and moved on, across the connecting bridge that took him past the chemistry laboratories, through the physics section and left into the block that housed on its five floors the business and professional students.

Robert Fanshaw was proud of his fitness and of the youthful spring of his step. When he had taken young Spedding as a fledgling HMI last year he'd been pleased to note that the thirty-five-year-old newcomer had kept pace with Fanshaw's long stride only with difficulty. And normally Fanshaw would always walk up the stairs in the business studies block.

But not this morning. Perhaps he felt tired, even though he would be the last to admit it. Perhaps he was short of breath. Perhaps it was merely the fact that a picture of West's overstrained heart lay at the back of his mind. Whatever it was, Fanshaw decided to take the lift. The staff lift, he noted, was rising, two floors above. So he stepped towards the student lift which wouldn't have been used this morning with all the students remaining outside, and pressed the call button. Thirty seconds later the lift slid up to him, the doors hissed open and Robert Fanshaw stepped inside.

When the doors closed soundlessly behind him, he was still standing rigidly, glaring in shock at the figure of the girl curled up on the floor. Her head was swathed in a woollen cardigan, roughly tied around her throat, her skirt had ridden up above her waist and she was wearing one shoe. None of this would be bothering her though. She was dead.

* * *

Chief Inspector Crow settled back in the car and stared moodily out of the window, watching the hedgerows flash past. Detective-Sergeant Wilson sat beside the driver, saying nothing. Crow savagely reflected that Wilson knew better than to speak before time. Crow had just completed an investigation in Bristol involving a particularly bad knifing case on Brandon Hill, and he'd been looking forward to getting home. It had been Wilson's task to inform him that he was to proceed straight to Burton — influenza and three other homicide cases had sent the Murder Squad rota haywire and Crow was to be involved in the field again, immediately. Martha hadn't seen him for three weeks and now there was Burton . . .

Crow brushed an angry hand over his domed skull and scowled at the pale reflection that glowered back at him in the window. It was a thoroughly bad-tempered reflection and his deep-sunk eyes looked like dark cavities in which embers of anger gleamed dully. But he shouldn't take out his bad temper on Wilson; the dour detective-sergeant was just doing his job.

'Better fill me in on the details,' Crow said, and tried to lever his long legs into a more comfortable position. Wilson glanced back briefly, and nodded.

'The subject was discovered this morning, sir, in the lift at Burton Polytechnic. The discovery was reported at once; a squad car was despatched immediately—'

'And I was dragged off my train.'

'Yes, sir. The local force decided the Murder Squad had better be called in at once. The subject has been identified as Rosemary Harland, and it seems she worked as secretary to the rector of the polytechnic. The rector is Dr Antony Peters.'

'How did the girl die?'

'It's reported as a head wound, sir, but the unit will be down there as soon as possible.'

'Time of death not yet pinpointed, I suppose?'

'No. The lab's been warned and the pathologists will be standing by.'

Crow settled back in the seat with a sigh.

He stared out at the trees moving past in the summer morning and he supposed this part of it, at least, was better than sitting in front of a desk piled high with reports and files. He wondered briefly about the Bristol case: in court yesterday, when the young man had been committed for trial at the next Assizes, there had been a sick, lost look about him that had made John Crow feel ill in his turn. It hadn't showed; Crow presented an image of cold efficiency, but even so he often felt a prey to inner doubts, even when a case seemed complete, all the ends tied up satisfactorily. The doubts arose because he recognized that the truth had many facets and could sometimes be nothing more than an illusion. And in the long run you never knew, you just never knew. Facts and reports and details could give a picture, build up a circumstantial case, and it could all lead to a conviction.

But deep down, you never really knew.

Wilson was looking at him, craning his head backwards to catch his eye. There was an unhappy and uncomfortable air about the stance and Crow felt a stab of trepidation.

'What's the matter?'

'Er . . . there's something I omitted to add, sir.'

'What is it?'

'Sedleigh Television; they're already there.'

'Already there! How on earth did they manage to get there before we did? You're not going to tell me that they've got their blasted cameras all tracking on that lift already!'

'Almost as bad as that, sir. It seems they were out there before nine this morning—'

Before the body was discovered?'

'Well, yes, you see they'd received information about a proposed student demonstration and they hoped to film it and conduct some interviews—'

'And as soon as they see that first squad car arrive they'll be on to us like a swarm of bees! Why can't life be simple, just for once?'

He subsided angrily, and Wilson turned his head to stare out at the road ahead. He knew better than to say any more. The inspector would want peace to growl to himself.

The squad car flashed under the railway bridge and proceeded at a smart pace towards the looming block of the Polytechnic. A few students were still walking towards the Administration buildings as the car reached the campus, but they seemed unaware of any startling developments. The sight of the police car caused several of them to break into a run, nevertheless, and two shook angry fists. Crow wondered briefly why the sight of the car should incense them; he received the answer within minutes.

As Crow's car swung around the bend and towards the car park in front of the Administration building he caught sight of the flashing blue light of the squad car that had already been despatched from Sedleigh. The blue light; that was all he could see, for the rest of the car was hidden from view by a surge of students. They surrounded the car, almost a hundred of them, Crow calculated swiftly, and from the rhythmic swaying at the core of the group he guessed they were trying to rock the car, upend it ignominiously on the tarmac.

'Siren!'

The driver complied and the wailing note caused heads to swing, white faces to stare open-mouthed at the approaching car. 'Close up to them!'

There was a scrambling and leaping as the police car's brakes screeched, and the vehicle itself slid in at considerable speed, skidding almost sideways onto the crowd of youths and girls tumbling away from the beleaguered squad car. The combination of screaming tyres and wailing siren seemed to have achieved the immediate objective; the small group of youths actively engaged in rocking the squad car were exposed, and with a natural reluctance to having their vulnerable flank nakedly displayed they hesitated, a few flitted back among the crowd, and a blue-uniformed figure emerged, struggling, from the car, hatless and empurpled in the face.

A straggling shout went up and two men tried to thrust him back, but with flailing arms he burst clear and ran, stumbling, in the direction of Crow's vehicle. Crow's driver was already out, hurrying forward; the detective-inspector was still trying to extricate himself from the back seat while Wilson ran around the front of the vehicle.

The squad car was again submerged by leather jackets, colourful shirts and kicking jeans, while verbal abuse buzzed around the ears of the retreating constable. The less valiant souls who had scattered at the hurtling approach of Crow's car were now reassembling, linking arms and advancing with a bold front, chanting as they came. Crow emerged, with a ferocious scowl occasioned more by his difficulty of exit than by his displeasure at the demonstration, but was duly rewarded with a nervous ripple in the front line. They came on, nevertheless, and Wilson stood in front of them, a stocky bear of a man waving his arms furiously. The sight provoked a shout of laughter and then the chant took form, sweeping over the small knot of policemen, the spearhead of the last word thrusting, jabbing like a physical blow.

'COPP . . . PERS . . . OUT! COPP . . . PERS . . . OUT!'

The press behind surged with the rhythm, and the students were swinging into a crescent, reaching out to the side of the police officers. Crow glanced quickly about him; Wilson, the driver, the man who had run across from the squad car. Over the head of the crowd advancing on him he could see the squad car and two more policemen, struggling to break a way through the back of the crowd and being held back by brawny youths in leather jackets.

The stormtroopers, Crow thought grimly.

He glowered at the advancing, chanting group. His glance swung along the line and they laughed at him, jeered at him as his eyes met theirs. One in particular, right in the centre, met his eyes boldly, challengingly, and Crow fixed his gaze on him. The young man was supported by two girls, right in the middle — he could be wrested out of there without too much resistance, Crow calculated. He just hoped that those silly girls wouldn't get hurt — but if they took part in demonstrations they could expect no easy passage. He stared at the boy in the centre and the mindless chant swelled out. He shouted above it.

'Wilson!'

'Sir!'

'Get that one!'

Wilson and the driver leapt forward smoothly. They each shouldered a girl aside and the front line broke, shuddering, swinging wildly; the youth thrashed out with his arms wildly for a moment and then Wilson and the police driver had him under the armpits and were dragging him out of the line towards Crow. There was a shocked quaver in the chanting and then it turned, suddenly, into a muted, animal growl. The line formed solidly at the centre, turned into a fist, and it thrust forward towards the four policemen and their struggling captive.

Crow stepped forward.

He was suddenly angry. It was not that he was against demonstrations in principle, but he was tired of seeing policemen being kicked, tired of reading complaints of officers who retaliated against mobs — mobs who would as well leave a man's face a bloody mess as listen to his arguments. It infuriated him now, in a way he was rarely angered, and the tiger of violence growled into life within his own breast so that he wanted to strike out at these young people, hurt them, injure them in the way they might well have already injured the officers at the other car.

Perhaps he said it; perhaps the mob heard him. Perhaps it was implicit in his face, in his gesture as he stood forward from the other officers and raised one clenched fist. Perhaps they felt it in the air, felt his anger and displeasure like a physical emotion. Whatever happened in that second, whether it was that he spoke or shouted or simply stood, they stopped. Not abruptly, but in a long, circling swell, surrounding the tall thin man with the predatory nose and great domed head, and the angry murmur rose, and drifted and died, slowly, lingeringly.

Crow lowered his hand. He was entirely surrounded, and cut off from his colleagues. He looked slowly around at the small crowd.

'I can't talk to all of you. I'm going to talk to him!'

His long bony finger stabbed in the direction of the young man still struggling with Wilson and the police driver. At the sound of Crow's grating voice the man stopped struggling and looked up, straightened and ceased pulling against the men who held him.

Crow pushed his way through the arguing mob and ambled towards the man held by Wilson.

'Name?'

'I don't see that as relevant.'

'*Name!*' Crow's voice was cold and hard and the young man jumped. The crowd was silent.

'Rhodes . . . Peter Rhodes.'

Crow pondered. The crowd had already quietened behind him and with the cooler atmosphere this whole affair would quickly get sorted out. He nodded to Wilson and the sergeant released the young man, who shuffled his shoulders with the assumed attitude that if they hadn't released him within another two seconds he'd have broken their arms. Crow observed him dispassionately: about nineteen, a broad, ingenuous and heavily freckled face, red hair that was short and curling on top, thick at the sides, long at the nape of the neck, blue eyes, medium build, dressed in faded jeans and open-necked shirt.

'Tell me, Mr Rhodes, what's this all about?'

'You tell *me* what the hell you're doing here!'

Crow was aware of a slight commotion at the edge of the crowd; a television cameraman, with a hand-held camera, jostling his way forward. Crow nodded towards him.

'You wanted *them* in on it, but not the police, is that so?'

'We see no reason why the Administration has to call in the fuzz on this demonstration. We've got a quarrel with the rector and with the Academic Board, but this is a peaceable demo and there's no need to start screaming for you lot. So the sooner you blow, the better we'll get on with what's to be done—'

'You tell 'em, Cecil boy!'

'That's my baby!'

A girl screeched in the crowd and Rhodes grew another inch.

'And another thing,' he began belligerently.

'No,' Crow replied in a low tone. Rhodes stared in surprise and the colour flooded to his face. He opened his mouth to continue but Crow forestalled him. 'Keep your mouth shut, Mr Rhodes, and do as you're told. I'm now going into the Administration building and my driver is going to park the car. No damage has been done to the squad car, I trust, so we'll put all this nonsense down to high spirits — though I'd remind you that if some slum kids behaved like this they'd be inside by now. Now get out of the way, and keep these other louts back. All right?'

Crow turned aside and Wilson stepped up beside him. For a moment the crowd broke as he marched forward, backed by Wilson and the two other policemen, and then Rhodes was running around in front of them, the crowd of students surging about in some verbal confusion.

'I tell you,' Rhodes shouted, red in the face, 'we're not having the fuzz sticking their noses in on our protests!'

Crow ignored him completely and proceeded to stride up the steps of the Administration block towards the great glass doors. Wilson butted along behind him throwing off restraining arms, and there was a howl as the larger body of students surged along in their wake. A few men raced ahead of them to line their passage up the steps and there was a hail of verbal abuse, whistling and catcalling. Rhodes was hopping impotently along beside Crow, his face mottled and strained, incoherent with anger, waving his fist and mouthing irrelevant slogans. Crow walked on with a grim face, and took the steps two at a time.

He had almost reached the top when the atmosphere changed. It changed with a shout that swelled into a cheer and the students poured forwards towards the doors. Crow caught a brief glimpse of Rhodes's face, swept with a mingled chagrin and relief, and then that young man was running forward with the rest, surging towards the entrance. Crow glanced at Wilson; the Yorkshireman's eyes told him plainly that in his estimation they were now in for trouble. The students were physically going to block their entrance to the Administration building. There must be about fifty of sixty of them; the original hundred-plus had dwindled in face of the blue uniforms of the squad car men and Crow's driver, but the hard core of troublemakers remained. Crow's face betrayed no expression other than indifference, and his stride in no way slackened. He plunged on towards the doors, straight at the struggling crowd of young men and women.

They parted to let him through.

For a moment Crow thought it was a trick to cut him off from his companions and evidently Wilson thought so too for he put one hand on Crow's shoulder. But it was no trick; all four policemen were allowed to move relatively unimpeded, up the last few steps and across the strip of concrete at the top towards the doors and the students merely surged around them, quietly. The shouting had stopped.

A moment later Crow saw why.

He was standing in the doorway of the Administration block. He was tall, and dark-skinned, with an aquiline cast to his features. His hair was jet-black and worn long, swept back, shining, and tied at the nape of his neck. He wore pale blue jeans and a casual sweater, with rope sandals on his feet. He was lounging with one shoulder against the door and he was smiling, a white, gleaming smile below the heavy drooping moustache he wore. His dark eyes were hard, belying the smile, or perhaps qualifying it, Crow thought to himself. He was barring Crow's path into the building. This was why the shouting had stopped.

Crow didn't stop. He strode across the concrete straight towards the smiling man in the doorway, determinedly giving the impression that if the man didn't move Crow would walk through and over him if necessary. There was to be no discussion.

The students were silent. Crow's shoes echoed on the concrete, and were backed by the hurried sound of his colleagues' steps. Only ten yards separated the silent, smiling figure from Crow. The young man eased himself from the doorpost with a lithe grace, Crow loomed up in front of him menacingly and then the man moved smoothly aside, bowing, extending his arm in an ironic sweeping gesture of welcome.

'Inspector Crow, I presume!'

It was a deep voice, clipped in its tones.

The man was still smiling. Crow stopped and stared at him, hard.

'What's your name?'

The man shrugged, and the smile faded but his eyes mocked the policeman. Arrogantly, he turned his back on Crow and moved away from the doors, throwing an arm across the nearest student and waving to the others.

'It's off,' he called in a high voice. 'The demonstration's off for the time being!'

A groan arose, and someone shouted.

'To hell with the fuzz! We're not scared of them! What's protest for!'

The man in the pale blue jeans swivelled to look back at the motionless Chief Inspector. He was smiling again.

'No, friends, the demonstration's off. These slaves of the Establishment are not here to suppress the student body. They have other fish to fry, and like good citizens it's our duty to disperse at this time.'

'What the hell's going on? Why are they here?'

Crow saw the television team scrambling forwards but there wasn't a thing he could do about it. It was far too late, the whole thing would blow, right now.

'Why are they here? The ultimate, man! They've arrived to investigate, no less, a murder!'

* * *

'It would seem you've had a brush with Sadruddin, Inspector.'

'Sadruddin?'

Dr Peters nodded and walked uneasily across to the windows. His handsome face was pale, and his hands were unsteady. One of those hands stole up on occasion to the distinguished grey sideburns he wore; it was a gesture born of nervousness and insecurity in face of an unexpected, unprecedented situation.

'Sadruddin Khan. He's a student who has been here since we were established two years ago. He's reading for a degree in Law, and he's president of the Student Union this year. Extremely popular, an impassioned orator, a charming and gifted young man. And a Marxist, or so he says. I suspect that he's really a Sadruddinist, if I may be excused such a remark. He's from Iraq, I believe, and the "Khan" is an affectation, in my opinion. I have obtained the impression that he uses it to suggest perhaps a nobility of character and qualities of valour that may be lacking within him in reality.'

'You don't like him.'

'He makes administration difficult.'

Crow considered. The last ten minutes with the rector had not been unproductive but there was work to be done. After a short silence he nodded and turned to walk to the door.

'All right, Dr Peters, thank you. I'll be back shortly to speak to you again. Sergeant Wilson will ask you for various details but I must first go along to take a look at the lift, and the body.'

The rector winced at the word and Crow was made aware that Peters could possibly be somewhat sensitive. But then, the girl had been his secretary. It was a natural reaction.

There was a police constable waiting outside the rector's room and he was quick to direct Crow towards the business block. A commotion near the enquiries desk drew Crow's attention — two students were arguing with the girl at the desk.

'What are *they* doing here?'

The constable jumped and quivered at the tone Crow employed.

'I'll get them out at once, sir!'

'Do that. And keep these corridors and the rest of the building cleared.'

Crow stumped off up the stairs and made his way across the bridge to the business block. He passed two constables at the head of the stairs and they pointed out the huddle of men near the student lifts as the scene-of-crime unit. Crow joined them. A fresh-faced young CID man made way for him to thrust past into the lift itself. A flash bulb exploded and Crow turned his head aside with an exclamation. The others moved aside for Crow to take a look at the girl.

Death had been cruel to her. She wouldn't have been more than nineteen or twenty and she'd been fairly pretty before the blood had trickled down into her right eye and her face had assumed that loose, slack-jawed expression. She was fully clothed apart from a missing shoe; her clothing was disarranged, but seemed not to be torn in any way.

'Her other shoe?'

Young Kennedy, the officer who was in charge of the unit, shuffled uncomfortably, and held out the object. Crow stared at it, then shifted his glance towards the disconcerted policeman.

'Where was it?'

'I'm sorry, sir, it was found down on the stairs on the floor below. A lab steward called Johnson saw it and picked it up. He brought it to us before anyone could warn him that it should have been left where it was.'

This was going to be a mess, Crow knew it in his bones. It had started badly with his mood and it was continuing the same way. He was having difficulty in controlling his temper and this was uncharacteristic. Martha knew how to soothe him when he was in a mood but this time he'd have to control himself.

'Statement taken from this man Johnson?'

'It's being done now, sir. He brought this up only a few minutes ago.'

'Why wasn't the whole area sealed off in the first place, as soon as the unit arrived?'

'Well, we sealed off this floor sir, and we thought—'

'You thought!' Crow fixed the wriggling young man with a cold eye. 'Where did this girl die?'

'Well, we don't know yet, sir. We—'

'Exactly. You don't know. You found her in this lift. So you seal off this floor. But you don't seal off the floors below. The whole of the college should have been sealed off. How long have you been on this unit? Never mind, don't tell me, I might be inclined to allow it to prejudice me.'

In a stiff, formal tone Kennedy replied: 'The whole of this block has been cleared now, sir, and I have three men searching the corridors below.'

Crow noted the formality and the veiled reproof. He took a deep breath; nothing was to be gained by losing his temper with these officers.

'Who found the body?'

'A man called Fanshaw, sir.'

'College staff?'

'No, sir. A civil servant.'

A civil servant — Crow had had more than enough to do with such men already. Oxbridge-trained, as often as not, red tape-tied, stuffy, inhibited, superior — and this one boasted the name of Fanshaw to boot!

'What was he doing in the building?'

'He's one of Her Majesty's Inspectors of Schools—'

'Schools?'

'That's the official designation, sir, but I understand he works in the Further Education sector which includes the polytechnics. I gather the polytechnics are still local authority colleges, unlike universities, which are independent. So he tells me.'

'I'll want to see him.'

'He's in the staff room, at the end of the corridor, sir.'

Crow nodded, took another slow look at the dead girl with the feeling that there was something missing, glanced around at the silent men in the lift, then turned to leave them to their job. This was the part of the investigation he hated. In a matter of days things would begin to appear a little more logical: names, places, events, times would begin to settle, to form an overall impression. People would begin to fit into a picture, sequences would start to form a pattern. But now it was all a mess, an untidy shuffling of cards in an unfamiliar pack; officers drifting around the building, asking, watching, searching and not quite knowing what they were doing. Bewildering names and faces, strangers, inexplicable actions, short tempers and refusals or inability to answer the simplest questions, all of these contributed to making the investigating officer's task an unenviable one. And over all the situation hung the inevitable reaction of the man who was questioned: what does this have to do with me, he'd be asking himself; why are the police questioning me, how dare they infer that I'm in any way connected with the death; wait till I tell the kids about this! Irrational fears, stupid pride, inconsequential excitement, unpleasant and prurient curiosity. Crow grunted his displeasure to an echoing empty corridor and it grunted back. The staff room lay at the end of the corridor.

Crow pushed past the broad back of the constable guarding the door and entered the room. It was a long, pleasant room, with light-coloured wallpaper, small, plain tables and comfortable easy chairs in strong primary colours, red, green, blue. It was quite empty but for one dark-suited man sitting at the far end. He made no attempt to look up as Crow entered. He affected a massive lack of interest, and he sipped quietly at his cup of tea. He had flowing, carefully groomed white hair and an Honours Tripos face, lean and sharp and administrative.

'You must be Fanshaw,' Crow said as he approached the quiet man in the corner. The head came up, and then was inclined elegantly. One inch of white shirt-cuff was displayed as Fanshaw replaced the cup on the table in front of him. He stood up. He was almost as tall as Crow.

'I see you managed to find some refreshment.'

Crow's tone caused Fanshaw to blink behind his rimless glasses, but there was no change in his expression. Quietly, the man said: 'The rector was kind enough to ask the office staff to bring a cup of tea up to me. I thought it best not to return downstairs: I understood that the police would want to speak to me. But the rector realised that I would be . . . ah . . . somewhat shocked, so . . .'

'Sit down, Mr Fanshaw. I gather from your shock you must have known the girl?'

'I would have been shocked to discover *any* person like this, Inspector . . . er . . .'

'Crow.'

'But you're right, I did know Rosemary. I had met her upon several occasions, whenever I came to the college in fact. She was the rector's secretary.'

'Did you visit regularly?'

'Irregularly. But on each occasion I pay my respects to Dr Peters, and always reach him through his secretary first — she would tell me whether Dr Peters was available. It's a matter of form, you understand.'

Crow nodded. He understood. Red tape again.

'How did you come to find her on *this* floor?'

He listened carefully while Fanshaw explained. There wasn't much that the man could tell him, but Crow listened to his smooth elegant tones and recognized the easy self-confidence in the man. Fanshaw was not of his world. He was of the Establishment — and as those students down below had shouted, what were the police but the servants of the Establishment? Crow had had dealings with the Home Office in the past and found himself wishing that these civil servants would show their easy superiority in less obvious ways than dress, and speech, and social ease. Particularly when they found a corpse. Not a grey hair had been turned on the elegant Fanshaw head by the discovery of a dead Rosemary Harland.

'Have you made a statement yet?'

'I've not been asked for one up till now, Inspector Crow.'

Crow called to the police constable at the door.

'Take Mr Fanshaw downstairs now, and take his statement. I'll be seeing you again, sir, and I'll probably have some more questions to ask. But that'll do for the time being.'

Crow watched Fanshaw stroll elegantly out after the constable and then he sat down in the chair vacated by the HMI. Civil servant! He stared at the ceiling. Collect thoughts, forget irrelevancies.

What did he have? . . . a dead girl, the HMI who had found her, the rector who had employed her, the office staff who worked with her . . . Sadruddin. How had Sadruddin known Crow's name?

Ten minutes later a frightened girl in the office gave him the answer.

'I was standing out near the main entrance, and he — Sadruddin, that is, came up to me, tapped me on the shoulder and asked what all the excitement was about. So I told him that Rosemary had been killed and he asked me what was going to happen. I said that the police had been called and that an Inspector Crow was expected any minute. A few minutes later you arrived, sir . . .'

Crow told the office staff that he would want to see all of them, individually, during the course of the day and asked them to hold themselves in readiness. One girl, with long dark hair and a frightened mouth, put up a hand as though she were back at school again. Crow stared at her, saw what she held in her other hand and knew what it was that had been missing from Rosemary Harland's body in the lift. Her handbag.

He took it from the dark-haired girl as she stammered that she'd found it in the general office and looked quickly through it. It contained the usual paraphernalia of things useful and useless, decorative and functional. No letters. A bunch of household keys. And one big key. He saw the stamp on it — it was the key she would have used to get in and out of the Polytechnic. She hadn't used it to get out last night. He walked back into the rector's office. Peters, his face still pale, sat behind his desk. Wilson looked up and rose as Crow entered. The notebook he held was covered with pencilled notes of his conversation with the rector.

'Dr Peters has let me have all the personal details concerning the murdered girl,' Wilson said. 'There wasn't a great deal in her file, really, since this was her first job.'

And her last, Crow thought grimly.

* * *

The day dragged on. Crow and Wilson went through the dreary motions of interviewing all the people on the college staff who had had contact with Rosemary Harland. They asked what sort of a girl she was, who her friends were, when she had last been seen by the person questioned, what their relationships had been. Finally, Crow came back to the rector.

'From what I gather,' he said, consulting his notebook, 'Rosemary Harland was a friendly, but fairly quiet girl. She was educated at Sedleigh Grammar School, took a Private Secretarial course at Sedleigh Branch College of Further Education and then took up her first appointment in the office here.'

'She was recommended to me personally by the Head of Department at the Branch College; I took her out of the general office after two weeks and she became my secretary.'

'She was only twenty when she died. Isn't it usual to have an older woman for a job such as personal secretary to the rector of a polytechnic?'

'She was a remarkably efficient girl.'

'And a pretty one.'

There was a moment's silence. Crow's remark had been delivered in a flat, expressionless tone and Peters now stared at him, obviously undecided whether Crow had meant to be offensive or not. Crow waited, watching for reaction from Peters; in the event, Peters remained silent. A point to consider: his silence could mean that he felt himself upon sufficiently insecure ground to remain quiet in ace of such provocation.

'Boy-friends?'

'I don't think so. But really, I wouldn't know. I had a very pleasant working relationship with Miss Harland, but it did not extend to discussing her private affairs with her.'

'Is that being evasive, Dr Peters?'

The lean face of the rector tightened and he drew his eyebrows together in a frown.

'I don't know what you're implying, Inspector Crow.'

'I'm not suggesting you discussed private matters with her. But you're rector of the Polytechnic; you know what goes on in this college. You would know, for instance, if your secretary had admirers — in the office, perhaps, or on the staff.'

'There are other duties incumbent upon the rector,' Peters said in a cold stiff voice, 'which would preclude his descending to gossip about his office staff.'

'Perhaps the Academic Registrar would know more about it?'

'Perhaps he would. I wouldn't know.' Antony Peters wasn't easy to ruffle; he had control of his emotions. Yet Crow felt there was something about his attitudes which suggested he was too prepared to accept innuendo, too prepared to accept professional slurs. It was curious. It could be that he was a timid man, but this Crow doubted. It was more likely that he wanted to avoid a fuss — and if that were the case, he would have a good reason for wanting to avoid it. In Crow's experience, the man who refused to take a baited insult already had another hook in his gullet and was too conscious of its bite to accept another. Crow wondered just what barb was inhibiting Peters's freedom of expression. He closed his notebook.

'I'll have a word with the registrar, then, see what he's got to say. I've now spoken to the office staff but there's the academic people too. Have you drawn up a list of the staff who most came into contact with the dead girl?'

An anxious finger stole up to his sideburn as Peters hesitated.

'It's a bit difficult, really. Rosemary was my secretary, and as such would come into contact with the academic staff only rarely, in the formal completion of her duties. But almost all will have met her. Anyone who came to see me — and I make. a point of seeing every member of staff on appointment — would first be dealt with by Rosemary. So, in a sense, everyone on the staff would have had contact with her.'

'I understand. But who in particular might have seen more than this of her?'

'Well, the heads of the Faculties, I suppose.They come to see me more regularly than the rest of the staff and we have faculty meetings where Rosemary used to sit in and take notes. The heads would then get to know her, but again, I hardly feel that an intimate relationship could develop upon such grounds.'

Intimate relationship? Peters must have been aware of the question in Crow's mind, for he stumbled over his next, hurried words.

'I . . . I . . . can certainly give you a short list of their names but I don't really see any relevance in it all.'

'Perhaps I should judge that matter, Dr Peters. The list, please.'

He read the names out aloud, and Peters was quick to supply details of each.

'J.R. Stevens.'

'He's the head of the Faculty which comprises Law, Economics and Professional Studies. He has a crippled wife.'

'So Redman.'

'Faculty head — Engineering. The faculty comprises four engineering departments. A good man — a Roman Catholic, I believe. He's been here for eight months.'

'P.R. Carliss.'

'Head of the Faculty of Science. He . . . er . . . he's a very able man.'

Delivered in a tone of voice which means, Crow thought to himself, that Carliss doesn't quite fit Peters's picture of what a Faculty head should be.

'O. Svensson.'

'Faculty of Architecture. A temporary post; we're advertising this summer for a man to take over.'

'V. West.'

'Mr West, yes, well he's the Faculty head who's concerned with Social Administration. Joined us six months ago. A quiet fellow, introverted.'

'And all these men will be available for interview this afternoon?'

'All but Mr West. I'm afraid he was taken ill yesterday afternoon. A heart attack, I understand. He's now in Sedleigh Hospital.'

'I see. Perhaps you'll ask the others to stand by, Dr Peters, so that I can speak to them this afternoon. I'll go in and see the registrar now.'

Crow gained little from the man. He was a willowy, inoffensive person who was probably quietly efficient in his office but remarkably uncommunicative with the police inspector. It wasn't that he refused to impart information; he had none to impart. He was an office automaton; a flick of his fingertips and he could produce statistical evidence on any student on the Burton registers, but this was all he was capable of doing. He obviously saw them not as people but as statistics; the office staff were machine operators, register collators, fee-collectors, but not individuals. He had nothing to say which could in any way colour the picture of Rosemary Harland. She had never existed for him as a person. He was as dead, Crow thought, as she was.

Wilson was waiting outside the registrar's office as he came out. He handed a sheet of paper to him.

'I've just had a word with the doc and he's fixed a time of death tentatively for us, though it'll be subject to the findings at the lab, of course. She died sometime last night — probably after ten. She received a nasty head wound and her neck was broken. There's no clue at the moment where she was murdered, but the doc thinks it certainly wasn't in the lift. Now, this paper gives the names of people who were teaching here last night in evening classes, and the names of the caretaking staff employed here. The list is fairly long, as you'll see, and includes some part-timers, but there is one point to remember. If she was killed after ten, few, if any, of these people will have been on the premises. The last class ended at nine p.m. The caretakers hope to be away each evening by nine-fifteen.'

'That cuts two ways,' Crow said morosely. 'The one who did stay — he might not have been observed if there were few people around.'

He walked past Wilson, tapped on the rector's door and entered. Peters looked up from his desk; he had regained some of his colour and the way his mouth tightened at Crow's entrance showed the inspector that he was beginning to get tired of answering questions.

'The five Faculty heads. I'd like to see their personal files, Dr Peters.'

The rector's chin came up, slowly. His eyes had narrowed.

'I see no reason why you need to pry into their personal files, Inspector.'

'I'm sorry. I have a murder investigation to conduct. I'd like to see the files, please.'

Peters hesitated, then rose and walked across to his filing cabinet. He extracted five folders, handed them to Crow, then without a word went back to his desk and sat down. His eyes didn't move from Crow's face but nothing was said. The eyes had carried a clear warning, nevertheless; don't push too far.

John Crow had never heeded warnings, particularly from people who had something to hide. Sensitive skins repaid scratching. 'You didn't let me finish, sir,' Wilson observed when Crow left Peters's office.

'I didn't?'

'The scene-of-crime unit upstairs have discovered nothing, but one of the constables on the second floor came up with a glove which he has now handed to Kennedy.'

'What sort of glove?'

'Driving glove; leather backing, string palm. A man's glove.'

'Anything to connect it with the girl?'

'No, sir.'

'Get it along for forensic tests — see what they can make of it at the lab.'

Crow made his way to the interview room. Heads turned as he entered. Three men stood in one corner, talking in low voices which stopped as he came in. Near the window Robert Fanshaw was in discussion with another man; Fanshaw saw Crow enter but finished his conversation. Crow paused.

'I shall want to see each of you in turn, gentlemen, one at a time. We'll use the room through there—' he gestured towards the anteroom, beyond the heavy door — 'and I should be grateful if you did not discuss the murder while you wait together here.'

Which was as good as saying don't breathe. Fanshaw was striding across the room.

'I take it you'll have finished with me, Inspector.'

Crow opened his mouth but Fanshaw went on cheerily.

'I've given my statement, and I've nothing to add to it at this stage so I see little point in continuing to sit around here. I have work to attend to so I'll be on my way. I shall be available, of course, if you want to discuss anything further with me and if I can be of any assistance at all I shall be only too pleased to help . . .'

Crow smiled thinly, and inclined his head. 'I don't think we need keep you any longer, Mr Fanshaw.'

'Dr Peters can let you have my address and that of my office. If you need to get in touch, the office will let you know where I am.'

He was gone. Crow watched the door close and then glanced at the other four men in the room. They shuffled their feet uneasily. 'Wilson!'

'Sir.'

'These gentlemen. One at a time.'

Crow took the personal files of the four Faculty heads into the anteroom. He sat down with his back to the window and he stared at the file covers thoughtfully.

Wilson was bringing in the first of the four Faculty heads.

The interviews were not unproductive. Stevens came in first. He was a youngish man, with fair, carefully nurtured hair. He sat on the edge of his chair, was extremely polite, and was given to talking a little too much. People who did so, in Crow's experience, had little to say. When he was asked about his relationship with Rosemary Harland he coloured a little and became somewhat evasive. Crow raised a query against his name, both as regards that relationship and as regards his whereabouts the previous night.

Redman came next. A tall, balding Scot with an equine face, he had trouble arranging his legs, which insisted on cramping under his chair. His wriggling irritated Crow and brought an edge to his tongue that had not been apparent with Stevens. Redman made no protest. Crow was surprised; Scots were often prickly.

Carliss wasn't a Scot, but he was prickly. He was from Penzance and had a mining and engineering background remarkably extensive for a man of his age. He was about forty-five, stocky, with thick stubby-fingered hands and an angry mouth. He was not prepared to take Crow's questions quietly.

'If you're trying to say that I knew Rosemary Harland outside this office you're nuts.'

'My sanity isn't in question.'

'Neither are my morals! All right, I've been married, and I'm getting a divorce but as far as I'm concerned that's got nothing to do with all this! My wife ran off with, of all things, a hairdresser from Stockport, but if you think that's made me start looking around here for women you can think again. I've better things to do with my time. Chase Stevens up if you like, but don't try to tar me with that kind of brush.'

'Why should I chase Stevens up with such a question?'

Carliss's broad face twisted into a sneer. 'He's the skirt-lifter in this college, haven't they told you that yet? He's the feller who's always up in the library chatting up the two assistants; he's the Casanova who's always drifting around on the social evenings; he's the Romeo who mingles with the Graduate Secretarial group on coffee mornings when staff and students get together. I tell you, man, there's not room for two characters like him in Burton!'

'You seem to keep a close eye on him.'

'He needs watching.'

'Why should you watch?'

Carliss shrugged and remained silent. His little eyes flickered away from the inspector and his pugnacious mouth settled in a thick line. He had talked too much; he was unwilling to say more.

'Where were you last night, Mr Carliss?'

'You want to know? The cinema.'

'Alone?'

'Yes.'

'You will, of course, be able to provide some corroboration — or tell me what film was showing and so on.'

Carliss scowled and then suddenly fished in the pocket of his jacket to produce a ticket stub, tightly rolled, half-shredded.

'A habit I have. I roll the ticket stub over and over, right through the time the film runs. I must have stuck this in my pocket last night, half way through.'

Crow took the proffered stub gingerly and inspected it, rolling it out with a twist of distaste to his mouth as shreds of paper fell from it. He handed it back in disdain.

'It could have been sold at any time; the number isn't visible.'

Carliss shrugged. 'That's your problem.'

'It may develop into a problem for you. But we'll see. Thank you, Mr Carliss. That'll be all for now.'

After Carliss had gone Crow smiled and his brown eyes were warm. Prickly men interested him — they were so unable to control their emotions that their motivations became transparent in quality. It could well be that Carliss was at the cinema while Rosemary Harland was being murdered, but the relationship between Carliss and Stevens needed looking at. They certainly were not friends.

The last man to enter was Svensson. He was a caricature of an academic; thin, pale, bespectacled and bald, his myopia seemed to extend to his memory and his grasp of events. He was as hazy on dates as he was on names and he had the curious capacity of making the most patently honest remark seem like prevarication. Yet reputedly, from his file, he was a mathematician and an architect of quality. Crow was glad to see him stumble from the room. Svensson embarrassed him; he was too weak to be true.

Stevens, Redman, Carliss, Svensson. And West. Crow thumbed through West's file; there seemed little point to it, but he supposed he'd better get around to the hospital some time tomorrow to have a word with West. If he was fit to speak to the police.

Crow leaned back in his chair and stared at the ceiling. The digging would have to start now, and it had better start with the rector. He had been Rosemary Harland's employer. Wilson could start with that. Crow would have a more unpleasant job to undertake while Wilson searched files and records. He'd have to go to see Rosemary Harland's parents.

Crow walked out of the anteroom and told Wilson that the Faculty heads could go. Then he walked out through the hall, past the rector's office and the enquiry office. A girl stared at him over her typewriter as he walked past, tall, gaunt, ungainly. He ignored her.

He stood in the glass doorway for a moment before stepping out on to the concrete apron. The campus was quiet in the late afternoon sunshine. The trees shone greenly, dipping their heavy branches in the light breeze and the sky was a deep blue. Crow noticed hardly any of this.

He was wondering what had happened to all the students.

There was not one student in sight. No lectures, all right, but no curiosity either? No poking-in of noses, no vicarious thrilling at the sight of the police marching around in their hunt for the murderer of Rosemary Harland? He stood there, and he wondered, and he heard a muted sound, a roar from the distance. Men shouting.

A sudden thought stretched itself across his mind, lazily, like a yawning cat. It was still half- formed when he walked back into the hall and made his way to the office of the Academic Registrar. The willowy man with the pale hair looked up as Crow entered.

'The caretakers,' Crow said slowly. 'They have keys to the building?'

'Certainly, Inspector.'

'Every part of the building — the business block?'

'Only the chief porter and one caretaker, Smith, will have keys to the business block.'

'You'll have access to the keys.'

'Yes, I have.'

'And Dr Peters?'

'Of course.'

Crow grimaced. Rosemary Harland had died probably some time after ten o'clock last night. The classes had ended, the lecturers had gone, the cleaners and caretakers had locked up and left. But someone had stayed. For some reason, Rosemary Harland had still been in the building, and there had been someone else here too. Someone who would probably have been able to get access to the business block.

His next question produced the answer he was seeking.

'Oh, yes, they'll have access, too. All five of them.'

Stevens, Redman, Carliss, Svensson. And West.

Chapter 2

In Robert Fanshaw's experience hospitals were unpleasant places. To a certain extent his view had been coloured by his recollection of the removal of a foreign body from his ankle. He had lain on an operating-table and watched the doctor cut off the supply of blood to his leg, then proceed to make a swift incision on the swollen ankle. It was not only the discharging fluid which had upset Fanshaw; it was also the glee in the doctor's face when he had prodded a pair of what Fanshaw assumed to be tweezers into his patient's face. Gripped by the tweezers had been a piece of bloody gristle.

'Souvenir?' the doctor had asked in a jolly voice. Fanshaw had been violently sick and he disliked being sick; it was an undignified reaction to stress. He had vomited since that occasion, of course, but with better reason. There had been the evening at the Conference in Scarborough, for instance, and again the Music Festival in Exeter. On the latter occasion the first violin had found him in full evening dress, asleep, bassoon clutched in his left hand, his left foot cocked up on the toilet-roll holder and a large lump on the back of his head. By way of explanation for his twelve-hour sojourn there, Fanshaw could only say that he had gained the drunken impression that he had been locked in the little cubicle. In an attempt to remove himself from his predicament he had placed his left foot on the toilet seat and, casting about for further support, his right foot upon the toilet roll. He had attempted to grasp the top of the cubicle wall, to climb out but this necessitated a transference of weight from toilet seat to toilet roll; unfortunately, true to its function, the latter rotated and Fanshaw was deposited, to lie snoring, on the tiled floor.

He gave an immaculate performance the following evening, he remembered.

But hospitals he disliked; the long, echoing, soulless corridors, the efficient, marching viragos in blue uniforms, the haughty, self-sufficient nurses, the casual doctors and subservient patients, and the odours. Nameless smells, tincture of chloroform and ether, poppy and blood and plasma, penicillin culture and eyeballs — the appalling words and images crowded in upon him whenever he thought of hospitals. When he was in one it was worse, and his sensitive soul cringed.

Nevertheless, Robert Fanshaw possessed a sense of duty also so he sat in the draughty corridor waiting for the sister to allow him into the ward and he kept his knees together and his pale, slim hands on his knees and his eyes fixed on the window in front of him.

Only when the echoing footsteps stopped beside his chair did he look up.

'Good morning, Inspector. This is a surprise.'

Inspector Crow also seemed surprised, and was not averse to expressing it.

'What are you doing here?'

An interesting man, Crow, an ungainly, ugly man, whose unprepossessing appearance was softened by warm, intelligent eyes that missed little of consequence. Fanshaw smiled his elegant smile and stood up.

'Mr West is here — but you'll know that already, of course. It will be why you've come, I expect. I thought that as general inspector of the college I ought to call in to pay a visit.'

'General inspector?'

'We have two functions — general and specialist. As a specialist — my own specialism is business studies — we hold a divisional responsibility and enter, in my case, business studies departments. But we are also given general duties which demand that we oversee the work of a whole college and Burton is one of mine. This is why I tend to know most of the staff at Burton, whereas elsewhere my acquaintance is likely to be less close.'

'This man West; do you know him well?'

'Reasonably so. I've had no dealings with him in my specialist function, for his Faculty is Social Administration, but he was given responsibility for re-organizing the democratic structure of the academic committees and I watched his work with interest.'

'What sort of man is he?'

Fanshaw paused and eyed the inspector curiously. The long white face was still but there was a calculating look in the brown eyes.

'Mr West came to Burton about six or eight months ago. He's a quiet, introverted sort of feller. Efficient, academically well-qualified, taught in Australia at a university for a number of years, then came over here and drifted into the technical colleges. I've not really understood that, because I feel sure he could have got into a university, but there you are: perhaps it was an emotional thing, I don't know. He's a good Faculty head, reasonable, organizes well.'

'Married?'

'I don't think so. He *was* married I think, but isn't now. He lives alone, I understand; doesn't mix particularly with the staff in a social situation. I like him.'

'Does he like you?'

Fanshaw raised his black eyebrows.

'I can't really say. Most educationists are polite to HMI but who is pleased to be inspected? The inspectorial function inevitably colours one's image, I fear, and it is too easy to take professional respect and equate it with personal regard. No, I think Mr West probably trusts me, professionally; whether he likes me as a person, I can't say.'

Old Charley Nixon, now, he was a different fish. He could take Robert Fanshaw for what he was, a friendly quaffer of ale in small quantities, a musician of sorts, a good listener to country tales, an inveterate sentimentalist as far as village life and village people were concerned. But Charley Nixon wasn't tied up in an educational world, he didn't see Robert Fanshaw in professional terms, and he could accept Robert Fanshaw for what he was.

'Would you say you knew the other heads pretty well too?'

Fanshaw raised an elegant, deprecating shoulder.

'Let me put it like this. Part of my job is to deal with people in a professional situation. I act as an adviser to my Department. In so doing there are occasions when I have to make recommendations to the Department. These must be based, in part, upon what I think of individuals. Therefore, it follows that part of my job is to make assessments of people, to make what may be called value-judgments .'

'So you could give me thumbnail sketches of the Burton staff?'

'The senior people, yes. Without prejudice, of course.'

'Without prejudice. All right, Mr Fanshaw — what about Stevens?'

An interesting exercise. Fanshaw pursed his lips and rocked slightly on his heels. He stared out through the window.

'Stevens, Head of the Faculty of Law, Economics and Professional Studies. A young man of promise. Ebullient, go-ahead in my view, and perhaps destined for a principalship himself within the next five or ten years. He's about forty.'

'Carliss?'

'Faculty of Science. A short-tempered, explosive feller, prickly, aggressive, with a considerable opinion of his own capabilities which is not shared by all his contemporaries. Ambition is present in his veins; it causes him to get purple in the face on occasion—'

'When he speaks of Stevens, perhaps?'

Fanshaw stared at Crow and a slow smile spread over his face.

'I congratulate you, Inspector. It was at least three months before I detected the presence of animosity between the two gentlemen. It's taken you, what? Twenty-four hours?'

'Less. But things accelerate under pressure of a murder investigation.'

'I believe you.'

'Why does Carliss dislike Stevens?'

'It's never been put in such crude terms, Inspector, and I would hesitate to so describe the . . . ah . . . situation between them. But it really comes to this: Dr Anthony Peters is rector of Burton Polytechnic. The post of assistant rector fell vacant just one year ago as a result of the retirement of its incumbent. No suitable applicants came forward for interview; there is a strong possibility that an internal appointment will be made though the governing body has not so intimated as yet. Stevens is a young man who is going places, to use the idiom. Carliss sees his own destination as possibly being the same as Stevens — hence a certain acrimony in social intercourse between them.'

'You mean they're both after the job of assistant rector?'

'I must protest at the directness of your statements, Inspector. No one has ever said this, or suggested it openly. It is my belief that each of them sees himself as the natural candidate. Inevitably this colours their judgment of each other. The colours have been sharpened by the attempts made by Stevens to influence the future academic development of the polytechnic, and the obstacles raised by Carliss at Academic Board level. Carliss also tends to be — ah — excessively industry-oriented. Stevens believes in freedom from entanglement with industrial interests. The two men disagree violently. In Carliss's case, at least, it might tend to spill over into vituperation, and even slanderous statements.'

'Such as the suggestion that Stevens is a womanizer?'

Fanshaw smiled and wriggled uncomfortably, smoothing the white hair at the side of his head.

'I do wish you wouldn't put things in such black and white terminology. I prefer the secondary colours myself. Stevens . . . it has come to my attention that he is not averse to female company in conversation. Beyond that I cannot comment.'

Crow smiled faintly and Fanshaw was aware that he was amused by the traditional caution of Her Majesty's Inspectorate. Yet Crow obviously understood the necessity for caution when statements could be interpreted as being other than personal.

'He trusts you, this man West.'

'Professionally, yes.'

'Would you like to be with me when I speak to him?'

'If you think it will help.' Fanshaw was surprised and his tone betrayed the emotion. 'But I hardly see—'

'I'm a stranger, and a policeman. West is ill. I don't want to upset him too much. If you're there it might make him calmer, and he might also be more inclined to speak freely. I'll also want your opinion of what he has to say.'

'I'm flattered.'

'It's not my intention to flatter you. You can help me, it's as simple as that.'

Fanshaw's face held an amused smile as he walked in behind Crow. The sister took them to Vernon West's bedside.

West was sitting up in bed. He looked no different to Fanshaw, except for a slight mottling of his features, and the sunshine picked out on his cheeks a fine tracing of veins, the network of experience, that Fanshaw had not noticed before. He sat quietly, with his hands resting on the bedcovers and he watched the two men approach him. His features were fleshy; he was heavy-jowled and he had a double chin but his mouth was firm and his glance keen. Fanshaw had never thought of him as a soft man, in spite of his heavy build; he possessed a strength of character which helped him considerably in his handling of Faculty affairs but Fanshaw had known at least one young lecturer who had mistaken West's air of quiet restraint for weakness and had paid the penalty accordingly. Vernon West was nobody's fool and was capable of reaching firm decisions on logically argued facts. But he never acted precipitately. He weighed up events, and acted when action became necessary, not before.

Crow ambled forward and stood over the man in the bed. Without preamble the policeman said: 'You'll have heard what happened at Burton. I'd like to ask you some questions.'

West's reaction was slight; a tongue moistening dry lips and a quick glance in Fanshaw's direction.

'Yes. I heard about . . . about Miss Harland over the radio this morning. Hello, Mr Fanshaw.'

Fanshaw nodded a greeting, and Crow continued.

'Rosemary Harland was killed about ten in the evening, on the college premises. Statements have already been taken from the other Faculty heads, who knew her fairly well. You knew her also. Would you like to tell me where you were at the relevant time?'

Fanshaw opened his mouth to speak, but stopped. West had glanced in his direction but again had made no

45

other reaction. He was not obviously disturbed by the direct nature of Crow's questions.

'I was at home, ill. There's no one who can corroborate that, of course.'

'Tell me precisely what happened.'

'I had experienced some pain during the morning; a sort of gripping pain in my chest. I suspected indigestion and went back home intending to have a light lunch. Once home, I felt quite unwell, and so I phoned the college and told them I'd be staying away for the afternoon. Then, about two in the afternoon, I had a heart attack. Or to be more medically precise, I suffered an attack of angina pectoris.'

'This would be a pain only. No crippling effect?'

'That occurred only later, about five in the afternoon. I had a second attack: this amounted to a lesion, I understand. I had an idea what was happening; I was upstairs at the time and I lay on my bed. I was too scared to go downstairs to the phone: I thought it was safer to keep still. That's what I did. I must have passed out then, because when I woke, it was close to dawn the next morning. I was feeling somewhat better, and I made my way, very gingerly, believe me, down to the phone, and called an ambulance. Then they brought me here.'

Crow sniffed and made a brief note in a book he fished out of his pocket. 'Do you drive?'

'A car? Yes.'

'Driving gloves?'

'I have some, yes. Why do you ask?'

'Keep them in your car?'

'I do. But why—'

'Were you friendly with Rosemary Harland?'

Fanshaw watched and listened with interest. He was beginning to wonder why Crow had suggested he come in with him, but it was interesting to see the policeman at work. The blunt, direct attack of his was hardly calculated to make things easier for a man who was ill, but at least

46

this method meant that the interview would be quickly over, and this would probably be best for West in the long run.

Fanshaw sat and listened sympathetically to West's answers. They were given in a low, quiet voice, with occasional surprised glances in Fanshaw's direction, as he puzzled at the drift of Crow's questions. No, he had not been friendly with the girl, he had not known her outside office hours. Yes, he did have a key to the building. They were all the answers that Fanshaw would have expected, the ones he knew would have come.

But then things changed suddenly.

'Have you anything to add? Anything you think might have some bearing upon her death?'

West said nothing but there was a curious tenseness in him that was communicated to both his visitors. Crow leaned forward.

'I should add,' he said, 'that if there is anything, you should divulge it. In a murder investigation loyalty is misplaced. Is there anything you can tell me? About the girl's relationships, for instance, with members of staff?'

West licked his lips and looked down at his hands. His eyes narrowed and the lines around his pouched eyes grew deeper.

'I'm not sure. It's not really for me to say. It's just that . . . there have been rumours . . .' He paused, and silence gathered conspiratorially around the three men. 'Rumours about Miss Harland . . . and . . . and the rector.'

Something cold touched Fanshaw's neck.

He stared at West but the man did not meet his glance. Crow said quietly, 'What sort of rumours?'

'I can't really say. Just . . . just veiled hints that there was some sort of relationship between them.'

'Sexual?'

'I can't . . . I don't know . . .'

'Who told you about this?'

'Again, I don't know. I mean, rumours, where do they start? How do they gain currency?' West's speech had begun to speed up, underlined as it was by a slight desperation as though he had found himself in an arena where he had no desire to be, and was facing a bull he had no desire to fight. 'All I know is that while I've been at Burton there have been rumours . . . drifting around, concerning Dr Peters and . . . and the girl.'

Fanshaw hardly listened to the rest. Crow continued to probe, press West for details but they were not forthcoming. West became shorter in his replies. His eyes had taken on a fixed deadness; the glass eyes of a mounted fox-head. It was obvious that he was already regretting what he had said. Finally Crow gave up, took his leave of West and walked out. Fanshaw followed him, after saying quietly to West that he'd be back in a few minutes.

In the corridor outside Crow swung around abruptly to face Fanshaw. 'Well?'

'Well what?'

'Was he lying?'

'A value-judgment about a man is one thing, but an ability to detect lies is another.'

'You said you knew West; that he trusted you. If he'd given you those answers would you have believed them?'

Fanshaw considered for a moment. This was the trouble with Crow — he expected directness, firm statements from which one could not later resile. Such remarks, and attitudes, were contrary to Fanshaw's character and inclinations.

'Let me put it like this, Inspector. From the evidence of West's hospitalization we know that he suffered a mild coronary — though he seems pretty well today and I understand that he'll be kept only a matter of days before he's allowed to convalesce at home. I believe his story to that extent.'

'But?'

'But I'm confused over his remarks concerning the rector.'

'You think the rector isn't capable of having an affair with his secretary?' Fanshaw winced at Crow's directness.

'I didn't say that. I'm in no position to make any such statement; I don't know the man well enough to be able to make such remarks or reach conclusions about his private life. No, my confusion arises over West himself.'

'How do you mean?'

'West is an introvert; a quiet, unassuming person who says little more than he needs to and keeps very much to himself. He is not a retailer of gossip, he is not the kind of man who listens to it, let alone passes it on.'

'But he heard rumours concerning Peters.'

'That's what I find confusing. First, that he should consciously hear such rumours; second, that he should place any credence upon them; third, that he should regurgitate them for what they are.'

Fanshaw sighed unhappily and looked at Crow with sad eyes.

'You took me in with you for my opinion, I gather. Well, my opinion is that Mr West was not being completely honest with you in his later remarks.'

Had he been of Crow's disposition and profession, Fanshaw thought, he'd have put it more crudely. No matter, he'd leave Crow now and go back in to West, pay his respects as he'd meant to on this visit.

He might then discover just why Vernon West had lied.

* * *

It was an unpretentious family house, red brick, grey-tiled roof, a curving, shaven lawn, rose-beds and flowering cherry trees in the front garden, shrubs and vegetable patch in the back. The sitting-room sported a piano on which were perched three photographs of a girl, taken at ages eight, fourteen and twenty; on the settee there had been a leather-backed album open at the third page. It contained some baby snaps. All of the same person, all of the same girl, the girl whose murder Crow was investigating.

He wasn't here to project sympathy, he was here to probe, to ask questions, to bring back to the minds of the parents the image of a daughter who had died only a matter of hours ago, and died violently. He had to ask them about her recent activities and her friends, suggest that they might look for significance in innocent actions and statements made by her during the last few days, and inevitably bring into their minds the seeds of a suspicion that they might never have known their daughter. This was the unpleasant part of an investigation: the inference that a close-knit family was yet composed of individuals who could and would hide from each other their inner thoughts and desires.

His own ghoulish appearance did nothing to alleviate the problems posed by his questioning, and at such times as this Crow felt himself to be very much a blunt instrument, lacking finesse and diplomacy, the syrup of a politician, the honey of an ambassador. He knew he would stumble over words and scrape raw nerves because the real sympathy he felt for these people would nevertheless have to be submerged by the necessities of his task — the ferreting of fact out of a welter of emotion and sentiment.

His presence would not be welcome.

Mr Harland was a portly, middle-aged accountant who worked for a respectable engineering firm in Sedleigh and his firmly middle-class situation rendered him incapable of coping with the inexplicable intrusion of murder, with all its unpleasant connotations of the underworld of which he knew nothing. Mrs Harland was fluffy, blonde gone grey, heartbroken and incapable of coherent speech for longer than two minutes, faced as she was by the shadows of her lost daughter — the photographs on the piano, the painting on the wall, the stitching on a cushion cover, the book on a shelf. They drifted in the room for her, the whispers of a girl's life, dying whispers, dead whispers, rustling like dry leaves in her mind. Crow tried to deal with these two saddened people, tried to ask them firm, logical questions but found himself faced with a dull, uncomprehending hostility from the man and stuttering tears from the woman. No, they did not know why Rosemary would have stayed behind at the college; no, they didn't worry when she failed to return for she sometimes stayed with her friend, Sally Woods, and they had been told that she was to do so that evening; no, there was no boyfriend as far as they knew for she wasn't that kind of girl and they resented the suggestion that she was. No. They could think of no reason why anyone, anyone at all, should want to kill their daughter.

It was only with considerable reluctance that they agreed to allow an officer to search through their daughter's room and possessions.

When Crow drove away it was with a sense of helplessness at his inability to help the couple in any positive way: the person who had existed at the centre of their lives was dead. Crow spent that evening sitting in the Sedleigh Arms with a glass of beer in front of him, pondering on the lines of enquiry that he'd be following the next day — but he had to make a conscious effort to do so, for the Harlands drifted unbidden into his mind. He was sorry for them, and in his job a man could afford little sympathy, for it clouded judgment.

The tasks for tomorrow had to be decided upon. First, there'd be the preliminary lab report which might give him something to work on. Then there'd be the sifting of statements from the Faculty heads and from the rector. He'd get Wilson working on the personal files he'd retained, and one of the constables on the background information on Dr Peters and the others. That was enough to get started with.

Stevens and Carliss; two possibilities.

Stevens for the fact that he might have been interested in Rosemary Harland, Carliss for his obvious desire to involve Stevens in the murder enquiry. But there was the other deliberate involvement which had seemed to puzzle that civil servant, Fanshaw — the involvement of the rector by Vernon West. It was an interesting question — why should West want to put the finger on Peters? It was certainly what Fanshaw had implied: he'd tended to discount West's statement as it stood.

West would stand some looking into.

* * *

It was the first thing that Crow did next morning. He rang Martin, the police surgeon at Sedleigh, and asked to see him. Martin was reluctantly available at eleven-thirty so Crow checked through his notes on West and then had some coffee before walking across from Headquarters to Martin's office. The little man with the bald head, blue suit and quick, nervy hands welcomed him briefly.

'What can I do for you, Inspector?

'Give me some medical information. I want to get sorted out on heart diseases.'

'And in particular . . . ?'

'Angina pectoris.'

The little man settled back in his chair and folded his hands over the delicate paunch he had developed. He put his head on one side like a blackbird eyeing a worm.

'Not a medical diagnosis, strictly speaking. It's a name we give to a symptom, a gripping pain that starts beneath the breastbone and radiates up to the throat and jaws. Sometimes it extends over the back, and down the arms.'

'Over suddenly?'

'It reaches a climax of intensity, and then diminishes slowly. It's caused by a temporary deprivation of part of the heart muscles of an adequate supply of blood. The pain often becomes apparent under conditions in which the oxygen requirement of the muscle is greater than usual.'

'You mean when some stress occurs?'

'That's right. The pain of angina pectoris is usually brought on by effort; it tends to subside when the patient rests for a while. In the course of time, however, the effort required to produce the pain may become less.'

'What sort of effort will bring it on?'

Dr Martin put his head back and stared at the ceiling thoughtfully. His fingers played with a gold watch-chain on his waistcoat spreading across his paunch. '

'Lots of examples I could give, Inspector. Any strain or exertion making demands upon the heart muscle for blood. Running, lifting, anything really, particularly if it is abnormal in nature as far as the patient is concerned. That's not to say the strain *must* be abnormal; I've seen a case where a fatal heart-attack was brought on by the patient concerned putting on the brakes of his car.'

'One moment — I'm not clear. You've now moved to *fatal* attacks. Angina pectoris can be fatal?'

Dr Martin smiled and flicked out his watch-chain, glanced at his watch, and shook his head.

'I've described one kind of anginal pain to you. There's another, which occurs in more severe degree and is longer in duration. It arises from a sudden reduction of the heart's blood supply by a blockage of one of the coronary arteries. This cuts off the supply of oxygen to that part of the muscle affected by the block. The first angina I mentioned arises because of the increase in the heart muscle's oxygen requirement — because of the exercise, you know. The one I now speak of arises because an artery, which has already been narrowed, has been blocked by a thrombus—'

'Thrombus?'

'Blood clot. It circulates slowly through the narrowed artery—'

'How did the artery get narrowed?'

Martin glanced again at his watch. He obviously felt that it was not part of his job to give medical lectures to policemen.

'Arterial disease. The walls of the artery get thicker, rougher, more tortuous. This in turn causes layers of clotted blood to cling and further narrow the width of the passage through which the blood must flow. It slows the flow, and the slower the flow the more easily the blood clots. It's a cumulative thing. Now, Inspector I really must—'

'What's the main difference between the two kinds of angina?'

'The latter tends to be more severe, and of longer duration. It can often be preceded by attacks of angina of effort. In the latter case, if the thrombus blocks one of the main arteries, or one of the large branches, it can cause the death of the patient.'

'Immediately?'

'Quite so. In less serious cases, the occlusion does not cause immediate death but gives rise to permanent death of a part of the heart muscle — a myocardial infarct. The pain of an acute occlusion,' Martin added, rising to his feet and slipping his watch-chain firmly back into his waistcoat, 'is more severe than in an attack of angina, usually lasts until it is relieved by analgesics of a powerful kind, arises frequently at rest, is not relieved by rest and gives rise to considerable shock. I have just realised, Inspector, that I have another appointment and though I trust I've been of assistance to you I fear I shall have to terminate this interview.'

'One more question, Dr Martin: in an attack of angina when does the pain pass away?'

'It passes off as soon as the exciting cause is removed — the effort, in other words. The patient then returns to his previous condition. The pain, you see, is a symptom of a temporary functional coronary inadequacy; the deprivation of a part of the heart muscle of the necessary supply of blood. No permanent damage to the heart or arteries results from the attack. Now you really must excuse me, Inspector.'

Within minutes Crow was entering Headquarters again. He returned to his desk and sat down, took out his notebook and looked at his account of West's statements. The man had suffered angina pectoris. Angina pectoris could be caused by abnormal effort.

Such as battering a woman to death?

The problem was, Vernon West had suffered his attack *before* Rosemary Harland had died. Crow sighed. He'd have to look at the whole thing again, but right now there were other problems too. Stevens, Carliss, Redman and Svensson. He walked over to his door and called to Wilson to come in. The sergeant picked up some papers on his desk and entered.

'Have you got the statements of the Faculty heads?'

'Yes, sir. West you already know—'

'I saw to him myself. What about the others?'

'Well, they're an awkward bunch, sir. Stevens, the one who's got a crippled wife, he states that he was at home all evening. A principal lecturer in his Faculty was undertaking a duty evening and Stevens stayed in.'

'Any corroboration of his statement?'

'His wife is crippled. She was upstairs. He says she can vouch for his presence.' Wilson hesitated. 'When I spoke to Carliss, however, he asked me about Stevens, asked what story I'd been given. Carliss laughed at the idea of Mrs Stevens corroborating any story of her husband's — Carliss claims that Mrs Stevens is so heavily sedated all the time she wouldn't know her . . . well, I won't use the phrase that Carliss used, sir.'

Crow had never thought of Yorkshire men as inhibited in their speech but he'd always recognized that there were some limits beyond which Wilson would not step.

'Go on.'

'Carliss — his account of his movements includes a visit to the cinema where he claims to have been at the relevant time. He's divorced, or about to be, anyway—' Wilson pinched his nostrils at this point in the disapproval of a long-married man for another cutting free — 'and says he's nothing else to do but go to the cinema often enough. States what he saw there and—'

'I've spoken to Carliss. Get all this checked out with the cinema manager. What about Redman?'

'Funny chap. He's a bachelor and a sort of culture-vulture, sir, with books, records, paintings all cluttering up his flat, but I get the impression that he's a good, solid type who keeps very much to himself and doesn't bother anyone. I gather he was listening to a radio programme — Beethoven's Fifth — that evening and I've checked in the radio programmes published in the paper—'

'Which is what *he* could have done.'

'Oh yes, sir, but I'm inclined to believe what he says and—'

'He's a Roman Catholic isn't he?'

'That's right. He lives with his mother, but she was out at the Bingo that evening so can't corroborate his presence at home.'

'Bingo! All part of the Redman cultural background?'

Wilson smiled. 'There's culture and culture, sir.'

'Right. That brings us to Svensson.'

'It looks as though he's in the clear. He was at the Anglo- Norwegian Club for the latter part of the evening and says that there are at least three people who can vouch for the fact.'

'Check it.'

'Yes, sir.'

And that left Crow waiting for the lab report. He sent Wilson out to his own desk to check whether the report was likely to come through that afternoon and he turned up the files on the rector. He himself had interviewed Peters yesterday and had taken down the details in his notebook. Now, out of interest, he looked through the personal file held by the college on Dr Peters.

It lacked the additional comments included in the other personal files on the Faculty heads but that was quite understandable; it was Peters himself who had annotated the other files. He was unlikely to place remarks on his own. The details, therefore, were bald. Antony Peters, born in 1925, son of a wine merchant, educated at Charterhouse, service in the Royal Marines during the Second World War, mentioned in despatches in 1944. Cambridge welcomed him in 1946 and he remained there as a research fellow in 1950. A brief spell in industry — 1953 to 1957 — and then a directorship in a chemical firm, with the creation of a management consultancy firm in 1962. Six years and several moves in the business and he had stepped into the education field by serving on two Royal Commissions on Education before become Principal of a College of Technology in the Midlands. From there he had been appointed first rector of the new Burton Polytechnic.

Crow pursed his lips. Bare bones, no flesh to show what the man's desires, weaknesses, strengths might be . . . He rose and walked across to the door, opened it and waited until Wilson looked up from his desk.

'Peters, the rector at Burton. Get Records to throw up anything they can on him. Just to fill in background.'

'All right, sir. I've been on to the lab, by the way; they'll be sending up a preliminary report in ten minutes.'

That was better than he'd hoped for. This would be one occasion at least when they'd have got their skates on. Crow went along to the canteen and a got a cup of tea for himself. There was a small group of officers sitting in one corner and they eyed him uncertainly but he made no attempt to join them. He sat away from them by himself and slowly stirred his tea. He wanted solitude, chance to think. The Harlands . . .

He finished the tea and walked out of the canteen, conscious of the silence as he ambled across the room, and the eyes of the other officers watching him as he left. Time to take a look at that lab report.

'Has it arrived?'

'On your desk, right now, sir,' Wilson said.

'Come on in.'

Wilson followed Crow into his office and closed the door quietly behind him. 'You've read it?'

'Yes, sir.'

Crow picked up the sheet of blue paper and read it through quickly. He replaced it on the desk and glanced across to Wilson. He pulled thoughtfully at his long chin.

'Well, who do we go after now, Wilson?'

'Looks pretty clear, sir.'

'But not quite clear enough, I think. I'll want all the detail I can get my hands on, so you'd better get over to the newspaper offices, and the library in Bank Street; take a couple of men with you. I want everything you can dig out on this man — everything, you understand? He's been enough of a public figure to make news on occasions. So I want it all, the Debrett bit, the lot. Understand?'

'Yes, sir.'

Crow nodded to him in dismissal and Wilson went out of the room. Crow returned to the paper and read it again, more slowly.

More details, and then he'd be able to go back to the Polytechnic and ask all the questions he wanted to ask. .

He wondered whether Dr Peters would be able to provide the answers.

* * *

Mr West was certainly looking better than Joan had anticipated. It was the first time she'd been able to get away to see how he was, though she had wanted to come earlier, as soon as she'd heard he'd been taken ill. She liked Mr West: he was a good Head of Faculty and a kindly one.

There had been occasions when she had caught him looking at her in a strange way — a way which she would have described as wistful had she been asked to categorize it, but it had been in no sense disturbing. It was certainly better than the looks she sometimes got from the male members of the Social Administration department when her husband wasn't around, and nowhere near as unpleasant as the openly lecherous glances she received in the Engineering Departments when she went there for her General Studies classes. But then, everyone knew that engineers were over-sexed — a reaction from dealing in rigid metals, heat combustion engines, pistons, and other phallus-oriented machinery. Their diseased imaginations even described various joints as male and female. It would have been all quite embarrassing to anyone other than a sociologist like herself. She took all their leering in her stride and allowed the apprentices no liberties, physical or verbal, while in the engineering staff room she kept her back to the wall. That way, she knew she was safe from assault.

Men in the other Departments tended to be more subtle, but no more successful in their approaches. In the Economics and Law Department there had been the gambit of testing her out with quips and suggestive remarks. The first had been the tale about the factory girl who had been leaning out of a window calling to a friend when a fellow worker had come up behind her, pinned her down with a lowered sash and worked his will upon her, whereupon after her pregnancy was over she had made a claim to benefits under the Industrial Injuries Acts. That leering story had brought no more success than the predatory pinching of the Principal Lecturer in Thermodynamics.

But Mr West was different; he looked at her but it wasn't a leer; he spoke to her, but it was in quiet, modulated tones, not in suggestive undertones; if he touched her it was lightly, a fatherly hand on her shoulder not a secretive stroking of her buttock. She liked him. She was sorry he'd been taken ill.

'It's kind of you to call in, Mrs Lambert.'

'I came as soon as I could. I hope you're feeling a little better.'

'Oh, I am indeed.' He smiled at her, a warm, friendly smile that contained a hint of affection. 'I should be able to leave the hospital tomorrow afternoon.'

'I'm pleased it isn't serious.'

'Well, they tell me it really amounts to a warning, you know. I had two attacks; the first prostrated and frightened me and the second, fortunately, flattened me! It meant I got some enforced rest — I was unconscious most of the night. I'd virtually recovered by the next day and while they've kept me in for observation they say I should be all right — as long as I heed this warning.'

'Have you had trouble before?'

'Just once — two years ago. But I shall be all right now. I won't be back to college for a couple of weeks, I think, but no doubt the Faculty will manage without me for a while.'

'At least you'll not have to concern yourself with the students and their pressure group for the democratization of the Polytechnic!'

West raised his eyebrows and put his head back on the pillow.

'You mean they're going to try to work outside the committee structure we've been establishing?'

'I believe so. They're a bit hazy, and their views are, as usual, somewhat amorphous, but they've arranged a meeting tonight. They organized a demonstration yesterday, but it sort of fizzled out when . . . when the news about Rosemary Harland came out. It hasn't stopped them calling a meeting tonight though; I'm on my way there, as a matter of fact. I just called in to see how you were, first.'

West's eyes narrowed and he pursed his lips. He looked anxious, in a paternal way. 'Why are *you* going to the meeting?'

Joan Lambert shrugged.

'It's always seemed to me that the rift between students and the administration isn't great — it's lack of communication that's the real trouble. Language itself — it's become a trap, a maze of changed meanings as the old idea of protective authority is faced with the emerging power of individual responsibility. The students want a democratic dialogue on an equal basis: they don't want paternalism. And, let's be frank, many of our teaching staff aren't prepared to recognize that the growing political awareness of the student body is a force to be reckoned with. They're still steeped in the Victorian ethos of hierarchies — they think they know what's best for other people.'

'You sound like your thesis.'

'Well, yes, I agree that one of my reasons for going is connected with my MA thesis.' She laughed, an embarrassed, throaty sound. 'But there's more to it than that, Mr West. I feel that the students have a point, and I feel that there's a great deal of constructive bridging to be done. The only people who can do it effectively are those who are able to speak the language of both sides. In the universities, the junior dons can do it, because they're newly out of the student body themselves, and haven't yet become immersed in the traditional authoritarianism of the university structure. The junior dons in the universities can do the bridge-building.'

'And in the polytechnics, people like you.'

She hesitated, looking at him soberly for a moment, and then she nodded.

'I think so.'

West sighed and shifted his bulk into a more comfortable position.

'To some extent you're right. If academic authority had been kinder to younger staff, I'm sure the outbreaks of student violence during the last two years would not have been so strong. But you know, I tend to look at it all with a jaundiced eye. I've seen it all before. The situation is no different now from twenty, forty, a hundred years ago. The lessons of revolutionary tyrannies throughout history tend to be brushed aside. Our student radicals don't remember Stalinism, the Hungarian Revolt, they may not even remember the Bay of Pigs and Dominica. But our radicals do see communists as victims, never as executioners. And they look to Che Guevara because he means improvisation, excitement, permanent revolution, the automatic destruction of an incipient organization.' He smiled, and glanced apologetically at Joan Lambert, listening quietly. 'Still, I'm sure you don't really want to spend your time sitting here listening to the views of a man of fifty-eight; at my time of life one doesn't see or feel the same burning desires for revolution as anything other than a vast expanse of hot air. You'll want to get to your meeting.'

Joan glanced at her watch and nodded.

'I shall have to fly, in fact; my husband's got the car this evening and he's at the college with an evening class; this means I have to take the bus. They're holding the meeting at Deercliffe Hall. So I'd better be on my way; it'll take an age to get across town.'

'I'm pleased you called, Mrs Lambert.'

'I'm only sorry it had to be such a flying visit. But I'm glad you're looking so well; I look forward to seeing you back at work but not too soon, eh? Goodbye for now, Mr West.'

On a sudden impulse she leaned forward and kissed him on the cheek. When she walked out of the ward she glanced back and waved and she saw that he was touching his cheek with his fingers. She had never seen anyone looking so sad.

She had to run for the bus; she caught sight of it as she came out of the hospital gates and the bus stop was some sixty or seventy yards up the street. The conductor was a young man, however, and was only too pleased to hold the bus until she arrived, breathlessly. He took the opportunity to hold her arm, helping her aboard. She wasn't in the least surprised that when he released her his hand brushed firmly against her breast.

She sat down, fighting to regain her breath. It was a heavy evening, with storm clouds piling up, darkening the sky, and as they passed under the railway bridge the interior of the bus was quite dim. She caught her reflection in the window; her fair hair curled across her forehead, somewhat windblown. She also saw the reflection of the man across the gangway, staring at her, noting the line of her neck, the swell of her breast. In a moment he'd get to her legs and she tucked them back under the seat. They were her least attractive asset anyway, and she was woman enough to resent his leering but ensure that he saw only her better points.

There had been a time when Bill, her husband, had laughed about her legs. There had been a time when Bill had laughed. He didn't these days; not when she was around. Just where was it, the old feeling of fun and excitement that they'd felt in each other's company? Had it become eroded during the three years they'd been man and wife, by the fact of their working together in the same establishment? Or was it simply that it had been part of the general corrosion of their marriage, where they saw less and less of each other, took fewer opportunities to be together, expanded their own personal interests and ignored the mutual pleasures they'd once enjoyed.

Even the basic mutual pleasure.

Perhaps it had been her fault. But she didn't think so. The honeymoon had been a disaster and Bill had been clumsy, brutal almost in his insistence. Even so, that was no excuse. In two years she should have been able to uncurl, defrost her emotions, enjoy sexual relations as she understood they should be enjoyed. It was a laugh, really; a sociologist, an observer of social *mores,* a commentator upon taboos, and desires, and motivations, and social institutions, she was all of these and yet the one basic institution to which she belonged was crumbling and the one basic desire she should enjoy was repulsive to her. Marriage and sex, disasters both.

Time to get off the bus.

In every sense, she thought grimly to herself as she walked down the street towards Deercliffe Hall. Students trickled in through the wide doors ahead of her and she dawdled for a few minutes on the steps; she didn't want to take up a too prominent position in the hall, otherwise her presence might become too obvious, and wrongful inferences drawn. She also wanted to choose her own spot at the back of the hall, where she could see everything that was going on — and avoid being too near any of her own students, who had made enough leering promises in the classroom to cause her to proceed with caution outside it. It was the penalty she paid for being five feet three inches tall and built upon lines which, she candidly admitted to herself, could easily become of a type described as overblown by the time she was thirty if she didn't take care of her figure. She intended taking care of her figure. And she intended to take care of her chastity.

Joan Lambert might look the roll-in-the-hay type but she wasn't. And that was that.

Someone was already speaking on the platform by the time she entered the hall as unobtrusively as possible. She found a chair for herself near the back, on the left-hand side, and sat down. There were about two hundred students present; it was a good turnout and she was somewhat surprised: militancy must be in the air, for this comprised a tenth of the student population. The young man on the platform was red of face and hair. He was punching a fist in the air to emphasize the points he was making. She recognized him, a young man called Rhodes, a member of the student committee, and a character who saw himself as an emergent revolutionary.

'Attempts to give workers a voice in administration are just subtle techniques by which tyranny hides its face and lulls its victims into a sense of euphoria in unhappiness. Technology cannot be isolated from the use to which it is put; the technological society is a system of domination which operates in the concept and construction of techniques. Technology cannot, therefore, be neutral.'

Joan smiled. Old hat; Neufeld had said it before him. But then, what hadn't been said before? She let her attention wander and stared about her. There was the usual motley collection of outlandish clothing, the usual unwashed females with wild, frizzed-out hair. She wondered what they felt they achieved by it: perhaps radical appearances were the new conformity for radical viewpoints. A question of drawing attention.

Rhodes had relinquished the microphone.

A succession of other, less fluent speakers followed, each shouting their own particular brand of anarchy. It was all so conventional, all so flattening. Joan began to wish that she hadn't come. There had been little else to do, on the other hand; she'd already ironed Bill's shirt for tomorrow, and he had a clean pair of socks on today. Her lessons were prepared and though she could have spent a little time on her notes for the lecture on the Family she supposed there had been little harm . . .

Her attention was directed back towards the platform. Something was happening in the hall. The young man behind the microphone was still talking, still struggling to retain the attention of his audience but it was a lost cause. Ripples ran through the front rows, murmurs of excitement and heads began to turn. A few voices rose, and some feet thumped on the floor. The few, straggling feet became a thunder that spread throughout the hall and became rhythmic, swelling violently to a crescendo and backed by a punctuation of hand clapping, urgent, insistent, demanding. At first she couldn't catch the chanting slogan, couldn't pick up the words.

Word.

Just one word, one word repeated, over and over. A magic word, a word of compulsion, and excitement. A word, a name.

'SAD-RUDD-IN!! SAD-RUDD-IN!'

The mindless, primitive sound rolled around the hall, echoed in confused eddies from the walls, pounded in the eardrums and it was like a drug in its effect. Joan felt the physical excitement of the name, became aware of something happening to her legs and her stomach and her chest and she sat up straight, craning to see the platform, and the name changed to a roar, a sweeping sound, animal in its intonation.

He was there, standing up. One clenched fist was raised. Sadruddin.

She had seen him before, on a number of occasions, but she'd never spoken to him. She had seen the way girls looked at him at the college; she had seen the little entourage which followed him, dogging his footsteps. He was Sadruddin, the firebrand, the student leader, the spokesman for the radical mass, the left-wingers, and the progressives.

For her his emergence upon the platform was a sociological revelation. She had watched student disturbances, and student debates; she had observed their formlessness, the swirling incongruity of their ideas, their slogan-chanting, their opposition to freedom of speech, the incompatibility of splinter groups aiming for the same goal. She had seen logic shouted down, common sense derided; she had seen the death of debate and the phoenix of mass violence arising from its immolation.

Always, hero-worship had been out.

The individuals had existed but they had always fought through spattering abuse, the expulsion of hecklers, the hurling of verbal stones. It had always been a case of the strongest conquering; the group with the greatest support won through by virtue of that support. But it wasn't that way here. Sadruddin was alone. There were no splinter groups. There was no heckling, no verbal abuse, no chanting of slogans.

They listened. They *all* listened. And they roared on those occasions when they were invited to roar. They applauded when called upon to applaud. They bayed like dogs when the quarry was pointed out.

'We all know marching doesn't achieve anything. We all know the sit-in gets us nowhere. People still get burned with napalm and germ warfare still flourishes because of the insensitivity of tiny administrative minds. But throw paint over a politician, get the action condemned by the Student Union, *that* receives attention from everyone and the columns of coverage in the newspapers, the hours the broadcasting authorities devote to discuss the phenomenon of student violence, all show us the way to power!'

He was saying little that was new; his words were words that had been used everywhere, for years. But the way he said them held his audiences captive and more: it sent nervous ripples of enthusiasm shuddering through the serried ranks of students. It electrified the atmosphere. He stood there, slight, dark, his teeth flashing white against his skin and she recognized the animal attraction he exuded in his deep, stabbing voice.

'The student body is an elite — the role of this elite is quite different from that of the revolutionary vanguard in traditional communism. Its role is to agitate and provoke the system until it reveals its true repressive and totalitarian nature. It will do this, eventually, by unleashing the police. Here, at this college, it came near to it yesterday. But the time for us was not ripe. When it is, when we provoke to the proper degree, then will these forces be unleashed against us and that very action will awaken more and more people, who will see that they are being hoodwinked and manipulated. Only in this way will there at last arise a spontaneous revolution.'

He was propounding a traditional philosophical justification for the deliberate provocation of the police and yet his audience was accepting his propositions with delight, with howling applause as though he delivered wisdom from heaven. Groups rose to their feet shaking their hands above their heads, calling to their new apostle.

A man with dark, shining hair swept back; a man whose white shirt, carelessly rolled back from his wrists, was open to the waist and stained with sweat, whose faded blue slacks clung to his thighs and calves, outlining them against the black cloth of the dais, whose rope sandals stamped against the boards with the vehemence of his words.

He was holding out his arms for silence, and it fell, suddenly and completely. There was an inexplicable tension in the room as Sadruddin stood there, and slowly drew from the pocket of his jeans a folded sheet of paper. His voice was low now, and his audience strained to catch his words.

'But all this is overshadowed by a new danger — and the evidence is here in my hand. Here — here I have proof that the administration of Burton has become so enmeshed with the power politics of the consumer capitalist society that it is actively twisting the purpose of the polytechnic and threatening its integrity. as an academic institution. The academic body itself is exhibiting a mere accommodation to the system — either that, or it is paralysed by fear of loss of employment.'

He waved the paper and a dangerous rumbling came from his audience, as he demanded action of them.

'They will say there is an organized conspiracy behind us, throughout the world, but they are blind. Do they not see we are simply all affected by the same issues? War in Vietnam, racial discrimination, consensus politics, an overstrained educational system; all these, and now, here, the attempted manipulation of academic administration and the prostitution of academic integrity by the forces of big business.'

Magnetism; a sheer animal magnetism and it stamped the hall into fervour, an unquestioning, roaring fervour that was almost frightening. She had seen old pre-war films of similar situations, on a larger scale, but film could not convey the physical side of it all, the sheer twisting of the stomach, the quivering of the thighs.

Her thighs were quivering too, as she stared at Sadruddin.

And suddenly it was over. The noise became fragmented, hands were raised and counted, a roar came for a vote, men swarmed to the platform, a few shrieks from over-excited females caused laughter and more shouting, and then students were jostling their way out of the entrance. Joan Lambert left her chair and stood against the wall. Her mouth was suddenly dry. She stood there quietly and waited, and the crowd thinned. No one took any notice of her. Until the last small group came up, the platform group, eight men and one woman talking and laughing. Joan Lambert stepped back into the shadow of a pillar but one pair of eyes saw her, dark, predatory eyes.

Then they had gone, and she was alone in Deercliffe Hall with the fetid air and the litter of paper and in a few minutes the caretakers would be around, sweeping up, putting out the lights. She walked slowly towards the door.

He was standing just outside, at the top of the steps. He was alone. 'Mrs Lambert?'

She hesitated.

'You know my name.'

'*You* know *mine.*'

'I could hardly fail to do so, the way it's been shouted tonight.'

'I suspect you knew it before. As I've known yours. I've seen you at the college; I asked your name.'

Her legs were quivering and her stomach muscles jumped spasmodically. She lowered her head, as though to hide her eyes from him. He put out a hand.

'This way.'

'What do you mean?'

'You have to travel across town. The buses will be full this evening, all the students returning home. They might even be somewhat boisterous. I'm offering you a lift.'

He smiled as he said it and he took her hand. She could not be sure that she didn't offer it. They were walking down the steps. She tried to overcome her nervousness by laughing at it.

'You have a car? That's a bourgeois possession for a radical like you, isn't it?'

'Everyone must accept the modern world, take it for what it is, reject some of its values — but the horseless carriage, now, that's a necessity.'

It was an old car, and the passenger seat sagged. She laughed again but her thighs were still quivering.

They drove across town and she was aware of the sheen of his dark arm under the lights of the street lamps, the curve of his muscled thigh as it almost touched hers. She tried to use words and thoughts to overcome her shaking body.

'I can't say that your ideas on the platform were world-shattering in their originality.'

'Truth is as old as the sun.'

'And to advocate violence — what's that got to do with the democratization of academic committees at Burton?'

'A quick end to discussion. That's all. I believe there is a natural right of resistance for oppressed and overpowered minorities to use extra-legal means if the legal ones have proved inadequate. If we use violence we do not start a new chain of violence; we simply try to break one already established.'

'Marcuse already said that in his *Repressive Tolerance*. '

'Does reiteration make it any less the truth?'

She made no reply. They had been driving west and had left the street lights behind. He had moved away from the town and the road was narrowing. This was not the way to her home, but she made no reference to this. Instead, she asked him about the paper he had waved to the meeting.

'It's a letter, written to the rector, by someone in the employ of Sir Humphrey Elliot.'

'The engineering magnate?'

'Right. He's reporting to the rector on various matters arising in a speech I gave last month.'

'I don't understand. Why should a businessman employ—'

'A spy?' Sadruddin sneered. 'You know Dr Peters has planned his polytechnic to be a "forward-looking institution" with close ties with industry and commerce, employing advanced methods of business management. Look at the Chairs that Sir Humphrey has endowed. No doubt he wants to ensure that his money is well spent.'

'That's what you meant in your speech about business interests destroying academic integrity?'

'Yes. And since you people won't act, it's up to the students to defend the intellectual integrity of the college.'

'You think the academic staff should support you,' she said slowly.

'You should, instead of clucking your tongues and shaking your heads. The capitalist society is destroying intellectual truth in Burton. By your silence you assist in that destruction.'

They said no more. The darkness of open moorland stretched around them and she could no longer ignore the significance of the route he had taken, nor the significance of her own lack of protest. She did not ask herself why she had failed to protest for the evidence and the answer lay in the physical state in which she found herself. She sat still and her heart was pounding and she could not control the quivering of her legs; her stomach felt weak, a lassitude stole over her body and breathing was suddenly difficult. He stopped the car under some tall black trees, turned off the engine, and the warm darkness rushed in on them. He turned to look at her. His hand touched her shoulder.

'No!' she said in a gasping voice.

He moved and his thigh was pressing against hers, his arms going around her. 'When I see what I saw in your eyes tonight, in that hall,' he said in a quiet, hard voice, 'I *know!*'

He was kissing her. The weakness was spreading throughout the whole of her body and she was shaking uncontrollably. She tried to break free but he was strong, and his arms were hard against her body. She was aware of the faint odour of his sweat-stained shirt as he pressed close to her and his knees forced her own apart, painfully, as she struggled against him. And then it was as though she was dropping into a well as any thought of resistance fell away; her body opened to him and she no longer fought.

There was the close darkness, the sound of his panting breath and she did everything he wanted, everything he asked, everything he demanded, and she was shaken by his strength and his urgent persistence and she was lying across the back seat and it had never been like this with Bill, never . . . never . . . never . . . as she shuddered into darkness, a vast, pulsating, driving darkness that ended in a peak of violence.

Then, there was only the drifting.

* * *

Chief Inspector Crow took most of the morning to familiarize himself with the details that Wilson and the two constables had provided on Peters. He wasn't sure yet just how much of it was going to be useful, but that was something you couldn't ever be sure of anyway. When you started probing, needling at a man, there were admissions he would make and some he would not; there'd be incidents he'd recall to mind, and some he'd hesitate over; there'd be names he'd remember, and some he'd insist on forgetting. But Crow needed them all, the facts, the incidents, the names. Their importance was something he couldn't yet calculate; their relative importance would emerge, he hoped, when he spoke to Dr Antony Peters.

'Wilson, get the squad car laid on. I'll want you to come with me to Burton, and I'll want you in the room while I question Peters.'

Wilson bustled away. Crow gathered up his notes and pushed them into a folder along with the lab report on Rosemary Harland. They were still preliminary findings but they were explosive enough to warrant his attempt to press Antony Peters.

When the squad car arrived Crow stumbled moodily into the back seat and remained silent throughout the drive. Wilson looked back twice, as though he were about to say something but on each occasion thought better of it and remained silent. There were few students about when the car swept on to the campus.

An attendant directed them to the places reserved for visitors. He had been conspicuously absent the last time they'd arrived. Crow respected his judgment; any uniforms could have been roughly handled on that morning once the police cars had shown up at Burton. But this morning there wasn't going to be any trouble. As Crow got out of his seat he lurched uncomfortably against the door of a family saloon parked next to the police car. He raised his eyebrows when he saw what was placed on the back seat: a black briefcase with gold embossing. Fanshaw was already here at Burton.

Crow ambled up the steps of the Administration building with Wilson just behind him. When they entered

73

the hall it was to see Robert Fanshaw engaged in conversation with a member of the teaching staff. Crow stopped near them as Wilson unobtrusively slipped away, briefcase under arm, to tell the rector's secretary that they were on the way. The Inspector's face was solemn.

'Here again, Mr Fanshaw?'

Fanshaw smiled and inclined his elegant grey head.

'Good morning, Inspector. I'm just on my way out, as a matter of fact.'

'Was it curiosity or business that brought you?'

'You're not conversant with the task of Her Majesty's Inspectorate, Inspector Crow. Our business is *based* on curiosity.'

'But not about murder.'

'As you say. The organization and management of a college and the teaching standards and innovations within it — these things are more our concern. Murder we leave to you. Er . . . have you established any . . . er . . . leads yet?'

Crow smiled gravely.

'As you say, Mr Fanshaw, that you must leave to us.'

Wilson was waiting with the rector's secretary at the door to Peters's office. He stood aside to allow Crow to enter the room first as she opened the door for them. Peters was rising from behind his desk to greet them as they came into the room.

'Good morning, gentlemen. Have you had coffee yet? Margaret, could you bring in three cups? And perhaps arrange for lunch for—'

'We won't be staying to lunch. And this isn't a social occasion. No coffee.'

Crow's tone was deliberately curt; without waiting for an invitation he took an upright chair from its station against the far wall, brought it near to Peters's desk and sat down. After a moment's hesitation Peters went back behind his desk and sat down also; Wilson took an easy chair to Crow's left and opened the briefcase that he carried, without bringing it up onto his knees.

Antony Peters settled back in his leather chair, swinging slightly from side to side. Crow stared at him, quietly, observing the man. The greying hair was carefully parted, the sideburns full but neatly edged and trimmed. The rector was a man who liked the sun; this was evident from the light tan he sported, and the backs of his hands were brown against the white cuffs of his shirt. A thumb and one finger caressed his square, positive chin while the other hand gently stroked the dark brown tie that so well matched his suit. Crow was aware of both gestures and wondered whether they were habitual or occasioned by a slight nervousness. Peters had been nervous the last time his office had been invaded by the police but perhaps that had been a natural reaction to the news of the murder of his secretary. Now . . .

'Have you managed to obtain any further information?'

There was something lying at the back of Peters's eyes, lurking, careful, watchful. He seemed calm enough at the moment apart from his gestures, but there was something in his glance that denoted wariness and it interested Crow. It decided things for him. He could have come straight out with what he had but now he knew what he was going to do. He was going to watch those eyes, watch whether what was lurking there would leap forth, in fear, or excitement, in panic or desperation. A slow probing was called for; Peters would have to be subjected to a sifting of the sands of his past.

'We do have a few things to help us in our investigation, but I'd like to leave those on one side for a moment. First of all I want you to tell me all about yourself, Dr Peters.'

The glance was evasive, the smile deprecating, the stroking gesture unaffected.

'Tell you about me? I hardly think there's much about me that can be regarded as relevant to this investigation.'

'That's for us to decide.'

'Yes, but surely—'

'One moment.' Crow's voice was sharp and cold as an ice-splinter. 'Let's get one thing straight. If you persist in a coy denial that your life and success story has nothing to do with this affair the only result is that I'll be here rather longer than I want to be, or need to be. The quicker the better. I've got a dossier on you, I just want the facts confirmed and we can go on from there. All right?'

Peters didn't like it. He didn't like being spoken to so sharply and he didn't like the assumption being made that his life story could have any effect upon the murder investigation. Yet he capitulated at once and this in itself gave Crow some food for thought. Peters shrugged.

'Well, all right, you've got a task to fulfil I suppose. I'll do as you say. I took this job here at Burton when the Polytechnic was established two years ago. You'll be aware, of course, that this was an additional college to the thirty or so that were originally designated—'

'One moment, please. Don't let's start with the job here. Let's go back earlier.'

'Earlier? But how far back do you want to go.'

'Twenty years?'

Peters licked his lips and stopped swinging the chair. He gave a short bark that affected amusement and passed for a laugh.

'I can see you're determined to be bored, Inspector, and though I can't see the point of it all I'll do as you suggest. Like most men, I am not averse to talking about myself. Now let me see, twenty years. . . I was about twenty-five then. Yes, well, I'd taken up an offer of research fellowship at Cambridge. I was involved in some work in the electronic engineering field — I won't bore you with the details unless you are passionately interested, but I spent three very pleasant years there. Towards the end of that time, late in 1952 I think it was, I made the acquaintance of Sir Steven Humphreys, who was director of an engineering company in Rugby and he offered me a post—'

'You had already done some work for them?'

'Well, yes, I had in a way. Part of the findings from my research project had a direct bearing on the work done at the plant and they asked me to do a bit of liaison work with their own people. I did this and—'

'Did you get paid for it?'

'Paid? Well, yes, I believe I did but I don't see—'

'Did that have anything to do with your leaving Cambridge and working for Humphreys?'

The hand had stopped stroking the tie; it remained still, pressing lightly against the lapel of his jacket.

'I don't understand what you're getting at, Inspector.'

The voice was dangerously controlled. 'I'm not getting at anything. I'm not inferring anything. And if you're wondering about libel actions, forget it. I'm just presenting facts to you. A research project at Cambridge, but no publication of research findings. A contact with Humphreys. A job with Humphreys. Where's the linking factor?'

'Your tone of voice suggests there is something improper in the facts you've stated.'

'It depends what you mean by improper.'

Peters was staring fixedly at the papers in Crow's lap. His expression quite clearly illustrated that he would have been more than pleased to read their contents. He sighed.

'You would seem to have researched *me* very carefully. I don't know why. But all right, I'll not spin this thing out longer than necessary. I'll say what you want me to say. I was involved in a research project at Cambridge; I was paid by the University; I made certain findings which were of interest to Sir Steven and made his acquaintance; I turned those findings over to his people; I later joined the firm and worked with his researchers. There's nothing illegal, or even unethical in all that.'

'The University didn't like it.'

'Understandably. But then, they just wanted an academic research paper, giving the findings to the world of science. It seemed more sensible to me to turn the facts over to Sir Steven.'

'Sensible . . . and profitable?'

Peters met Crow's glance calmly. He flicked his fingers, accepting the point contemptuously.

'If you say so. Yes, all right, I handed the findings over to Sir Steven and he paid me more than the University could do and he gave me a job also. But I really would like to know what this has to do with the murder of Rosemary Harland.'

Crow consulted the notes on his lap. 'Perhaps nothing but we'll come to that later. So you joined Humphreys. What then?'

'I stayed with him for three years. Then I left the firm and became director of a chemical firm. After that—'

'Wait a minute. You were with him four, not three years.'

'I believe you're right,' Peters replied in a mocking tone. 'But then, you have the facts before you. I just have my memory.'

'We won't leave Humphreys just yet, if you don't mind. That four years span — did it see the firm expanding?'

'Somewhat.'

'How did you leave it?'

'I don't understand.'

'How did you leave it — in a blaze of glory, or like a sinking ship?'

There was a short silence and Peters's jaw was stiff, his mouth set in a grim line. Wilson sat stolidly in his chair. He knew what Crow's tactics were: unsettle Peters with a brutal directness and let anger and anxiety lead the man into admissions. Peters leaned forward and placed both hands on the desk in front of him.

'I can't say that I care for the tone in your voice—'

'The inference, you mean, not the tone. You did, though, didn't you — you did leave the ship sinking, like a fleeing rat? Isn't it true that Humphreys was in liquidation within a year of your leaving him?'

'That's so, but it had nothing to do with me. I had a good offer from—'

'From Eugene Garland, head of Munson Chemicals, I know; it's here. Let me tell you what else is here. In 1956 management consultants were called in to the Humphreys firm and they recommended certain changes; some of these were of a confidential nature and involved the development of a new computerized purchasing, distribution and sales system. Humphreys never installed that system, because the necessary program had been written by an American organization and it was bought and killed by a rival firm, who then put the squeeze on Humphreys and within a year forced him into liquidation.'

'I think you have the facts about right,' he said quietly. 'But this is all a matter of public record.'

'That's right. It's also a matter of record that when you left Humphreys you took the offer of a directorship in the chemical firm Munson Chemicals, Ltd. A big firm?'

'Big enough.'

'Salary of seven and half thousand.'

'Also a few perks — *that* won't appear in the record.'

The chair had begun to swing again, gently, and the fingers caressed the thin lips. Peters peered at Crow with narrowed eyes.

'You were doing well. But tell me this. What was the name of the rival firm that squeezed out Humphreys?'

'I suspect,' Peters said in a cold voice, 'that particular information is already in your possession. But I'll play your game. It was a firm called International Electronics, Ltd.'

'Yes. And can you tell me who owned Munson Chemicals?'

There was a fractional hesitation before Peters replied.

'I'm not sure whether I understand your question. The shareholders would not be known to—'

'I'd appreciate a straight answer. You know perfectly well that seventy per cent of the equity in Munson Chemicals was owned by another company. And that company was Continental Industries Ltd.'

'So?'

Crow smiled, but it was an unpleasant smile with an edge of distaste.

'Continental Industries is a holding company — it does not undertake any business in its own right at all. It owns a number of other trading companies, one of which is Munson Chemicals. Another of its subsidiaries is none other than International Electronics!'

Peters raised his head, staring vacantly past Crow's long face to the blank doorway. His hands were still on the desk, but there was a pinched look about his nostrils now, and he swallowed, twice, before he spoke.

'I seem to remember a scurrilous article being written some years ago—'

'Yes. It's from that article I got most of this information. But it didn't name names, of course, or people might have been forced to sue. I say *forced*, because they wouldn't really have *wanted* to sue, would they, Dr Peters?'

The rector was silent.

'All right, let's get on then, let's draw our conclusions from all this. Humphreys is in business but needs sales and distribution reorganization if he's to keep his share of the market. The program he needs to keep solvent is bought up by International Electronics and Humphreys goes bust. An employee of Humphreys enters the employment of Munson Chemicals shortly before the blow-up. Both Munson Chemicals and International Electronics are subsidiaries of Continental Industries, Ltd. The inference? Maybe that the employee in question gave some useful information to International Electronics — information which enabled them to squeeze out Humphreys, their rival. That employee couldn't be rewarded with a job in International Electronics, for then the whole thing would smell; instead, he could be given a job with a firm, another subsidiary in the group owned by Continental Industries. Now, just how *did* you get your directorship in Munson Chemicals, Dr Peters?'

The rector shook his head. His face was expressionless as he rose, walked across to the window and stared out across the campus. His shoulders were set firm, his back arrogantly, confidently stiff.

'All these innuendoes, these inferences you draw and try to attribute to me, Inspector, I don't see what you're driving at. I deny that there's any truth in it at all, but then, I don't need to deny anything really because you're not investigating my past. You're investigating the murder of Rosemary Harland.'

'Mm. I thought you wouldn't take exception to my remarks. I thought you wouldn't have the courage even to *threaten* suing me for slander.'

Peters whirled angrily from the window.

His face was suffused with an anger that up till now he had carefully controlled.

'What the hell do you mean by that! Are you trying to say that I'm afraid to challenge the imputations, the slanderous imputations you make?'

'Aren't you?' Crow's tone was cool and he stared at Peters with contempt. 'You've too much to lose, haven't you? That's why you never attacked the writer of this article in 1964.'

Peters hesitated for a moment, then crossed to his desk and reached for the telephone.

'I think it's time I contacted my solicitor.'

Crow nodded casually, stroking his lugubrious chin.

'I wondered whether you'd get around to that soon. This article I speak of, it was written about a year after you got married wasn't it? But about *three* years after you *first* got engaged, isn't that so?'

The hand clamped on the telephone made no attempt to lift it from the receiver. Peters stared at Crow; he remained quite still for a moment and then in a strangled voice he said,

'Make no attempt to involve my wife in this, Crow-I'll have your hide, if you do!'

'Friends in high places?' Crow laughed openly. 'Don't you realise they don't count for much when a murder investigation is in the wind? They won't want to *know* you, Dr Peters, when that becomes apparent.'

'You've got nothing to link me with Miss Harland's death.'

Crow's eyes were fixed on the whitening knuckles above the fingers grasping the telephone. After a short silence Peters noted the direction of Crow's gaze and reluctantly he released the telephone and sat down. Crow bent over his notes.

'You married Miss Sarah Fine-Jensen in 1963. You were engaged to her in the summer of 1962. You obtained several directorships after your engagement and you started a management consultancy firm — with money and backing from Sir William Fine-Jensen, who was only too keen to look after the financial interests of his son-in-law. He's not too well these days, I understand. How old is he now, eighty? Time gets on . . .'

Peters sat rigidly behind his desk. There was an open animosity in his eyes now, but the other things were there too, the wariness, the watchfulness, the lurking fear. For that was what it was, Crow could see now; fear. Crow still needed to discover what prompted it, which of the needles he had slipped into the man had caused the fear to be displayed nakedly in this way.

'Yes . . . you married Miss Sarah in 1963 after what might be described in her circles as a whirlwind courtship. The chinless wonders usually take longer than you did, but then you had some good red blood didn't you? Red blood, and a burning desire to get on in the world, fast, and you had experience too. Experience of women, I mean. For your engagement to Miss Sarah in 1962 — it wasn't the first time you'd been engaged, was it?'

'Crow—'

'You'd been engaged once before, about eight months before you hooked Miss Sarah Fine-Jensen! You'd been engaged to another girl, a Miss Valerie White. What happened to *that* lady, eh? Not enough money? Not enough prospects? What happened to her, eh, what happened to her?'

Antony Peters had turned white. He stood upright again and the violence of his movement sent the chair rocking backwards, swinging wildly. His teeth were clenched and the look he directed towards the police inspector was compounded of anger and hatred. His voice was thick and his tone nasal.

'I'll tell you what happened, Crow! I'll tell you exactly what happened! Valerie was killed, do you understand? She was in a car, stalled on a railway crossing, and she was hit by an express train travelling at almost ninety miles an hour! Now, is that what you wanted to hear? Well, *is it?*'

Wilson sat very stiffly in his chair and Crow was silent. He had received an answer, but not the one he had expected and momentarily it reversed their roles, with Peters as the aggressor. And with reason, perhaps. But Crow could not allow the flicker of sympathy he felt for the rector to blind him to the other facts in his possession, to make him hold back from his questions. Doggedly he went on, refusing to acknowledge the sickness that rose to his throat.

'No. It isn't what I wanted to hear. I wanted to hear you'd thrown her over in favour of a better prospect.'

Peters was still standing and he was stiff with indignation; his fingers were reaching for the telephone again.

'I'll have your skin for this, Crow.' His tone was scored with a sudden malevolence. 'I'll have you stripped of your rank.'

'No you won't. You'll have too much explaining to do. Too much explaining about Rosemary Harland.'

Again the hand wavered over the telephone; yet again it was withdrawn. There was a break in Peters's voice when he spoke. 'What the hell are you getting at?'

'Perhaps it's time I began to put some of my cards on the table. I've been delving into your background for a reason, Dr Peters, a reason connected with this investigation into the girl's death. And what do I find? I find a man who would seem to have an impeccable background but who would also seem to have used strange methods to get where he is. A man who's always had an eye for the main chance; a man who gave up academic honours for cash; who sold out to a higher bidder when the market hotted up, and got a directorship for his betrayal; a man who used his position as the son-in-law of a wealthy industrialist to burrow into respectable fields of endeavour — education, where he could earn pin-money and have a great deal of community respect and perhaps one day even make the House of Lords as a solid citizen! Oh yes, I know why you used Fine-Jensen to push you onto Royal Commissions. You and your wife, you'll have more money than you can use once the old man's dead. You've never been keen on industry, but education — that's another matter! A backwater, free from strife, plenty of delegation to the people who'll do the real work. What'll be next? Vice-Chancellor of a University — or the House of Lords, as I suggested?'

'Crow—'

'No, let me finish! The shadows I saw in the past, the Munson Chemicals, the Cambridge affair—'

'You can't prove any of that; it's just not true!'

'I wouldn't have to *prove* it — that's why you never sued the writer of that article in 1964. Proof is irrelevant, for a mere slander action in court would be enough to make some of the smears stick and that's the sort of publicity you wouldn't want. And the girl, too, the girl you were once engaged to, you wouldn't want that to become common knowledge because it wouldn't suit your image.'

'There was nothing in that . . . situation that reflected any discredit on me.'

Peters passed a hand over his forehead and ran a finger down one side of his nose. He was blinking and frowning, as though troubled with something. Crow made no allowance for the man's distress, but pressed on ruthlessly.

'All these questions, these shadows from your past, they helped me build up a picture of a man who wanted to climb in the world, and who had done so. A man who had an eye for the main chance, who was prepared to do what he felt necessary in order to achieve what he wanted. And now he's got it: a splendid marriage, money behind him, an academic post of distinction — and I ask myself what would he do if it were all threatened? To what lengths would he go if the whole edifice around him were in danger of crumbling?'

'I don't understand what you mean.'

Peters's voice was thick and strangled. He turned away from his desk and stumbled past Wilson's chair as the sergeant rose, looking towards Crow. The detective-inspector rose to his feet also, doggedly, his glance staying on Peters's white face.

'And why did I ask these questions? I'll tell you, Peters, after you tell me where you were the night Rosemary Harland died.'

Peters had his hands on a water jug.

Crow's last words were followed by a rattling, clinking noise: an involuntary shaking of Peters's hand caused the

85

jug to clatter against the metal tray. He turned an ashen face towards Crow.

'I've already told you! I left the college here at about eight-forty. I drove home—'

'And didn't arrive until eleven-fifteen.'

'But I explained to you! I had a flat tyre. I tried to change the wheel, but the nuts were too tight and it took me over an hour to get the damn thing done. I shoved the deflated tyre into the back and then drove home, after stopping for a drink and wash-up in the Blue Anchor.'

'Your story's been checked, Dr Peters. That deflated tyre — there was no gash, no hole in it. The publican of the Blue Anchor, well, he saw you, but not until ten forty-five. He doesn't remember you appearing at all dirty or unkempt.'

'I'd washed by then, and was having a drink.' Peters's voice had risen a key in protest and he passed a hand across his forehead again as though brushing away cobwebs of uncertainty. 'But I don't in any case understand why you should be bringing all this up again.'

He turned his back to Crow and poured himself a glassful of water. Crow watched him impassively, waited until the rector walked back across to the desk and sat down. Then Crow said in a level and expressionless tone:

'Your story as to your whereabouts sounds thin. Your background shows you might well take desperate measures to achieve your ends. You might even get very dangerous if your life's ambitions were threatened.'

'Threatened?' Peters shook his head contemptuously and opened the drawer in front of him. 'I don't understand. What threat was being made, and who was making it?'

'Rosemary Harland?'

Peters had taken a small white box from the drawer. Now in the act of opening it he stopped, staring at Crow with a mouth slack with surprise.

'You must be mad!'

'I've now had a preliminary lab report on the girl, and on her clothing, and on an article which was found in the college. Have you seen this before?'

Crow gestured towards Wilson and the sergeant pulled out of the briefcase a man's driving glove, leather-backed, string-faced. Peters stared at it. He made no reply.

'Miss Harland,' Crow said harshly, 'wore make-up, a foundation cream which she had applied to her face and throat. The lab report tells me that there are traces of a similar cream impregnating the string of that glove. It is suggested that the killer of Rosemary Harland, the man who killed her, wore that glove.' He paused, weighing his words carefully, and watching Peters's face. 'I have reason to believe that this glove belongs to you.'

Peters began to shake his head slowly.

Crow forestalled his next words.

'We found its companion in the glove compartment of your car.'

Peters was still staring at the glove in Wilson's hand. His face was grey, his breathing difficult and there was a pained frown on his face. Almost automatically he fumbled in the little box with a forefinger and thumb.

'Just because that glove belongs to me, you can't—'

'The glove is yours, and your whereabouts at the relevant time, the time she died, are unsubstantiated.'

'But there's no reason, no reason on earth why I should want to kill her.'

'The lab report points out two more things. The first is that she died of a broken neck and a skull injury caused by a heavy blow on the side of the head. She didn't die in the lift, she was dragged there.'

'All right, all right, but I don't see why or how you connect this with me!'

'You're a married man; your wife and your father-in-law are rich; you hold an eminent position in the community; you had a great deal to lose. Rosemary Harland was your secretary.' Crow paused reflectively.

'The lab report also tells me that Rosemary Harland was pregnant.'

'What!'

Peters stood up slowly, his amazed glance travelling from Crow to Wilson and back again. Then he was suddenly smiling, but it was a mirthless, death's-head grimace that lacked humour or joy.

'You're mad! Mad! You're actually suggesting that I seduced my secretary, got her pregnant, and then murdered her to keep the whole thing quiet.' A spasm of annoyance crossed his features and he brushed the back of his hand against his nose again.

'Something like that, sir,' Crow said quietly.

Peters gave him a look that should have shrivelled him on the spot but Crow had received worse and survived. There was a moment's silence, then Peters reached for the telephone, for the third time. This time he picked it up.

'Margaret? Get me Mr Andrews, of Andrews, Martin and Sweet. As soon as you can.'

He replaced the telephone and glared at Crow, his eyes brilliant with dislike.

'I should have done that as soon as you came bursting in here. I've telephoned for my solicitor.'

'That's your privilege, sir. I take it you're not prepared to make any answer to the questions I raise?'

'They're so damned silly they won't need answering,' Peters replied with spirit, taking a small capsule from the box in his hand and reaching for the glass of water. 'I tell you, Crow, I'll break you into little pieces for this, for the things you've said to me in here this morning.'

He shot a malignant, triumphant glance towards the detective-inspector, sipped at the glass of water, swallowed and then placed the capsule angrily in his mouth, clamping down on it. He was raising the glass to his mouth a second time when he suddenly choked, gasped, and with a strangled exclamation threw the glass away from his lips. It shattered on the table edge, showering water over the carpet. Peters gave a hissing, throaty sound.

Next moment he fell forward across his broad polished desk, one hand clutching at his mouth.

Chapter 3

He was spitting violently and crying out in pain. Wilson was already leaping forward and he reached Peters before Crow could stumble to his feet. Wilson was grabbing at Peters's face and twisting his head around as the remains of the half-bitten capsule were ejected on the desk.

'Burning of the mouth,' Wilson said urgently. 'Corrosive poison of some sort.'

'An emetic?'

'For God's sake no, sir! Salt, in water.'

He was pushing Peters back into a chair, and Crow rushed to the door, shouting to the girl to get as much salt as she could, and quickly. He returned to Peters and Wilson; the rector lay back in his seat, moaning, and Crow saw the staining around his mouth. He glanced at Wilson and the sergeant shook his head quietly.

'Not serious, sir. Nasty burns, but I don't think he's really swallowed any of the stuff.' Peters was glaring at them both and holding his mouth wide open as though seeking air to cool the burns that he had suffered inside his lips. Crow leaned across the desk and looked at the small capsule lying on the blotter. It had been half-bitten through and some of the contents must have caused the burning of the rector's mouth. He stood staring at it silently until Margaret came in, her eyes wide with fright, bearing a small block of cooking salt. Her eyes widened still further as she caught sight of Peters's anguished face. 'Oooh! What's happened to Dr Peters?'

Wilson was already dissolving some of the salt in the jug of water and within moments he forced Peters to drink the water, straight from the jug, without ceremony. Half of the liquid spilled on the rector's jacket and he was spluttering for breath but Wilson doggedly forced him to continue.

'I'll get him through to the washroom now,' he said to Crow, and the Inspector nodded. Margaret fluttered her hands unhappily as Wilson dragged Peters to his feet and led him across the room, half stumbling, to the door leading to the washroom, while Crow remained staring at the capsule on the desk.

'What's happened, sir?' she asked.

'An accident,' Crow said shortly. 'Ring the doctor at once, will you, and get him to come—'

'There's one on the campus this afternoon, sir. Shall I get him?'

'At once.'

'He's carrying out some student medicals,' she explained nervously as she waited to be connected by telephone. 'He and the vicar, they come once a week.'

A fateful combination, thought Crow to himself. He waited until she had contacted the doctor and stressed the urgent necessity for his presence and then he pointed to the box of capsules on the desk.

'What are those?'

'Those capsules? They're Dr Peters's — he suffers from some sort of allergy, gives him nose trouble, you know, gets all stuffed up, especially when he's tired, or overworked.' Or subjected to stress, thought Crow. The girl hesitated, then continued slowly, 'He takes them to get rid of the congestion, you know. It . . . it isn't them that's made him ill, is it?'

'No,' Crow said reflectively, 'they haven't made him ill.' He slid a sheet of paper from the desk under the half-bitten capsule and turned to the girl. 'Have you got an envelope?'

* * *

The following Monday morning Crow called a conference in his office. Wilson sat immediately in front of Crow's desk, square-shouldered, quiet; on his left sat Framwell, the detective-constable who had been sent out to look through Rosemary's things and speak again with her parents; on Wilson's right was Detective-Constable Gates, who had been doing the foot-slogging check upon times and dates and explanations of where particular people had been at particular times during the previous week. Crow understood the nervous tension suffered by Gates and Framwell: they were based with the Sedleigh division and this would be their first experience of working with a man from the Murder Squad.

'All right, Gates, what have you got?'

Detective-Constable Gates leaned forward in his chair. He had a young, fleshy face that tended to emphasize that his raw-boned frame could well undergo a metamorphosis in time.

'Which do you want first, sir?'

'No matter.'

'Well, Svensson then, sir. I checked with the Anglo-Norwegian Club and it looks as though Svensson's in the clear. On the night the girl died he was at the Club all right, most of the evening. He left at about ten and walked home.'

'Where was the meeting held?'

'Elton Road.'

'That's what — about ten minutes' walk from Burton Polytechnic?'

'Yes, sir. I suppose there's just the outside chance that Svensson could have left the meeting, walked back to the Polytechnic and killed the girl. The lab's approximation of the time of death, I understand, is sufficiently unspecific to allow for the possibility.'

'Mm. The college heating was on, and the lift itself was relatively warm. The preliminary lab report just says ten to ten-thirty for the murder. Right, so we don't rule out Svensson entirely. Redman?'

'Nothing new at all, sir. Don't see how we can check his story further than we have; there certainly was a Beethoven programme on that night, and though he has no corroboration — I've checked, his mother was at Bingo that night — there's nothing to suggest he might have been lying. He's very much a home bird too, no whisper of any association with women, no Saturday night drinking, no nothing. Very steady chap.'

Crow asked Gates whether he'd checked on Carliss.

'His case is rather like Redman's as far as an alibi goes. He claims he didn't leave the cinema until ten-thirty but can't produce corroboration—'

'Other than a filthy piece of shredded paper.'

'Beg your pardon, sir? Er — yes, well, no one to back up his story but no evidence to disprove it either.'

'Any known contact with the girl outside work?'

'Not as far as Carliss is concerned, sir. It's possible, of course, but the impression I got was that he's not exactly a man who's fond of women. He's about to get a divorce — on the grounds of his wife's misconduct — and he's quite openly malicious about it. I mean, his wife doesn't really want it; the correspondent has no intention of marrying her apparently, but Carliss is keen to cut her right off. His attitude is quite . . . well . . . nasty, you know, sir? He's got reason, of course, but he *enjoys* having the right to do this to her, it seems to me.'

Crow squinted at Gates reflectively.

'It's facts we want, not impressions.' Even as he said it he knew it was an unfair remark to make, for he himself had gained some insight into Carliss's character that was now being reinforced by what Gates had to say. But he didn't say this to Gates. Instead, he asked: 'Did your "impressions" extend to the relationship between Carliss and Stevens?'

Gates's fleshy face had gained a little colour and he seemed peeved. He sat very upright in his chair and looked Crow in the eye.

'Yes, sir. It was quite obvious to me that. Carliss didn't like Stevens and was quite prepared to hint that Stevens might be implicated in the Harland murder. That was my "impression", sir.'

Crow caught Wilson's faint nod of approval at the way Gates stuck to his guns. He smiled quietly.

'All right. Go on. What about Stevens?'

'Your notes suggested that Stevens's alibi might not stand up, sir, so I went out to see Mrs Stevens and it's as Carliss suggested to you. She's a woman of about forty-eight, older than Stevens, and she's crippled with osteo-arthritis. She seems to be in considerable pain most of the time and she's sedated. I believe she also drinks fairly heavily although Stevens didn't tell me this. I think it's been one of those situations when a man marries a woman older than himself because he's attracted to maturity, and the maturity suddenly changes into age.'

'You fascinate me,' Crow interrupted ironically with a twitch of his eyebrows. 'Tell me, what would be the result of this change as far as Stevens was concerned?'

Pinkly, but determinedly, Gates went on. 'I think Stevens married her for the reasons I state, and perhaps the security of the house she owned — she'd been married before, incidentally, and widowed. Once ensconced in the marriage, he rapidly realised it was turning sour, but accepted its security. It meant he had a base from which to work—'

'I don't follow you.'

'Stevens is a womanizer, with no great record of success, but a ladies' man nevertheless. He's safe: a crippled wife at home, divorce out of the question, the chance to have his affairs kept quiet — if he can get them started. It's possible there have been one or two and he certainly tries hard enough. A sort of Casanova *manque.*'

Crow observed the young officer for a moment and then in a serious tone he said, 'You're new to this Division. Where did you spend the last few months?'

'Training school, sir.'

Crow glanced towards Wilson and when he caught the twinkle in the sergeant's eye he found difficulty in restraining a smile. He was saved by a light knock at the door. Wilson rose and walked across to open it. A young policewoman with a tray entered. Four cups of tea; Crow sipped his reflectively behind his desk while the other three men murmured among themselves. Just once Wilson looked at Crow questioningly but the Chief Inspector ignored the glance. It was unusual for Crow to arrange for tea in the middle of a conference like this, but so what? A privilege of office. He'd just felt that he might need a cup of tea after listening to reports from these young constables.

Crow put down his cup abruptly. It rattled on his desk.

'All right. A Casanova *manque.* Did he seduce Rosemary Harland?'

Gates gulped a mouthful of tea and leaned forward to put his cup and saucer on Crow's desk. Catching sight of the Inspector's wooden expression he changed his mind and carefully placed them on the floor beside his chair.

'There's no evidence to suggest he did seduce her, sir. I've spoken to a number of people at the college and they all agree that Stevens gets around — the library staff, the women in the Economics Department, even the kitchen staff have come to his attention. In there,' he said with a slight smile, 'it seems to descend to a bit of verbal slap and tickle.'

Crow showed no amusement and Gates hurried on.

'He had certainly visited the girl more often than other heads of Faculty and I would imagine that this is because of his nature — he would be more than interested in becoming friendly with her—'

'Did he get her to bed?'

'There's nothing to suggest that, no, sir.' Crow leaned back in his chair. 'This leaves us still at the starting point. Svensson could have got to the college in time, Carliss, Redman and Stevens all have stories that could be holed, but they haven't sprung a leak yet. Nothing to connect them with the dead girl, nothing in particular, but we know she was pregnant! Framwell, what did you get out at her home?'

Framwell brushed a nervous hand over a thinning hairline. He was twenty-six and looked ten years older. He had a yellow pustule on his chin and Crow avoided looking at it.

'I searched her room and belongings, sir, but found nothing that was in any way significant. However, I did send her clothing to the lab for analysis, just in case — the clothing she'd worn that morning, that is.'

'She'd changed during the day?'

'Yes, sir. Apparently she'd been given an assignment that involved going to a Trustee Bank — she was involved with the Student Union as Treasurer — and this meant that she was able to slip home for lunch. She changed while she was there before returning to college. It was the last time her parents saw her.'

So she might have arranged to go somewhere that evening. With someone.

'This student thing — explain it to me.'

'The Student Union has a committee which is composed almost entirely of students, but there are two officers who are members of the teaching staff -- they act in an advisory and auditing capacity — and two members of the office staff also assist. One does the minuting of official meetings; the other — that was Rosemary Harland — acted as Treasurer. It overcame the problems that would otherwise arise with a shifting student population.'

'So she would have considerable contact with the students?'

'No, I don't think so. This was a possibility that occurred to me, sir, and I followed it up — even though it was beyond your instructions. I interviewed some of the committee and it seems that Rosemary Harland kept very much to herself on these occasions. She did attend two student functions just recently, but on each occasion she arrived and left with a girl-friend — Sally Woods.'

Crow frowned.

'All right. Tell me more about the Harland girl.'

'I spoke to her parents, sir, and to some of the neighbours. I interviewed the office staff and the student committee. For the record, she was five feet five inches tall, brunette, blue eyes, weight about eight stone, a good-looking girl by all accounts, good-looking without being really attractive. The college office was her first job and her efficiency, backed by secretarial training she had previously undergone, brought her early promotion to the job of the rector's secretary—'

And that still raised questions in Crow's mind. Peters had an eye for a woman, he was sure of it.

'-her parents insist that she was a good girl, and were horrified to learn that she was pregnant—'

Crow could see their middle-class hands raised in unbelieving stupefaction. It would have been a shock almost greater than news of her death.

'-they can give no lead as to who might have been responsible for her pregnancy. They insist that she had no boy-friends, other than some local lads who occasionally called at the house. 1 checked these sir, and they are pretty obviously not involved — they deny ever having been alone with Rosemary. The Harlands say that she was very rarely away from home overnight, and when she was she always telephoned them before eleven to let them know she was all right.'

Crow pounced on the inference.

'She didn't phone the night she died?'

'No, sir. But they didn't worry about that. She'd already told them she was staying with Sally Woods and they received a call from Miss Woods earlier that evening to say that Rosemary was with her.'

Crow stroked his blue-shadowed chin and Framwell waited nervously.

'It didn't occur to you to ask them why this Woods girl should phone, rather than Rosemary herself?'

'I thought it better to ask the girl herself, sir.'

'What did the Woods girl have to say?'

'I didn't see her. She was shocked by the news, her mother said over the telephone went away for the weekend. She'll be back this afternoon. I intend going around there this—'

'Don't bother, I'll do it.' Crow was interested in Sally Woods. There might be something about the relationship between her and Rosemary Harland that could provide a key to a few problems. 'What did the neighbours have to say about the dead girl?'

'Nothing untoward, sir. They regarded Rosemary Harland as a good girl too, quiet, self-effacing, pleasant enough, passed the time of day and so on. No suggestion that she was running around with boys or anything, and I think that in a small middle-class community like that anything of that kind of conduct would very quickly have become the cause for comment. Moreover, I obtained the impression that—'

'Yes, all right.' One like Gates was enough. 'So there were no obvious boy-friends. A brick wall, again. What do *you* think, Wilson?'

98

'About the possibility of Peters having an affair with Rosemary Harland? I don't know . . .'

'You think it unlikely?'

'All we've got so far is the fact that Peters took her on when she was still rather inexperienced—'

'Which could mean he was attracted.'

'But after that there's nothing.'

'Except that she was pregnant when she died, she was murdered in his college, his glove was stained with foundation cream she used, he had a key giving him access to the whole building, his alibi for the relevant time is far from strong—'

'That deflated tyre,' Wilson interrupted firmly, 'was certainly not cut, but the garage say there's a slow puncture in the valve and it could just have gone down over a period of hours. Peters's story could be right.'

'His alibi for the relevant time,' Crow insisted, 'is far from strong, and if he had got her pregnant he certainly had enough motive to get her out of the way.'

Wilson's expression told Crow quite clearly what he thought of *that*. It was one thing to say that a man *might* have sold his research findings, *might* have betrayed industrial confidences to get a better job, *might* have married a woman for her money and her father's influence — but it was all stretching the coincidences a bit far along with the suppositions if this was regarded as leading up to murder. Circumstantial evidence could clash the prison gates in a man's face, but though there was plenty of it pointing towards Peters there was one vital piece missing — the evidence of a clear link between him and the girl.

Wilson was a good man to have around.

He could bring Crow back to earth with a thump.

'How is Dr Peters, anyway?'

Wilson shrugged his broad shoulders. 'Mouth burns only. If he had swallowed that capsule he could have been dead now. The lab confirmed that it was a corrosive poison. He must have spat it out when the burning started as he put the glass up to his lips. He was released from hospital yesterday; detention was just for shock, really.'

'And I suppose he has us to thank.'

'Sir?'

'For getting him angry in the first instance. Normally he would have swallowed that capsule and it would have dissolved in his stomach, but in his fury at our insinuations he must have bitten at it, instinctively. The burning sensation made him eject the capsule almost immediately.'

'He was lucky,' Wilson said stolidly.

'Or clever.' A silence fell and the three men looked at Crow expectantly. He pursed his lips and stared out of the window. 'Let's look at the facts,' he continued. 'Those capsules in the box were ordinary anti-histamine in their contents, but it's easy enough to open the capsules — they're made in two gelatin sections, one fitting inside the other. Slide the gelatin sections apart, replace some of the granulated contents with poison, and there you are. But who did this, and how did the capsule get in the box? Accidentally, or deliberately?'

His deep-sunk eyes flickered a glance in the direction of the three silent officers. 'Peters could have done it himself, or it could have been done by someone else. The result, accordingly, could have been accident, attempted murder, attempted suicide or attempted subterfuge.'

'I don't quite follow, sir.'

'If we rule out mistake — the contents were, after all, a mixture of anti-histamine and a corrosive poison — the capsule was placed there deliberately. If Peters had placed it there it would have been attempted suicide—'

'But sir—'

'I agree, we can rule that out. It's illogical. But think of this . . . if he killed Rosemary Harland, and expected to be questioned, he might have placed that capsule there with the idea of diverting suspicion from himself, casting our attention elsewhere, drawing a lovely red herring across our path. We press him on the Harland murder and he throws a spanner in the works by making us think someone is after him as well. He'd be viewed as a victim then, not a villain.'

Wilson was shaking his head doubtfully. 'It sounds a bit far-fetched, sir.'

'I'm propounding it as a possibility, Wilson, just a possibility. After all, he didn't *swallow* the capsule, did he? Minor burns of the mouth — that's all he suffered. And what about the other unlikelihoods, if he didn't place the capsule there himself?'

'You mean two murders on the same campus?'

'Isn't it pushing coincidences a bit?'

'Could be the same person.'

'And the motives for killing both Peters and his secretary?' Crow smiled suddenly and turned towards the two constables. 'You see, gentlemen, there are several possibilities. Nothing is what it seems . . . perhaps. But college-trained detectives like yourselves might have some other, psychological suggestions to bring up?'

Gates flushed, and Framwell wriggled but neither spoke. After a moment Crow nodded.

'All right. It seems to me no one is in the clear yet — Svensson, Redman, Carliss, Stevens and Peters too, they could, anyone of them, be implicated. We'll not lose sight of the possibility of someone trying to kill Peters, but we don't just pursue *that* line. What we do hammer at is the discovery of Rosemary Harland's lover. If her lover wasn't one of these men, we want to find out who he was.'

'You've left out West, sir.'

Crow smiled at Gates.

'He seems to be clear. I spoke with the hospital registrar and I was shown the cardiograph results. West collapsed all right, and a heart attack is somewhat crippling in its effect. But Fanshaw did suggest that West was lying when he hinted at a possible liaison between Peters and the girl. If he was, I can't see his motives. I agree, nevertheless, we mustn't rule West out completely.'

He rose, stretching his long arms.

'All right, that'll do for now. Gates, keep checking on Peters's background and draw up a timetable of the precise movements of these people we've been discussing. Framwell, you check the dead girl's movements through the day and as far as possible her activities during the last few weeks. That'll do for now.'

Framwell and Gates scuttered out of the room like rabbits. After the door closed behind them Wilson smiled at Crow.

'You frightened them.'

'They'll be all right. Make good officers.'

'When they stop psycho-analysing?'

'There's a lot to be said for it, Sergeant, as long as one doesn't carry it too far. Anyway, I'll want you with me this afternoon — we'll get out to see this Woods girl.'

'There's one chap we haven't looked at, sir. That civil servant, Fanshaw.'

'You think he'll repay checking?'

'We don't know that he won't.'

Crow smiled. There were occasions when the direct Yorkshireman could sound like a reproving conscience. And when he did he was usually right.

* * *

Accountants, bankers, solicitors, building society managers, doctors with small practices, and architects employed by local authorities lived in Edgerton Lane, cheek by reluctant jowl with the two actors engaged in television commercials, a self-styled Italian prince, and three brothers with Bermondsey accents and incomes, the sources of which were a complete mystery to HM Inspector of Taxes. The actors, the prince and the Bermondsey brothers provided a splash of scarlet in the even brown tones of Edgerton Lane lives, and the vicarious thrill that sparkled into dull coffee mornings was directly attributable to the presence among the eminently respectable of these slightly, and not so slightly, disreputable.

Myra Woods' home was a particular favourite for the coffee-morning sessions that lasted from ten till three, since it afforded an across-the-garden glimpse of the prince himself as he prowled through the summer mornings, all brown skin and black hair and white, sharp-cut slacks. They would have loved to have him over for coffee but *imagine* what Joe would say!

'Bloody gigolo.'

But that's what Joe said about anyone he didn't like. Well, almost anyone. He didn't say it about the brothers from Bermondsey. He might have thought it, he might have whispered it to himself inside his head but he never said it because Joe was a careful man who ran his branch of the bank with pride and skill and never took chances with a customer. Not that the Bermondsey brothers were customers; Joe doubted whether they would ever entrust their money to a bank. It would be against their professional ethics. That would have been a good joke for Joe to make, but Myra knew he'd never make it. Joe was careful even about jokes: funny remarks had a habit of rebounding and another person's discomfort could so easily become your own.

Joe was a very careful man.

He did pass the time of day with the two actors and so did Myra on occasions because there was something steady about them in spite of the fact that they were homosexuals. They used Joe's bank, for instance, and they had seven standing orders, two of some magnitude. Of course, one could hardly invite them around in the evening for a drink, and on the occasion when Karen Steiner had said the women ought to invite at least one of the actors to their coffee-morning round Myra hadn't laughed because she didn't approve of dirty jokes. But when she'd related it to Joe that night he'd laughed. He was like that, Joe; he had a crude streak. But then, didn't all men have crude streaks?

So the coffee-morning cups rattled, and the tongues clacked and the men laughed their deep laughs over evening cocktails and suggestive jokes, and the actors and the prince and the brothers from Bermondsey continued to provide topics for amused conversation, and it was all so peaceful and remote from reality in the cocooned existence they lived behind their four walls, until the real world outside suddenly came home to them, to Myra and Joe Woods. In the first instance it came home to them through the fact that they had known Rosemary Harland personally, and she had been a friend of Sally's. This was a cause for wonder and excited chatter and false sincerity in their tones as they telephoned their condolences to Mr and Mrs Harland, for they couldn't keep the thrill out of their voices. But in the second instance the intrusion of the outside world into their tidy, well-ordered home was not in the least exciting for Joe and Myra, and in no way thrilling in the pleasurable connotations that these words had assumed for them. It was merely distressing, for no other house in Edgerton Lane had received an official visit from the police and one didn't like to have a police car with an infernal flashing blue light parked outside one's drive. Moreover, there was the gaunt, skeletal police inspector who seemed to have no regard for Joe's status or Myra's feelings.

It hadn't started too badly, nevertheless; it just so happened that Joe was home that afternoon so when the doorbell rang and Myra prinked her hair briefly in front of the hall mirror before opening the door she wasn't unduly worried. Her stomach lifted under her corset when she caught sight of the car and she experienced one of those unpleasant burning feelings around her heart, the kind that lobster usually visited upon her, when she observed the grim expression upon the face of the gentleman in plain clothes accompanying the blue-uniformed man, but Joe was home after all, and she was sure it was something he could take care of.

'Joseph?' she called in a weak, fluffy voice with one hand firmly controlling her midriff and her head and shoulders drawn back to lift the line of her matronly bosom. 'Joseph, there's some gentlemen . . .'

She wasn't to know that they weren't gentlemen then, of course. Joe came out of the sitting-room, buttoning up the jacket which he had taken off as he sneaked forty winks in front of the television and the golf programme from Royal and Ancient.

'Who is it, dear?' he asked.

'The police, Joseph,' Myra replied in her weak, cultured voice. 'They'd like to come in to talk to us.'

Joe summed up the situation in a flash; Myra could see that, from the way he jerked his arm as he did whenever a client came to the branch, and he exposed a fraction of his white cuff; he gestured backwards towards the sitting-room.

'Then come in here, where we'll be comfortable.'

As always, Joe was right, of course; after all, it would hardly do for the neighbours to see them gossiping on the doorstep with the police. Uncivilized. Treat the whole thing with the panache expected of a bank manager and his family. After all, they were all professionals. Joe was right as usual.

But, she thought, as she watched her husband wave the two policemen to the easy chairs in the sitting-room, she wished he would take a little more care over his personal appearance. Not his suits — though amply proportioned, they were well cut and expensive — but his fingernails and his teeth and his nose. She'd told him, years ago, to stop biting his nails when he was angry and clean his teeth in the morning. And stop attacking his nose. He had just bitten his nails in anger at her and refused to clean his teeth. And he had squeezed at his nose until little white dirt-worms wriggled out of the enlarged pores and he had rubbed them off with a thumbnail and stared at them in fascinated contemplation, lying white and soft on his nail. She hadn't bothered to discuss it with him for years. Now he smiled and she saw the yellowing dentures, and he stuck one hand in his jacket pocket with thumb protruding so she could see the rough cuticle and the jagged, black-edged nail and she could remember all those dead, white, soft little worms emerging from his reddened flesh. She sighed, took a seat and the two policemen sat down also, the young one in the uniform waiting until the tall, gaunt one was seated before he took a chair.

'Well, gentlemen, how can we help you?' The gaunt man in plain clothes was looking at Joe as he stood with his back to the fireplace. There was no fire there; Myra lit it only after October the thirty-first.

'We'd like to talk to your daughter, Sally.'

'Ah. I see. It's about the Harland affair. Well, I'm afraid you've wasted your time ... er ...'

'Detective-Inspector Crow.'

'Yes. The fact is, Sally is hardly likely to be able to help you. She's been away for the weekend, you know, for a rest, because the news about Rosemary was a tremendous shock to her ... to us too, of course, though I can't imagine that it would be anyone in their circle who would want to, or even could possibly—'

'I'd like to see your daughter.'

Myra saw Joe's back stiffen and she was proud of him.

'I'm sorry. I don't think she should be disturbed. I took the afternoon off today to fetch her from the station, and she's still not recovered, in spite of her weekend away. She's up in her room now, lying down, and I'm sure there's nothing she can say that will be of any assistance.'

'I'd be grateful, nevertheless, if we could speak with her.'

Joe wouldn't like such a virtual contradiction. He'd soon cut this policeman down to size. She wondered whether the man knew that Joe was manager of the branch bank.

'Who's your superior officer, my man?'

'*I'm* in charge of this case, Mr Woods, I'm conducting a murder enquiry and your daughter may be able to give me information which will assist me. I would like to speak to her here, but if you prefer, I can ask to see her down at the station.' His voice was deceptively quiet as he added, 'And if you stop me seeing her I can ask *you* to come to the station.'

Joe gasped. 'What on earth—'

'You'd be obstructing me in the line of my duty.'

When Sally was five Myra had bought her two goldfish. She suddenly realised that there were occasions when Joe looked remarkably like the larger of those fish, and this was one of those occasions. He was glancing towards her and his mouth opened and shut ineffectively several times before the words eventually emerged. 'Get her, Myra!'

Myra was hurt. It wasn't her fault, after all.

She sniffed her disapproval of the way they were conducting themselves, deprecated the atmosphere with a delicate arching of her eyebrow and rose, left the room, climbed the stairs, tapped delicately at her daughter's bedroom door and called softly, 'Sally? Could you come downstairs for a few minutes? There's some . . . gentlemen to see you.' There was a short silence and she added, 'About Rosemary,' and a few moments later the door opened and Sally appeared.

She hadn't been looking well for weeks but Myra had put that down to a surfeit of dieting and the general way youngsters seemed to carry on these days. Sally hadn't told them, for instance, where she'd gone this weekend. She could have gone off with a man, perhaps, but Myra didn't think so. After all, Sally was a little unfortunate in that she would never possess the firm bustline and slim waist that had been Myra's when she was in her twenties; but that was Joe's fault, for he was inclined towards corpulence and this was why Sally's figure tended to be somewhat, well, thick and straight. One had to be honest with oneself, even about one's own daughter. Of course, Sally had rather nice eyes, if one liked eyes, and a smooth complexion, if one overlooked that silly little mole on her chin, and Myra had heard other women say that Sally had a very nice smile but that was just said to flatter Myra really. Myra preferred the truth about these things; she knew Sally's smile couldn't match her own.

But it was nice of her friends to try in their wrongly phrased way to please her.

She preceded Sally down the stairs. She wasn't displeased that Sally was wearing slacks for she personally did not approve of the short dresses Sally wore. Just because she had legs that had been commented upon favourably, that was no reason to wear these horrid mini-dresses and skirts. Myra sniffed. It was all so *low*.

She glided into the room and waved a negligent hand in the direction of the young constable and Inspector Crow, both rising to their feet.

'Please remain seated, gentlemen. Here is my daughter.'

Joe rocked on his heels, his hands locked behind his back, and he lowered his head to peer at Sally.

'These policemen would like to ask a few questions, Sally, but I've already explained you've nothing to tell them. The quicker it's over, the better, so just say to them that—'

Crow remained standing and now Myra saw the long face interposed between herself and Joe. The movement also had the effect of cutting father off from daughter and Myra saw Joe hop sideways to maintain sight of Sally. Crow was addressing the girl.

'I'd like to have a few words with you about Rosemary Harland.'

'She was my friend.' Sally's voice was flat, but then, Myra had always felt that Sally's voice lacked the musical quality of her own. When she was young, people had said—

'I understand she visited you here on occasions.'

'On occasions, yes.'

'But she's not been here recently, has she, Sally?' Joe strutted forward, his hands still locked behind his back, like a fat little captain on his quarterdeck. 'It must be at least three weeks since you've seen her.'

Crow glanced over his shoulder at Joe but Sally replied in a quiet voice that served to emphasize the stillness of her bearing.

'How would *you* know? It's either bridge, newspapers or snoring in front of the television for you! You wouldn't have noticed if she *was* here!'

'Sally!' An ecstatic thrill of displeasure surged through Myra's ample bosom and she turned to look at her daughter. 'How can you speak to your father like that?' She was amazed, and perturbed too, to see that Sally was smiling contemptuously.

'You mean that truth and words with meaning shouldn't be used in this house? I know they haven't been, for years!'

'Sally!' Joe's voice carried a fierce warning and he tried to shuffle his way past the detective-inspector but Crow moved almost as though by accident, barring the way.

'Is there a room where I can speak to your daughter in private?'

'I insist that I be present when you speak with her!'

'Mr Woods, I can *ensure* privacy at the station.'

Joe was puffing as though he were out of breath and Myra revised her impression; he wasn't a goldfish at all but a bullfrog suffering from glandular fever. She said not a word as Sally shrugged and turned away.

'Come on through to the dining-room. You can ask me your questions there.'

She was nineteen. And she was ignoring Joe and she was ignoring Myra and these two policemen were walking after her into the dining-room and Joe was puffing away in front of the fireplace and Myra sat down.

'How can they . . .' Joe expostulated. 'What's got into that girl . . .?'

'How did she behave coming home in the car?'

'Well, I don't know, we didn't have much to say, really, I was listening to the golf on the radio and I suppose she just sat there staring out of the window. I did ask her how she was when she got in and she said all right and I just switched on the radio.'

'I see.'

'Well, I didn't know she was going to behave like this, when these policemen came, did I?'

Myra sneaked a glance towards the window; there was a movement of white at the window across the garden. The Italian prince was returning the compliments paid him by the coffee-morning clique.

'Shall I make a cup of tea, dear?'

Joe shrugged helplessly. Myra went out and made a cup of tea. He was still standing, red-faced, in front of the fireplace, when she returned with the tray and the bone china tea service. Five cups; she poured out two cups of tea, one for herself, and one for Joe.

'I hope they won't mind if we don't wait. Do you think they'd like a cucumber sandwich?'

Joe shrugged again, equally helplessly.

Myra sipped at her tea and hoped they'd come out of the dining-room soon while the tea was still hot. They did. To her dismay the inspector smiled, refused the tea offered and made off with the young constable in train. When the door closed behind them she could hear Joe shouting at Sally in the sitting-room.

'What did they say to you? What did they want? You had nothing to tell them, of course, because you hadn't seen Rosemary Harland for some time, had you, she'd not been here anyway and if you ask me there must have been something funny going on for her to get herself killed like that! I mean, respectable girls don't get killed like that, do they? You had nothing to say to them did you?'

'Oh, shut up!'

'What did you say?'

Myra swept into the room on a great bow wave of excited pleasure.

'Don't speak to your father like that!'

'I'm surprised he heard me.'

'Sally!'

'He never does. He just hears himself, all the time, no one else. And you, you hear only what you want to. Only when it's flattery, isn't it, Mother? The rest is silence.'

Myra sat down, deliciously weak at the knees.

'What on earth do you mean?'

'Sally—' warned Joe in a menacing growl.

Sally began to walk towards the hallway and the stairs. 'Sally,' Joe called, 'you stay here, do you hear me? We've got to have words, you and I!'

'As one door closes,' Sally said in a dreamy voice, 'so another shuts.'

'Eh? What do you mean by that?'

'Nothing. But it is about as important a statement as most of yours.'

'What the hell are you talking about?' Joe's voice had risen and his neck was corded in anger; Myra scrambled out of her chair in a manner quite undignified, with a quick peek out of the window.

'Joe—' she began tremulously, but Sally's voice cut across hers. Its inflection was icy. 'Mother! People who live in glass houses . . . shouldn't.'

'Shouldn't what?'

Sally just stared at her contemptuously.

Myra had never seen contempt in someone's eyes before, not a naked contempt like that. It quivered right down to her lower stomach, gave her a strange feeling that she hadn't experienced for years, and never with Joe, but just once when the bank clerk had come across to the house for Joe's briefcase and had looked at her as she'd handed it to him and had said—

Sally had turned away again. Joe barked at her, a harsh sound that roughened his voice to a rasp-like quality.

'I've told you! Stay here, until we've had this out! What's got into you, girl?'

Sally stood by the door. Her hands were hanging limply at her sides. She was taller than Myra, as tall as Joe, but in her pale blue sweater she looked rather dumpy. Her face was stiff and lacking in expression as she stared at Joe and Myra but her voice was powered with a bitter anger that Myra had never heard before.

'I'll tell you what's got into me. Rosemary's dead, and she was my friend and she was just a bit older than me and you don't give a damn, either of you. Tomorrow you'll have forgotten she even existed, and right now if I was to walk out of the house the only emotion you'd feel is embarrassment about what the neighbours would think. You're non-people, you know that? You don't live, I doubt if you even *exist* other than within yourselves. Well, I'm opting out, I'm getting out and leaving you to it. Rosemary's dead and I'm nineteen; I'm going to live the way I want to live, as far away from. this disinfected atmosphere as I can get. And what the neighbours think, that's your problem. It's the only problem I'll leave you, I know that.'

'Sally! This nonsense — there was a young man at the station — it's got something to do with that young man who left you there, hasn't it!'

Sally's lip was curling as Myra sat shivering with inexplicable excitement.

'If you like,' she sneered. 'After all, as they say, a bird on the sand is worth two who are bushed.'

She left Joe and Myra in a stunned and uncomprehending silence. They were incapable of uttering even a platitude.

* * *

He opened the car door for her and Joan ran across the dark pavement from the shop doorway, with a scarf draped over her hair. She told herself it was protection from the spattered rain but she knew that other motives dictated her action: she had no desire to be recognized. The car door slammed behind her; the warm distinctive smell of damp leather came to her and she shrugged off the scarf to look at him. The windscreen wipers beat a slow steady rhythm, outpaced by the quickness of her pulse.

There was no smile on his face. He was taking out a cigarette; the paper pack was battered and twisted. He lit the match and the glow in the car gave his saturnine features a devilish cast, lean and cruel. But she remembered the warm urgency of his mouth and the fierceness of his body and she took the cigarette from his lips and put her arm around his neck and kissed him. His hair was wet, and droplets touched her cheek. Her body stirred.

'Where to?' he asked as he broke away from her embrace, and recovered his cigarette.

'Anywhere.'

'Your place?'

She opened her eyes as a tremor of shock and fear shot through her. He couldn't be serious!

'My . . . my place?' she repeated in stupefaction.

'Why not?' His tone was careless as though the answer, or any of this, were of little importance to him. She was hurt. She shook her head.

'But that's rather foolish . . . and dangerous, isn't it, to go to my home?'

'Why?'

'Well . . . Bill, what if Bill should come home when . .
.'

Her voice died away. He shrugged carelessly and drew on his cigarette, staring forward through the streaming windscreen. 'You said he'd be out this evening. But no matter.'

She waited. He said nothing more and she continued to wait until she knew that there'd be no words from him until she spoke again. There had been that one glorious evening with him, when he had made her behave in a way that still brought colour to her cheeks when she thought of it. She thought of it often, almost hourly during the day since it had happened. She thought of how it had been, the things he had made her do, the things he had done to her, and she remembered how he had hardly spoken, made no display of affection, how he had made no suggestion for another meeting but had simply fallen in with her wishes, her approaches. There had been no affection in him, just a wild, yet calculated violence when he took her, but she couldn't help that; she had wanted him then and she wanted him again. Tonight.

'Can't we . . .' She faltered, and then plucked up courage. 'Can't we just drive somewhere?'

He just looked at her for a moment, turning his head and staring at her, and then he drew on his cigarette again, once, before flicking it out with a thumbnail and pushing the stub into the top pocket of his leather jacket. Without a word he engaged first gear, released the handbrake and they jerked forward spasmodically. The engine roared and they lurched down the street as the rain came at them in needle points, white under the soft headlights. Sadruddin drove through the town and she half expected him to take the side road up towards the moor where they had gone the evening after the student meeting, but he drove on. This time he was taking the road to her home.

He stopped the car in the roadway outside the house. She glanced up to the second floor where their flat, hers and Bill's, was situated, and there was no light. She had been expecting none.

'I'll see you.'

His tone was flat and harsh. Worse, it was indifferent. The engine was still running. She stared at him and caught the line of his profile and she put out a hand, but he turned his face aside like a child, avoiding her hand. Yet it was not a childish gesture; it was a cold one, a vicious one. He wasn't looking at her.

'I'll see you around.'

Wordlessly he switched off the engine. The silence crept around them and the windscreen wipers were frozen into streaming immobility. She leaned over and kissed him slowly but his lips were cold. She broke away, got out of the car and slammed the door. She ran around to the pavement and the rain dashed against her body and her face and soaked her hair as she fumbled for the keys to the front door. When she finally opened the door she paused and stood there in the doorway, holding the door wide, and looking back to him.

With a jerk the car door was opened; the car lights were switched off, and the road was dark under the drumming rain.

Inside the house he shook himself like a dog and made no attempt at silence as he mounted the stairs behind her. She stood aside at the door to let him enter the flat first and then she followed and closed the door behind them. He was standing in the dimness with his back to her and she came up behind him, put her arms around him, strained the softness of her body against him and he turned and switched on the light. He grinned. 'Nice.'

She drew the curtains and lit the gas-fire.

Sadruddin stood with his legs braced apart, staring around him at the flat. The sitting-room was small, with two easy chairs, a settee, a radiogram and two bookcases, both crammed with paperbacks on sociological topics with a creaming of light fiction. Joan caught her reflection in

115

the mirror as she straightened up from the fire: her hair was damp and sticking to her forehead but her eyes were warm and excited and there was a flush to her cheek. She turned and looked at Sadruddin and he was grinning again, his teeth white under the black moustache, lines appearing along his lean jaw. The humour in his eyes held a hint of malice, nevertheless.

'Come here,' he ordered and held out his arms. She went to him quickly and his arms were tight around her, locking against her spine, so tight that her head fell back until she was looking up at him involuntarily. He kissed her; she didn't like the contempt in the kiss and struggled against him.

'You're hurting me!'

'Isn't it what you want?'

'I don't want you to—'

'You had no objection the other evening, when I hurt you. And you haven't forgotten it, Joan, have you?'

She hadn't forgotten it. He had hurt her, a tearing hurt, but she hadn't fought against it for it had been at the height of her excitement. This was different, more cold, more deliberate, but even so the thought of the other evening softened her now and she pushed her head against his chest, feeling her limbs tremble. He released her and she stared at him for a moment before taking his hand to lead him across to the settee.

She lay back and looked up at him and he smiled, shaking his head.

'No. Not here.'

She was puzzled. She sat up and he pulled at her arm.

'I want you in there.'

In her bed. Bill's bed. Their bed.

Her resistance to the suggestion was simply overcome, by the slightest pressure on her arm. She wanted this man, wanted to experience the wild urgency of the previous occasion. She stood quite still in the bedroom while he removed her clothes, expertly, slowly, and she shut her mind to Bill and the flat and their bed and the two years of their married life, and she waited only for the slow rise of excitement in her stomach to change to a flowing heat that would thrust her into that shuddering darkness again.

She felt the coldness of the sheets against her skin and the warmth of Sadruddin's thighs. Then there was the pain, and the harshness of his breathing and the exciting, culminating surge once more.

Later, much later, in the darkness she whispered to him.

'We must go, now.'

He stirred, threw an arm across her breasts.

She smiled at the dark head beside her and pushed at his arm.

'No, we must get up. It's late. You'll have to go, and I'll straighten things up.'

He grunted, turning slowly towards her and his hand grasped her shoulder, his body moved against hers. She laughed, pleasurably.

'You're never satisfied! Don't tell me you want—'

He was crushing her. Suddenly she struggled because it was late and she didn't want him again, and he was coming at her angrily, like an animal, but he was strong and she couldn't control him and then, in a few moments, she could no longer control herself either as the heat and the movement and the desire mingled into a threshing that was timeless and endless and surging on a sea of pain.

Until light was bright and white in her eyes and she could see the blackness of Sadruddin's sweat-soaked hair and feel the crazy laughter bubbling up in his chest, against her breast. He rolled back from her and he was laughing and she sat up. Her breasts were damp and the air struck cold against them outside the sheets and Bill was standing in the doorway with one hand still on the light switch and his mouth wide open, gaping in his broad, soft face.

Sadruddin stopped laughing and sat there, supporting himself on his hands, staring amusedly at her as she stared at Bill and Bill stared at both of them, naked in the marital bed.

Then Bill said one word and charged. Sadruddin moved with speed, cackling hysterically. He snatched up the pillow and threw it with accuracy, straight at Bill and it hit him in the midriff. Joan saw her husband stagger sideways and then come on forward again as Sadruddin rolled out of bed. Bill sprawled across her thighs, his suffused face below hers, his hands grabbing for the man who had just left her. Sadruddin skipped up across the room, still laughing, and Joan was reminded of all those crazy 1920s comedies but this was different, for this was Bill, enraged, and this was Sadruddin. She stared wildly at him as he laughed. His body was lean, and young, and brown, and his movements were uninhibited, graceful as a young jungle cat. She had never seen anything more beautiful in her life.

Bill gasped obscenities at them both and lurched up to face Sadruddin. The naked Arab faced the raincoated, irate husband and they took up similar stances, leaning forward watchfully, but while Bill's face was puffed with anger Sadruddin's was still twitching with the laughter that bubbled uncontrollably from his lips. It had the effect of further angering, yet confusing Bill and he glanced back towards Joan, and again at Sadruddin. The student spat contemptuously and said something in Arabic and a spasm shook Bill Lambert's body.

Next moment he turned and his hand swept back and lashed Joan across the cheek. She screamed, more in surprise than pain, and threw herself back on the bed. Bill was staring at Sadruddin again and Sadruddin was grinning. Neither moved.

Joan knew her husband was afraid of the Arab.

'Get out!'

118

The words came in a snarl but Joan and Sadruddin and Bill Lambert knew it was a gesture only. It was only because Sadruddin felt that there was nothing to keep him there that he was prepared to accept the order.

'Like this?' he said, pointing to his body and grinning infuriatingly, but Bill made no reply. Sadruddin waved a hand at Joan and moved across to the pile of clothing on the floor beside the bed. He began to dress, whipping his long legs into his narrow trousers with insolent, provocative jerks. He grinned continually, his eyes flickering from the naked woman to the angry husband. He buttoned his shirt.

'Don't take it hard, Mr Lambert. I've just been indulging in what we might call a sociological survey. Some of the findings . . .'

A growl started in Lambert's throat but it died again as Sadruddin's eyes changed from mockery to malice. Again, Lambert recognized his ineffectuality and lashed out at his wife, verbally this time.

'You whore!' She stared at him, clutching the bedclothes to her as though reluctant to allow her husband to see her breasts, mottled from contact with her lover's body. 'You whore — sleeping with an Arab!'

Sadruddin straightened slowly. He slipped on his shoes. The smile remained on his face but his glance was cold.

'Racial prejudice is a funny thing. Curious classifications, each with shades of meaning, eh?' The smile expanded and it was the smile of a tiger. 'I'll allow you that one epithet, Mr Lambert, because I'm still the gainer, eh, Mrs Lambert?'

He slung his leather jacket over his shoulder and began to walk towards the door with an insolent swagger. He had just reached it when Lambert lost control and started for him. The Arab whirled around to face his assailant and his hand swung up from his waist. There was a light in his face, the glow of blood lust. A knife flickered in his hand.

'Come on then, let me cut your horns!'

Lambert stopped dead in his tracks and his enraged face paled visibly. He stared at the knife in silence and the two men remained immobile, half-crouching, stiff-legged. The knife began to move slightly from side to side and Lambert's eyes followed the flicker, fascinated, until with a casual relaxation, Sadruddin straightened from his crouching stance and sniggered.

'I thought not.' He winked mockingly at Joan. 'Till next time, then?' With a studied contempt he turned his back and walked through the bedroom doorway. Lambert expelled his breath in an anguished sigh and then turned to face his wife. His mouth twisted. He swore at her, an obscene flood of words. Sadruddin's voice floated back from the sitting-room.

'Don't be too hard on her, Lambert! After all, who are you to talk?'

Joan saw the way Bill stiffened and clenched his fists but then the door slammed and Sadruddin was gone and Bill was glaring at her. He seemed to be struggling with himself as he stood there and she was suddenly aware that she was naked from the waist up. She'd released the bedclothes involuntarily — now she made a convulsive grab at them but the movement angered her husband and brought a furious desire leaping to his eyes.

'I'll show you, damn you!'

He tore off his coat, threw it on the floor and knelt on the bed, grabbing for her, swearing and tearing at her. She fought him with far more determination than she had thought she possessed. She'd never known him like this and she kept him at bay, hitting him about the head and shoulders as he scrabbled at her, kicked his way on to her, and she rolled and scratched and bit like a wildcat. In spite of his strength she succeeded. She kept him off, in spite of the numbness of her face where he'd hit her, in spite of the scrambling urgency of his attack. And once she knew he was beaten she cooled; once she knew he couldn't take her against her will, she felt the cold power in her veins.

But it wasn't until there were red clawmarks on his face, his angry vicious desire was spent in the violent attack upon her body, and he was sobbing in self-pity, and remorse, and emotional collapse, that she asked him.

In a cold contempt she asked him and he told her. And she discovered what Sadruddin had meant.

* * *

Next morning the sky had that pale, washedout look that was typical of a morning after heavy rain. In Sedleigh a blocked drain had overflowed into a bakery and short-circuited the electricity. Half of the town had been blacked out and there were three incidents involving burglary which could be put down to the blackout. Two youths had been taken into custody for the first of the burglaries: it had been an on-the-spot decision for them, and their lack of planning had contributed to their downfall. The other two jobs had not been bungled and though all the local villains who were known to indulge in such activities had been checked or were being checked there was some doubt at Headquarters that the CID would get much joy out of the exercise.

But Crow could leave all that to the local force. He was tied to the Harland murder and he was devoting his whole attention to it. His concentration was producing few results, nevertheless.

The Woods girl, for instance. She'd not been in a good humour when he'd followed her into the dining-room because those stupid parents had nettled her. The father had been a pompous fool, one used to the sound of his own voice in his own home, and Crow had little patience with such men. Mrs Woods was an affected, simpering nonentity whose main concern seemed to be that the middle-class gentility she fostered was to be maintained under any stress whatsoever. It hadn't been an auspicious start for an interview.

Only with difficulty had Crow managed to get a few facts from her, facts that were of some assistance in filling in the background on Rosemary Harland. She'd known Rosemary for five years — Rosemary had been ahead of her at school but they had met socially at the youth club and Sally had admired Rosemary. Rosemary Harland had been rather quiet, it would seem, and had been quite happy to spend her time with the younger girl at the club. She'd had little truck with the lads who hung around there and she'd remained friendly with Sally after she started her secretarial course at the Branch College of Further Education.

There had been more facts than this, but still there was something missing. Crow hadn't been able to put his finger on it but there was something. He knew what the trouble was, of course; he was a good police officer as far as results were concerned but he knew his limitations — and one of them was interviewing young women. Perhaps it was that he was too conscious of his unprepossessing appearance, and gaucheness. Sally Woods had answered his questions, given him a number of facts he needed, but he felt he'd not got all he wanted from her.

He'd had to press her considerably over the question of the times when Rosemary had stayed with her. Sally had agreed that Rosemary had stayed at the Woods's home from time to time but was vague on dates. Only when Crow insisted did she finally come out with what he wanted.

'All right, all right. Have it your own way! I suppose there were occasions when she said she was staying with us but she wasn't with us at all. Yes, and I suppose the night she was killed I did phone her mother to say she wouldn't be coming home and would be staying with me. No, I wasn't worried when she didn't come to my house, but that's because I didn't expect her anyway. The fact is, she rang me up about four-thirty at work and said that she had a date that evening and didn't want to go home. She asked me to ring her mother and say she would be staying overnight with me. So that's what I did. I waited till early evening and then I phoned her home, told her mother that Rosemary would be staying the night and was already with me and that was that. And it's no good asking me who she had a date with, or how many times she'd seen him, or anything else. We were friends and I talked to her sometimes about my men but she never told me a word about hers. Or even if there was more than one. She was tightlipped. And now she's dead and I wish you'd stop asking me all these bloody questions!'

It was all there in Crow's notebook. Three dates in recent weeks when Rosemary Harland had told her parents she would be staying with Sally Woods; three dates when she had in fact stayed elsewhere. But where? And with whom? She had told Sally she had a date; she had a man, a boyfriend, but that was all Sally knew. Or was saying. Because Crow still felt there was something Sally hadn't said, something she was keeping back. He'd been aware of the tense replies to his questions, the anxiety lurking in her manner, the way her eyes rarely met his. It could have been due to the thought of Rosemary's death, for it had hit Sally Woods hard, but Crow was sure there was more to it than that. He'd have to see the girl again.

* * *

Crow walked into Wilson's room and watched the sergeant crouched over a typewriter, painfully picking his way with one finger among the keys. His tongue was clenched between his teeth and his lips writhed back. He looked distinctly anguished.

'I'm just finishing the report on Fanshaw, sir. I'll let you have it in a few minutes.'

Fanshaw. Crow stuck his hands in his pockets. He'd intended looking into the civil servant himself, taking

Wilson to the Woods' home with him, but at the last moment he'd decided otherwise.

'Is he clean?'

'As a whistle, sir. The night the girl died he was sitting all evening in the Blackbird Inn at Arnleigh village, you know, just outside Sedleigh. He spent much of his time in the company of an old man called Charles Nixon, with whom he had a cup of tea before leaving for home at eleven. No. Robert Fanshaw may have found Rosemary Harland, but he didn't push her down those stairs.'

'What do you mean, push her down the stairs?'

'The unit's report is on your desk, sir. They found a scored mark on the tiles at the top of the stairs on the first floor which could have been caused by her heel, they found skin and smeared blood, most of it wiped off, on the guardrail below. They concluded that she was thrown down the stairs, struck her head, died there and was dragged to the lift with the cardigan wrapped around her head to prevent blood smears.'

'Hell's bells.'

'Yes, sir.'

Crow frowned at the impassive Yorkshireman.

'Could she have slipped there, or tripped and fallen accidentally?'

'Possible, sir. But she wasn't running away from nothing, and she didn't drag herself to the lift.'

Crow grimaced and touched his thick underlip with a doubtful finger.

'Anything else?'

'The lab now has a number of items of clothing belonging to the dead girl and brought from her home. They'll be analysing them today and tomorrow.'

'Good.'

Crow nodded and walked back into his office. There was a pile of papers on his desk, the reports already made by the officers working with him. He sat down and began to read them. The telephone jangled before he'd got through three.

'Inspector Crow? There's a young woman to see you, sir. Says it's connected with the Harland enquiry.'

'Name?'

'Mrs Lambert, sir.'

'Send her in.'

He didn't know her; her name had not come to light so far but she could be anyone as far as he was concerned. He rose as she entered and managed to keep the surprise out of his face only with difficulty. He motioned her to a seat and signalled to the constable to stay with him. He stared again at the young woman.

Her head was lowered and she did not look at him. He wasn't surprised. She had fair hair and a good figure, well-rounded and well-proportioned, but something had happened to her face. She had a swelling on her cheek, just below her left eye, and the discolouration extended down to her cheekbone and nose. There was a livid scratch on her throat as though a fingernail had torn at her. A red blotch on the side of her neck was of the kind he had seen made by fingers. He frowned.

'You've been in the wars, Mrs Lambert.'

She flashed an angry look at him and he wasn't sure the anger arose because of his statement or the memories it aroused. 'You're investigating the death of the Harland girl?'

'Yes.'

'I've got some information for you.'

'I see. Your name?'

'Joan Lambert. I'm a lecturer at Burton Polytechnic — sociology.'

'And you knew Miss Harland?'

'No. My husband did.'

'Ahh . . .' Crow sat back and stared at the woman facing him. The anger in her eyes, he knew now, was not for the directness of his questions. It was for her husband.

'It was your husband who did this to you?' he suggested, motioning towards her face. She nodded.

'We . . . we had a quarrel last night. He got . . . violent. Later, when I questioned him, he told me about Rosemary Harland.'

'What did he tell you?'

'That he'd been seeing her . . . going out with her.'

'Sleeping with her?'

'I don't know. I suppose so. We didn't discuss . . . details.'

'But you think it's a possibility.'

'I don't know. Maybe. Hell, yes, I suppose it is, why should I protect him? Yes, I think he's been sleeping with her.'

'And you decided to tell me about it.'

'We quarrelled.'

'Did you know, or suspect, he'd been having an affair with this girl?'

'No. I knew nothing until last night. I suspected nothing. But we haven't been, well, hitting it off too happily for some time.'

'Did he tell you how long he'd been seeing her?'

'No. But I gather it's been going on for some time.'

Crow hesitated. Rosemary Harland had been pregnant; she had taken a lover. She had made an assignation for the night she died. And Joan Lambert's husband had been seeing her. To date there had been no whisper that Rosemary Harland went out with a man, no clue, no lead. And suddenly here it was. Crow reached for his notes. In a casual voice he asked, 'How could he take her out without your knowing? Wouldn't you have noticed his absence — I mean, did he ever stay away nights?'

Joan Lambert shrugged.

'We've led our own lives to some extent. There are occasions when I'm away from home; and he sometimes attends Economic Conferences. He could have seen someone . . . her . . . then, I suppose. I didn't question him for details.'

Crow picked out the dates with his forefinger.

'Were you home overnight on April 15 and 27?'

Joan Lambert frowned. She opened her handbag and almost involuntarily glanced at the mirror inside before angrily rummaging past it. After a few moments she pulled out a small green-backed diary. She consulted it, turning the pages over quickly.

'On April 15 and April 27 I was in London. On each occasion. I'd gone up to see Professor Kroger — he's my tutor for the thesis I'm doing. It's an MA in—'

'And what about May 14?'

Joan Lambert consulted her diary again and in a slightly offended tone replied: 'I was home that night.'

'I see. And your husband?'

'Was he home, you mean? Er . . . I'm not sure. No, wait a minute, I remember now. He didn't stay at home that night — he attended a moderating committee meeting in London that afternoon and didn't return until the morning train. He went straight to college off the train.'

'How long is the journey from London — only about an hour, isn't it?'

'Yes, but both of us, if we have reason to go to London, we tend to take the chance to go see a show and then stay overnight. We can then get a train back at seven-thirty, in the morning, which gets us in at Sedleigh in good time for the first classes at Burton. We've both done it regularly.'

'Together?'

'And separately.'

'And this is what Mr Lambert did on May 14. What about the night Miss Harland died?'

Joan Lambert's eyes grew round. She had quarrelled with her husband and she had learned of his affair with Rosemary Harland and she'd wanted to tell someone in authority about it all. She had a need to feel hurt, play the part of the wronged wife. Crow could see that; he could appreciate but wasn't concerned with her other motivations. He could see that his questioning had now shown her the way his mind was working and this was something she'd hardly bargained for.

'You . . . you don't think that Bill . . .'

'Mrs Lambert. I shall be calling a press conference this afternoon, to issue a first statement. I see no reason why I can't tell you what I'm going to say. I'm going to say that Rosemary Harland was murdered. I'm going to say that she died about ten-thirty. I'm going to say there was no sign of sexual interference. I'm also going to say she was pregnant.'

'Pregnant! Bill? But he wouldn't . . . you don't think Bill would kill her, because of that! He's not that sort—'

'From your appearance,' Crow interrupted quietly, 'it would seem that your husband is not opposed to violent solutions.'

She shook her head disbelievingly.

'Where was he the night she died?' Crow asked in a patient tone. 'He . . . he was home.'

'All evening?'

'No . . . He had an evening class that he . . .' She paused, and stared at Crow's face. He saw the doubt begin to spread across her features, saw it turn into conviction, a horrified conviction.

'He had an evening class that night, but he told me he had a meeting to attend, an advisory committee meeting somewhere in London. So he'd arranged a stand-in for his class that particular night.' The words came rushing out now, falling over each other in their horrified haste. 'He went off at teatime and I drove him to the station. I didn't see him get on the train before I left. Then I heard him coming back home late that night and I was surprised—'

'What time was it?'

'About eleven-thirty, I think. I was in bed. I called his name. He came into the bedroom and he didn't turn on

128

the light. He told me that the meeting had ended sooner than he'd expected and there was nothing much on so he'd decided to come straight back home. He told me he'd got the ten o'clock train back from London and took a taxi from the station.'

Her voice died away into a fascinated whisper. 'Do you really think he killed her?'

'You've got that?' Crow asked the constable.

'Yes, sir.'

'You don't really think he killed her, do you?'

'We've got some checking to do now, Mrs Lambert. And I'll have to see your husband. Where can I find him?'

'I don't know. He . . . he walked out last night.'

'Walked out? Where did he go?'

Joan Lambert shook her head dully. She looked tired. Things were moving too fast for her, and in a direction different from that she'd anticipated.

'I don't know. He may be at college this morning. But I doubt it.'

Crow turned to the constable.

'Get Wilson in here! I'll want someone around to the college as soon as possible!' He came from behind his desk as Wilson came through the doorway in response to the constable's call. 'I want this lady's husband picked up for questioning. If he's not home, or at the college, I want a general call put out. Now then, Mrs Lambert, we'll want a description of your husband.'

She stood up. The blue-black swelling on her face was caught by the sunlight and she averted her head slightly.

'He's about five feet eight. His hair is sort of brown and he's got blue eyes. He's a bit on the chubby side.'

'What was he wearing?'

'Last night . . . a dark grey suit and a raincoat. He'd been at an evening class you see, and—'

'Get that description issued. I doubt whether we'll catch him at the college. If he's got any sense he'll have skipped. Was he distressed when he left you last night?' Crow asked, turning back to Mrs Lambert.

'Mad,' she replied grimly, 'rather than distressed.' Crow's urgency seemed to have made her pull herself together and she opened her handbag again. 'You might find it useful to have his photograph, as well as his description. If he did kill that poor girl . . .'

Crow glanced at the photograph. It showed Joan Lambert in a bikini on a sunlit beach, seated. Kneeling beside her was a chubby young man with hair that flopped over his forehead. He had a broad smile. One hand was placed possessively on his wife's shoulder. Crow handed the photograph to Wilson and glanced at Joan Lambert. She had seemed happy in that photograph.

'You won't have difficulty recognizing him when you see him,' she said with quiet malevolence. 'He's got scratches all down his face.'

Chapter 4

The hotel was no more than an hour's drive from Sedleigh, but that had been necessary for their arrangements: it meant they could spend the maximum time in each other's company and yet not run the risk of their arriving back late at their respective homes, or at work. It was a small hotel, with low ceilinged bedrooms, creaking floors and twisting stairs: there was a funny, ancient atmosphere about the place that gave a romantic tang to it for lovers. As they had been.

Five times they'd stayed there. Five glorious occasions when they kissed and loved and held hands and walked in the sunshine and felt the whole world coming alive for them. The first time had been late autumn, last year, and on that first afternoon at the hotel they had walked out, nervously, hands touching, too aware of each other to be at ease, and they'd gone down to the small stretch of open fenland, treading lightly as shadows between the pools of black gaseous ooze fringed by moss and bleached tassels of horsetails. The pennant leaves of the reeds had been streaked with gold, and guelder rose bushes had reached up like pillars of crimson flame. She had chattered to him,

131

over-anxious to appear natural, and they had brushed past the great seed-heads of water docks, rust-red among the rushes and he had told her that he loved her. He had known then that what he felt for her meant a permanency, a flowering of affection and love. Soon, they went back to the hotel.

They had come again, four times after that; the last occasion had been just recently and they had walked to the fen once more. It had been an exhilarating time and they had wrapped their arms around each other and laughed and kissed away the enforced partings that had occurred during the last weeks. She pointed out the March bedstraw to him: she likened it to their love. When they had first come to the hotel and the fen, the bedstraw had been black with seeds, sprawling in a great confused tangle supported by taller sedges and reeds, but now, in the early summer, it was bright with minute white starry flowers. So had their love been confused and sprawling, disoriented, she had said, where now it was shining and happy and alive. That had been only a week ago, days ago, hours ago in his mind.

But now she was dead.

The white flowers were trampled under his feet and Rosemary was dead. He turned and trudged back across the fen towards the hotel. The air was cool in the late afternoon and the weight in his chest, the dull ache of distress and disillusionment, was heavy to bear. He crossed the field, his hands thrust deep in his pockets and he came out into the lane where he and Rosemary had walked and leaned against the wall and kissed in the spring evening.

She was dead.

On the path the flints moved and scraped under his feet. He came down through the village, a stocky, chubby figure in his raincoat — it had looked a gloomy day when he went out — and turned the corner at the grocery store to head for the hotel. There was a car parked outside the hotel, next to his own, knife blades of sunlight flashing from its polished chrome. It was a police car.

He stopped walking. He hesitated, felt the keys in his pocket. His luggage was still in the room in the hotel, on the second floor. If he went in the receptionist would be certain to point him out to the police: he had no doubt that it would be he the police were looking for. They'd got here faster than he'd expected. Yet he felt he still could not face them, and flight was the obvious answer. Again and again and again.

The car. Could he get to the car without being noticed? Could he climb into the driving seat and get away before anyone came out to apprehend him?

The alternatives were non-existent. There was a railway station a half-mile away but the services were few and far between, and besides, he had little money and nowhere to go. Not by train, anyway. If he could reach the car, there was the chance of further respite: there was even the possibility that he could get away, sell the car, obtain another job, perhaps a new identity, and hide from the whole dreadful mess of Rosemary and Joan and . . . and that bloody Arab. He walked towards the car.

His luck seemed to be in. There was no one standing on the hotel steps and he could see no one inside the main doors. Casually he walked forward to the car and took the keys from his pocket. It was remarkable the way his hand displayed no tremor in spite of the quickness of his pulse. He inserted the key in the lock and turned it; there was the familiar holding, the resistance which he had sworn for months that he'd see to with a drop of oil, and then the lock clicked and turned and he pulled out the key, opening the car door with the other hand. He slid into the driving seat.

'Excuse me, sir!'

There was a man in a blue uniform walking down the hotel steps. The key slipped into the ignition hastily and was twisted: the engine coughed and died. 'One moment, sir, please!'

The blue uniform was hastening down the steps now, only a matter of feet away. He should never have parked so near to the hotel front. The engine coughed again, roared into life and there was a horrible grating scream as he tried unsuccessfully to engage reverse gear. There was a shout, a gloved hand seized the door handle as the gears bit and the car lurched backwards; he heard the policeman yelling and was aware of other men running down the hotel steps but the car was swinging wildly as he tore at the wheel, shooting backwards, and the first policeman was lying in the road, raising an arm. The gears screamed again as he slammed into second; the car stopped, he thrust down the accelerator and let out the clutch with a slow calm that was completely out of tune with the heat in his blood. The car swung around and nosed forward into the street and everyone was shouting and people were coming to their doors and the policeman on the ground was trying to rise, assisted by another, and there were three men waving their arms wildly, barring his progress. Three men in plain clothes.

The car leapt at them and they jumped for their lives. He thought for a moment that he hit one of them but he had no time to be certain. He was in the road, tyres screaming as he took the corner and the milk float came around that corner, trundling away on the wrong side of the road, the driver almost ready to get out of his seat to deliver a crate to the grocer's wife standing on the pavement.

After the crash there was a quiet ticking noise, metal cooling; the white spreading stain of the milk ran across the pavement down into the gutter and the woman on the step of the grocer's shop was screaming in a flat monotone. The car door was wrenched open and he looked up, dully; a white sleeve appeared and a fist took him heavily between the eyes and there was pain, and blood and at last nothing.

It was old-fashioned smelling salts that brought him round. He was sitting on the pavement. Some men were discussing in desultory fashion how the car and the float should be moved; a policeman was talking to the driver of the milk float. A hand took his shoulder, shook him roughly.

'William Lambert?'

He looked up and the light hurt his eyes. The greyness of the afternoon had gone and there was a red flush in the sky, a yellow streak above the curling cloud. He was reminded of the yellow iris pods in the fen, splitting into long, drifting lobes, shedding their brown seeds.

'Yes,' he said in a strangled voice.

'All right. Get up. Come on.'

They took him to the police car and they said not a word throughout the drive. Not to him at least; they talked briefly among themselves, but directed no words to him. He was thankful. He just lay back and closed his eyes and forgot. Forgot everything. Rosemary. Joan. Sadruddin. The college. Everything. But there was no pleasure in it, just an empty river, and he knew that there were limits and boundaries to the safe shallows, and outside those limits, prowling like piranha, were the questions that would tear at him, shred his emotions, strip his nerves to an exposed state where he would be unable to speak for the pain and the anguish and the horror of it all.

They took him to police headquarters at Sedleigh.

* * *

Inspector Crow stood over the man slumped in the chair in the interview room. The prisoner's tie was pulled to one side, there was a tear in his jacket and reddish-brown bloodstains on his shirt collar. His eye and cheekbone, on the left side, were puffy and reddish in colour; the right side of his face bore the scratches Joan

Lambert had spoken of and there was dried blood on his upper lip. Crow glanced at Wilson and asked,

'Who did this?'

'None of our men, sir.' Wilson was quick to dispel Crow's doubts because he knew what could happen to a case if police enthusiasm got out of hand — or in the papers. 'He tried to get away in his car — Jenkins was knocked down, but not injured, thank heaven, but as Lambert drove around the corner he was in a collision — with a milk float. I gather the driver wasn't very happy about it and came right out of his cab, dragged Lambert out and hit him a couple of times before our boys got to him to stop it. He was from Belfast.'

Wilson added the remark as though it explained everything.

'Make sure that they get a statement from that driver; we don't want allegations of police brutality or anything like that.'

'The statement's been taken, sir.'

Crow nodded his satisfaction and stared at Lambert. The young man's eyes were lowered; it was almost as though he were in a stupor. There was no report of drinking, however; perhaps he was just a bit dazed by the handling he'd received. It made no difference as far as Crow was concerned. He had questions of some urgency to ask.

'Why did you try to run away, Lambert?' There was a pause before the man in the chair stirred and sighed. He looked up, his eyes focusing upon the Inspector. He blinked as though he were hardly aware of his surroundings, or the reason why he should be here.

'What did you say?'

'Why did you try to run away?'

'I didn't.'

'Don't talk such bloody rubbish!'

Silence fell. Crow waited. They were not going to get far if Lambert argued everything. The man couldn't deny this last incident with any hope of getting away with it: he'd been trying to escape all right. Perhaps he was still a bit dazed.

'Are you all right?'

'I think so, yes. Run away . . . I wasn't, not at first, I just wanted to return to . . . to the hotel. You know.'

'I don't. Tell me.'

Lambert shrugged. 'What's there to tell? It's a mess. She's dead.'

'And you killed her!'

It pumped adrenalin into Lambert and he showed more signs of interest in his surroundings.

'Me? I killed her? You're mad! Kill her — I loved her!'

'You were also married. And you killed her, when she told you she was pregnant.'

'What?' Lambert sat up in his chair, his eyes round in disbelief, his mouth gaping. *Pregnant?*'

'You'll be telling me now that you didn't know she was pregnant. You'll be telling me that you never even touched her.' Crow stood up and away from the desk and pushed his hands in his pockets. 'Come on. Let's have the whole sorry tale.'

'But it's true! I didn't know she was pregnant — honestly, I didn't know. It's possible she didn't know either — I'm sure she'd have told me.'

'Perhaps she'd have told you that night she died,' Crow suggested casually.

'I don't know. She did sound nervous when she . . .'

Lambert's voice died away disconsolately and he stared at Crow with a curiously reproachful expression in his eyes. But this wasn't a game and there were no rules, and no kindnesses and no fair play. This was a murder enquiry.

'You were going to say that she sounded nervous when she agreed to meet you that night.'

Lambert stared at the floor.

'I don't know what you mean. I wasn't going to say that at all.'

'All right. What *were* you going to say?'

Lambert shook his head. Crow glanced at Wilson and gestured for the papers the sergeant was holding. Wilson handed them across and Crow read them once more quickly, before addressing Lambert again.

'It's no good, you know. We've got it all here, your pitiful attempts to lay a false trail. You told your wife you were going to an advisory committee meeting in London. There was no such meeting, in fact. You said you caught the ten o'clock train from London; only five people got off that train at Sedleigh, and the ticket collector is prepared to swear that none of them was a youngish man answering your description. In the course of time we'll probably be able to get all five passengers to come forward. I've no doubt there won't be a single taxi driver able to support your claim that you took a taxi home from the station. So you weren't in London, and you have been carrying on with the Harland girl and she had told her friend that she had a date that night. The girl was to cover up for her while she met you, went off to your love-nest again. So don't try to tell me you didn't meet her. And don't try to tell me she didn't inform you of her pregnancy.'

'All right, all right, all right! I had arranged to meet her; we were to go to the hotel! But she didn't turn up. And I didn't know she was pregnant.'

The vehemence of the outburst could have denoted an innocent man; it could equally have denoted a panic-stricken killer who felt the walls closing in on him. There was no way of telling which was the truth. Yet. Crow went behind his desk and sat down, motioning to Wilson to take a seat also.

'All right, Lambert, you'd better tell us all about it.'

'About . . . about Rosemary and me?'

'Everything.'

Lambert licked his lips and twisted one hand into his jacket pocket. His eyes failed to meet Crow's. He was a distressed, unhappy man who seemed to have lost his foothold on life, and was slipping he knew not where. Crow waited.

'I hardly know where to start,' Lambert said. 'It's not simple, you see. I could give you facts, but it's more than facts. Rosemary and me, well, it all started not just because we were two people who were physically attracted to each other. I mean, it wasn't as simple as that. We both needed something, we both wanted something that we weren't even aware of before we met each other. And then, suddenly, there it was. And there we were . . . I'm not explaining this very well.'

'I'm trying to follow,' Crow said drily. 'If you deal in facts only, perhaps we'll get somewhere. To start with, where did you meet her, and when did the romance start?'

Lambert's chubby face crumpled and he seemed almost about to burst into tears, but he pulled himself together with an effort.

'I met her at college; I danced with her at a college function, the first term she was at Burton. We were both attracted, but nothing really happened until I met her in the car park last autumn, as I was coming away. We began to talk . . .' His eyes came up to Crow's, appealingly. 'She was an only child you see, and she was shy, even though her poise and her carriage led people to believe otherwise. And I, well, Joan — my wife — and I, we hadn't been hitting it off and . . .'

'And you seduced her.'

'It wasn't like that! We were in love!'

'You started to take her to a hotel.'

'How did you discover the hotel? I didn't expect you to come there today and find me—'

'Your sentiment overrode your judgment, Lambert. Tucked in a pocket in a coat of yours at home was a receipted account for one of your nights at the hotel. Mr and Mrs Lambert. But your wife had never been there.'

'I took Rosemary there,' Lambert agreed miserably. 'We were in love.'

'You said that. So why did you push her down the stairs?'

'Push her? What do you mean?'

'We've now completed our investigation at Burton. The scene-of-crime unit discovered a smear of blood on the stair-rail. The rest had been wiped away. We can now assume that Rosemary Harland was pushed from the top of the stairs; that she struck her head on the rail, and broke her neck; that her killer dragged her, hid the body in the lift and placed one of the gloves he used in Peters's office and the other in his car. We think that she was killed by her lover—'

'I tell you I didn't kill her! I agree we had arranged to meet that night and it was supposed to be for eight, at the George Hotel car park. She was working late, and she told me that she might not be able to get away even then. It was something to do with examination papers — she was helping the office staff with their processing, or something. So when she didn't come at eight, and eight-thirty, I wasn't unduly worried. I guessed she'd been delayed. It wasn't until nine or nine-fifteen that I decided I'd better go and look for her. I went up to Burton and got there at nine-thirty or thereabouts; there were lights on in the Administration block so I thought she might still be there. I didn't worry too much, and I didn't go in because I had arranged a stand-in for my lecture and I didn't want to be seen on the premises when I was supposed to be at a meeting in London.'

'How long did you stay outside?'

'Only about ten minutes. I suddenly realised I was being silly. I'd arranged to meet her at the George; we could have passed on my way up to Burton. So I hared back to the George to see if she'd arrived in the meanwhile. She hadn't. I hung around there, in the car park, until ten-thirty. I knew then she wasn't coming.'

'You didn't get home until much later.'

'I had to keep the pretence up, that I was in London, I mean. I couldn't go home too early, or Joan would have been suspicious.' Crow frowned and ran a hand over his bald head.

'So you say she never told you she was pregnant, you didn't see her that night, you didn't kill her. . . I suppose the first you heard about it all was next morning?'

'At the college. We . . . we all heard the news.'

'Tell me this, Mr Lambert. You were Rosemary's lover, you'd arranged to meet her that evening, you were expecting to go to your usual hotel — and then, next morning after your disappointment at not seeing her, you suddenly discover she's dead. I find it rather curious that I've received no report of your shock. I mean, you *loved* her! Your wife noticed no change in your demeanour; the other members of staff, the office, no one, it would seem, noticed any change in you at all. What's the reason for that, Mr Lambert? Are you just a hard man or a man capable of restraining his emotions, or was it just that you *already knew she was dead because you killed her?*'

'You keep saying that!' Lambert jumped to his feet and Wilson rose also, quickly, to place one warning hand on the young man's shoulder. Lambert cast a distraught glance at the sergeant and then subsided, sat down in his chair again. 'You keep saying that, but it's not true. I can't explain, I can't answer the questions you raise. The fact is I was more than shocked; I was numb with disbelief. I couldn't understand it, I just couldn't understand or believe it. I went through the day somehow, but automatically — you know? I wasn't aware what I was doing, and you'll remember classes were cancelled anyway and I just sat with the others in the common room and they chatted in blasted sepulchral tones but I didn't really hear them. I was just numb.'

'Your wife noticed nothing when you got home.'

'Joan has come to notice very little about me during the last year.' There was a bitter note in his voice. 'I discovered the reason why the other night, when I came home unexpectedly.'

'That was when you attacked her?'

'She was in bed with a bloody Arab!' Crow stared at the man. He couldn't be certain which of the two facts had really made Lambert angry — the fact that his wife had taken a lover, or the fact that the lover was an Arab and a student to boot. Lambert could hardly complain if she had taken a lover, for he himself had been conducting an affair with Rosemary Harland, so it had to be the knowledge he was sharing his wife with a coloured student that had driven him to a violent frenzy.

'You went straight to the hotel the night you left home?'

'After I caught Joan? Yes. I went to pieces, I felt horrible. It was another shock, you know, coming after Rosemary's death. I felt as though my whole world was crumbling — that sounds theatrical, I know, but my marriage and my love had both been destroyed, all at once. I ran out, I got the car, I drove around, slept in the car that night and next day I went to . . . to our hotel. I was there for two days. Until your policemen came.'

A strained silence fell as the two policemen stared at the lecturer in the chair.

'Tell me,' Crow asked curiously, 'if you loved Miss Harland, why didn't you leave your wife?'

Lambert stared at him. He was silent for several seconds. Then his glance fell away and he shrugged despondently.

'We talked about it; I would have done eventually. But it wasn't the appropriate time. Rosemary . . . she wasn't twenty-one yet and her parents, they're very middle-class, you know, and her mother has a weak heart. Rosemary

142

didn't want to distress her. And there was Joan's thesis, as well—'

'What?'

Lambert had a hangdog look about him as he shook his head.

'Well, Joan was busy with her thesis and it was a difficult time for her and I didn't think it was the occasion to worry her . . .' His voice died away as Crow stared in bafflement at Wilson. The sergeant didn't meet his eye.

'So the reason why you didn't leave your wife was that she was doing a thesis?'

Crow shook his head sadly.

'Can I go?' Lambert asked pathetically, after a short silence.

'You're not serious! Charge him, Wilson, you've got enough on him to throw him in the cells, after that fracas at the hotel. That'll do for a start. We can get on with the murder stuff later.'

'You mean you *still* think I did it, that I killed Rosemary?'

Crow wrinkled his nose in distaste as though he were confronted by a plate of fish in an advanced state of decomposition. 'It's not beyond the bounds of possibility.'

When the stocky Yorkshire sergeant returned a few minutes later he wore a doubtful expression on his craggy face.

'We've charged him with assault and battery, driving without due care and attention, obstructing the police in the execution of their duty and if those charges don't hold him in the cells for a while we could try attempted murder too. He drove that car straight at the boys.'

'That should be enough. So why are you looking so damned miserable?'

'If I may say so, sir, I think we'll have trouble making the murder of the Harland girl stick with Lambert.'

'Tell me.'

'Well, if he didn't know she was pregnant — and *we'd* have to show that he did — and if there's no physical evidence to link him with the college that night, it's not going to be easy. He doesn't have a key to the premises, like the Heads of Faculty and the Rector do. How could he have got in and out?'

'Perhaps he's a resourceful man. You're telling me nothing I haven't recognized, Wilson. There's a strong chance he did do it, but I know it isn't going to be easy to prove it. But when the hell is it easy, anyway?'

He leaned back in his chair and locked his hands behind his head, to stare morosely at the ceiling. He had Rosemary Harland's lover, who might possibly have wanted her out of the way if he knew she was pregnant, and if he wanted to keep his wife — and if he could have got into the building to kill her. Too many 'ifs' for comfort. Then he had the five men who had had access to the building — Stevens, Redman, Carliss, Svensson and West — but who seemed to have no motive to kill the girl. Unless one of them also had been Rosemary's lover. An unlikely contingency, and he could imagine the violent protest that would have come from Lambert had he suggested the possibility. But then, every lover was the same, he would always feel that he and he alone provided the functional and emotional centre of his mistress's life.

Then there was the rector. Crow couldn't make up his mind about Peters. He was convinced the man was unscrupulous and would stop at little to achieve his ends. But why would he have wanted to kill the girl, his secretary. His secretary . . .

'Wilson,' he said thoughtfully, 'I wonder whether Rosemary Harland could have found out something about Peters? Something he wouldn't have wanted noised about. Lambert says the girl arranged to meet him at eight. But she stayed late at Burton. None of the other staff did. What was she doing there? Was she confronting Peters about something she'd discovered in his files? Was that an occasion when they could have argued, and he killed her?'

Wilson looked wary. He was encumbered with a greater respect for authority and influence than Crow.

'I think we ought to go carefully there, sir. After that last interview, and Dr Peters's accident—'

Crow dismissed it with a snort. He wasn't prepared to let Peters off the hook that easily. The rector had been the one at the college to know Rosemary best, after all, if one discounted Lambert.

'I think we'll have to get all Peters's files checked. Just to make sure. And will you chase up the lab again, about the girl's clothes?'

Wilson nodded and left the room. Crow sat on for a while, then went to the canteen and obtained a cup of tea. Tiny pieces of leaf swirled around and around the surface of the tea, little black specks, circling aimlessly like the questions in his head, going around and around and ending up where they began. Nowhere. There was one central big leaf swirling in the cup but in the Harland investigation no one seemed to be out in front leading the others, not even Lambert. Crow was an experienced officer, and in his opinion there had been an element of truth in Lambert's protestations. Crow was also sufficiently experienced to discount the formation of opinion based on insufficient evidence.

So it all left him back where he'd started.

He had a murder case on his hands and there were too many questions to be answered, too many to see the right one, the necessary one. Too many trees to see the wood.

Someone was standing at his table. He looked up, surprised. It was Wilson. His expression told Crow that he had something of importance to impart. Crow waited.

'Sorry to disturb you, sir, but I rang the lab like you said and I thought you'd want to know straight away.'

'Well?'

'It's another complication, I'm afraid, sir.'

'Well?'

'They've been looking through her clothes, the stuff she'd been wearing the last few weeks. Nothing much came to light at all except in her raincoat. And even with that they're not absolutely sure — they insisted that this was merely a preliminary report, and they don't think there's really enough to go on but—'

Wilson paused and Crow leaned forward. '-but you'll be interested to know they found minute traces of a substance in the pocket of the raincoat, sir. Or to be more exact, traces of two substances. One was a dusting from a mixture of amphetamine and barbiturate.'

'And the other?'

'Cannabis.'

* * *

Lambert had denied all knowledge of it, of course. But then, he'd now got to the stage where he was denying everything and screaming for a lawyer as soon as Crow or Wilson came anywhere near him. He denied having seen Rosemary that night, he denied having killed her, he denied knowing she was pregnant and he absolutely denied knowing that she had been in possession of drugs. More, he didn't believe it. He started bawling like a young calf at Crow, insisting that the police must have planted it in Rosemary's raincoat.

The Harlands would scream too, Crow had no doubt about that. Crow decided not to interview them himself: the last experience had been one he had no desire to repeat and Wilson could probably handle this one more tactfully than he. Besides, Crow doubted whether they'd be able to shed much light on this issue, for in his experience parents rarely knew what their sons or daughters were up to. The barrier that existed between the two generations was certainly effective as far as matters such as drugs were concerned: parents could not and did not understand why young people took drugs, and more often than not they simply did not believe that their children came into the drug-taking category. The Harlands wouldn't believe it, of that Crow was certain.

Perhaps Antony Peters would. Perhaps Antony Peters would know how Rosemary Harland came into possession of cannabis.

The desk sergeant checked that Peters was at the Polytechnic before Crow left Headquarters. When he arrived at Burton, Crow was surprised and a little nettled to be kept waiting, particularly since Peters had been informed in advance that the Inspector was coming to see him. Crow waited for a few minutes in the anteroom and then wandered out into the hallway. There were a few students walking up the stairs with books under their arms and there was a small group standing near some public telephones stationed in one corner of the hallway.

Among the group were two people he recognized.

As he stared at them one of the two looked up and caught sight of him standing there grimly. The student grinned, and said something to the others before detaching himself from the group to walk towards Crow. The second man whom Crow had recognized followed him. Sadruddin and Peter Rhodes.

Sadruddin's lean face was creased by a wide smile. He possessed considerable charm, this young man, but underneath it Crow sensed the sting of a scorpion. This man could be smooth and persuasive and friendly but he could not be trusted.

'Good morning, Inspector. A courtesy visit?'

'You might say that.'

'You've already met my friend, Peter Rhodes? Of course you have, the morning of the demo, wasn't it?'

Rhodes wasn't smiling. His freckled face was sullen and as he stood there with one hand tucked into the belt of his jeans there was studied insolence in his manner.

'Are you planning another one of those demonstrations?'

'Something like that,' Sadruddin said easily. 'But we're being very constitutional about it, Inspector. That's our action committee over there — though you can't get much real action to draw the necessary attention to ourselves. You know, the press, television, and the fuzz of course. We got to keep the fuzz informed!'

'Why don't you just do what you're supposed to do at college?'

'Don't be a drag, man. This is the day of student power, and we want our rights as citizens.' Sadruddin was smiling as he spoke and Crow gained the impression that the man had little conviction that his words were meaningful — they were attitudes that he found convenient to adopt for purposes of his own. 'We're out to democratize the institutions of higher learning. We're out to give youth a chance to air its views, we're out to revolutionize, man! The lecture room, ha, that's for the birds.'

He glanced at Rhodes and grinned but Rhodes was still staring resentfully at Crow. The Inspector suspected that Rhodes was still angry about the way Crow had treated him the morning of the demonstration. Perhaps Rhodes saw himself as an emergent leader, and Crow recalled that Sadruddin hadn't been around when the demonstration started; it had been Rhodes's chance to show his mettle but he had been browbeaten by the police inspector. He was still sore about it, still sore at having been shown up as lacking in steel. Sadruddin . . . now Sadruddin hadn't been bested that morning. He'd given way, certainly, but in an insolent, devil-may-care way that had in no sense detracted from his public image with the students.

'Anyway, how's your scene, Inspector? What's with the killing bit?'

Crow's glance flickered from Rhodes to Sadruddin.

'Why do you ask?'

'Interest, real, pure interest! I'm a law student, didn't you know, and it's penology and criminology for me once I graduate. So the chance to observe the fuzz at work, close at hand, it's not to be missed.'

'It may well be,' Crow said, turning on his heel to walk away, 'that you'll get the chance to observe it even more closely, from the inside of a cell, if you keep on the way you are.'

'Well said, Inspector!' Sadruddin jeered. 'You want to join our right-wing compatriots? They'll welcome an Establishment figure like you with open arms.'

Crow ignored the jibe and went back into the anteroom. He stuck his head through the doorway to speak to Peters's secretary but even as he did so he heard the door to the anteroom open. He looked back and a man in a dark grey suit was entering, carrying a briefcase. His face was round, chubby, with a skin as fuzzy as brushed nylon.

'Good morning, Inspector Crow.'

Crow nodded as the man went straight into Peters's office. A few moments later the man reappeared and said pleasantly, 'You can come in now, Inspector.'

Peters was standing in front of the desk.

His face was grim and stiffened by dislike.

'Good morning,' he said curtly. 'As you will see, I decided that I would not meet you this time until my solicitor was present also. This is Mr Andrews.'

'This is most careful of you, Dr Peters. You needn't have bothered, though.'

'That remains to be seen. What is it you want? I might say right at the start that I've discussed your last visit with Mr Andrews and he's informed me that you have no right to press me with questions about my background. So if that's the reason for your visit, we can conclude it even before it starts.'

'It seems you're in no great haste to help the police.'

Andrews smiled, a lawyer's smile, false, cunning, its meaning far divorced from its appearance.

'Not at all, Inspector, we're only too pleased, and indeed *eager* to help the police as far as we are able, but we must draw the line at personal questions which have no direct bearing upon the case.'

'Or answers which might incriminate your client.'

'Statements such as that are dangerous,' Andrews replied, still smiling, 'and a careful man would be well advised not to make them. Innuendoes, you know . . .'

'What is it you want, Crow?'

Peters at least was making no pretence at politeness. He stood with his back to his desk, his arms folded, a heavy frown on his handsome features. He bore no signs of his recent 'accident', apart from a reddish patch of skin near his lips but he spoke as though his mouth were full of pebbles and was obviously still suffering from some soreness of the tongue.

'I have some further questions to ask about Miss Harland.'

'I don't see how I can help you.'

'You haven't heard the questions yet.'

'What is it you want to know, Inspector?' Andrews interposed sweetly. Crow hesitated, then turned to Peters.

'Miss Harland — was she a moody girl? Subject to fits of depression?'

'She always seemed a balanced, pleasant personality to me. I don't understand what you mean.'

'There weren't occasions when she seemed to think she was super-efficient, or otherwise depressed; no occasions when she seemed hazy, over-excited, over-confident, prone to take things lightly?'

'I've already told you she was efficient, quiet, and well-balanced. There's nothing I can add to that.'

'All right. Then tell me this: have you had any trouble with the students as far as "pot" is concerned?'

' "Pot"? Drugs, you mean? Good heavens, no. It's true that last term there was an occasion when—'

'One moment, Dr Peters, I think we'd better get to the point of the Inspector's question.'

Crow ignored the solicitor and said quietly, 'You were about to say that last term you had an occasion when . . .'

'No, Dr Peters was about to make no admission which might leave him open to a charge of failing to inform the police that an offence of a criminal nature had been committed in the college. He was about to say no such thing, were you, Dr Peters?'

The rector opened his mouth, and closed it again. He stared thoughtfully at Crow. Andrews smiled again.

'Now just what is this all about?'

Crow hesitated. He was angry. He realised he wasn't going to get far with the solicitor there but there was no way he could get round the problem. All right, if Peters wanted it this way Crow could play rough too.

'I have reason to believe that there might be a charge relating to the possession of narcotics arising in this college, as well as murder. I have reason to believe that some drugs were in the possession of Rosemary Harland. Since she spent a great deal of time here in this office and in this college it's possible that she obtained the drugs here rather than from some "pusher" outside. It doesn't look as though I'm going to get much co-operation from you, so I have no alternative but to inform you that I shall be getting a warrant sworn out for these premises to be searched. In addition, all your files will have to be handed over to my officers. Forthwith.'

Peters straightened and protested angrily with his slim hands waving in front of him. 'You can't do that! You can't just walk in here and—'

Andrews interrupted him quickly with one hand on his arm. The solicitor stared at Crow, a mongoose watching a snake.

'I've no doubt, Inspector, you've got grounds for asking for a warrant.'

'I've got grounds.'

'Then I don't think we need to go to those lengths, getting a warrant, I mean. I'm sure that Dr Peters is only too pleased to render any assistance he can in the circumstances.'

'But I don't see—'

Andrews waved the rector to silence. He turned back to Crow. The speculative look remained in his eye.

'I should be grateful if one of my clerks were present while Dr Peters's files are scrutinized, and they will not be removed from the premises, of course. Not without the rector's permission, that is.'

'You afraid we'll plant something on him?'

'You're a very direct man, Inspector.' Crow was getting what he wanted, access to Peters's files and the right to search the premises without fuss, but there was little joy in it for him. He would have liked the rector to put up a fight, so that he could have hammered him into the ground, verbally. Andrews had forestalled it, and it would now appear to everyone that Peters was more than willing to help the police. When Crow stomped from the rector's office he was in an unpleasant frame of mind.

There was someone in the anteroom, talking to Peters's secretary. He had his back to Crow and the girl was just saying ' . . . much better, but he's decided not to keep his appointment with Mr Fanshaw this morning—' when he turned and Crow saw who it was.

'Mr West. Are you back at work now?' The heavy, serious face was touched with the ghost of a smile. West nodded slowly, and his jowls quivered.

'Not completely, I suppose. I'm back, but my principal lecturers are really doing all the work. I feel almost supernumerary and it makes me wonder whether I need be here at all, at any time.'

'Hmph. But you're feeling better.'

'I feel quite well, though I'm told I must take things easily.'

'It wasn't as serious as you made out, then?'

The pouched eyes met his calmly.

'It would seem not.'

Crow nodded and moved past West and out into the hallway. He crossed to the main doors and stood there a moment blinking in the sunlight before he went out and walked down to his car. A few students lounged under the trees, but it was all very quiet. The English academic scene. It had been somewhat different the last time he was here.

The next call that Crow had to make was out at Edgerton Lane. Mrs Woods wouldn't like the police car outside her door for a second time but that was just hard luck. He wanted another word with Sally Woods. The last time he had spoken to her she had been withdrawn, evasive in her replies without actually holding back the answers he demanded of her. He was beginning to wonder now whether he had asked the right questions.

This time he wasn't to suffer the pomposity of Joseph Woods at least. Through the frosted glass he saw Mrs Woods come to the door and as it opened he heard the murmur of voices from the sitting-room. She must be having guests to tea. She looked suitably upset when she opened the door, one hand fluttering theatrically to her ample breast.

'I'd like to see Sally, please. There are some more questions I'd like to ask.'

Mrs Woods's eyes were round as blue-centred white-edged saucers.

'I'm afraid she's not here, Inspector.'

'Where can I reach her?'

'I . . . I'm afraid I don't know. She's left home.'

* * *

When Crow walked back into the office he spoke to Wilson, playing as usual with his typewriter like a

153

tremulous virgin with a kinky magazine, fascinated but unable to cope.

'Have you been to see the Harlands?'

'Yes, sir. They can't believe that Rosemary had any connection with drugs at all.'

'You mean they *refuse* to believe it.'

'That's about the size of it.'

'Well, you'd better get on to the Woods girl now. She's left home, and her parents don't know where she's gone. Mrs Woods suspects she might have gone off with some lad — she might have spent last weekend with him, and she thinks that her husband's seen the man. So get down to the bank, have a word with Joseph Woods and get a description of the man he saw with Sally. And send Gates in here.'

The detective-constable entered hurriedly a few minutes later. Crow looked up at the raw-boned young man.

'A chance for you to gain some further impressions.'

Gates's face became a little pink at the gibe.

'I want you and Framwell to get out to Burton Polytechnic. I want you to go through the offices, any place where Rosemary Harland might have worked, with a fine toothcomb. And I want you to go through every file that she might have had access to, and particularly every file in Peters's office. All right?'

'Yes, sir. '

'Did you get anything more out of your check on Peters's background?'

'Nothing new, sir. Just more detail than we had previously. But I don't think there's anything which is useful to us.'

'That's for me to decide,' Crow said bleakly. 'Is that the file there?'

'Yes sir.' Gates handed the file to Crow and waited for a moment. 'Is that all, sir?'

Crow was already reading the file. He raised his head.

'Eh . . . what? Yes, get on with it!'

Gates left, trailing a comet tail of affronted efficiency. Crow was unaware of it. He was reading the file on Peters and, as Gates had said, there was nothing new in it. Some details on the year before Peters had married his Lady Sarah caught his attention. The girl to whom Peters had been engaged was called Valerie White. She had been living with her mother and stepfather, whose name she had taken. It would seem that her mother had divorced her first husband, four years before Valerie died. There was a photostat copy of a newspaper report of the girl's death — she'd been driving a car which stalled on a railway crossing. When the London express hit the car she hadn't had a chance. There were some details of her background . . . employed as a secretary at Munson Chemicals (that would be where Peters had met her, probably, and she might even have been his secretary). There was nothing there that could be of any use for him.

Unless Valerie White's death had not been accidental. It would certainly have suited Antony Peters to have her out of the way — he got engaged to Lady Sarah within a year of Valerie White's death. But such supposition was fanciful. Crow rose and prowled restlessly around the room. Lambert locked up in the cells, the Faculty heads still under suspicion, the drugs thing getting complicated by Sally Woods running away from home, and he was still wondering about Peters.

He glanced at his watch. Six-fifteen. Time to get out, get some air, obtain a meal at the hotel. He closed the office door quietly behind him as he went out.

* * *

At six-eighteen Fanshaw finally got through to the desk sergeant.

'Chief Inspector Crow? I'm afraid he's just left the station, sir. Is there anything I can do . . . anyone else I can put you in touch with?'

Fanshaw hesitated.

'No, thank you, I don't think so. It's the Chief Inspector I wanted to speak to, about the Harland case, but it can wait until tomorrow. I'll ring again in the morning.'

Fanshaw replaced the receiver and stood in the hallway of his bungalow, peeling off his driving gloves. He dropped them beside the telephone and bent to pick up the pile of mail, consisting mainly of official OHMS envelopes, from the mat. He flicked through the envelopes as he walked towards the sitting-room, then placed them on the table before taking off his coat and helping himself to a glass of sherry from the decanter on the sideboard. He sat down and sipped at the sherry.

He could have spoken to someone else at the station, that Sergeant Wilson perhaps, but he had felt a curious disinclination to do so. He was one of Her Majesty's Inspectors of Schools and the activity he'd been indulging in was hardy consonant with his position or his status. He had allowed his curiosity to get the better of him and he had started behaving in a most Lord Peter Wimsey fashion, the amateur thinking he could do better than the professional policeman. Perhaps that was why he wanted to speak to Crow, and only Crow, for he felt that from Crow, he would get a sympathetic hearing.

After all, he had discovered nothing *definite*.

Interesting, certainly, and suggestive, but not definite. It could be that Crow would snort in derision at his theorizing, but he didn't think so. The Chief Inspector might present a forbidding appearance but Fanshaw felt that the man had a warmth and a liking for human beings that was cloaked by that gaunt exterior — Crow was not a man who would sneer, or deride. Even the efforts of an amateur detective!

Fanshaw smiled. It really was too ridiculous, a man of his age and status getting excited and intrigued by a situation to such an extent that he spent time — even *official* time! — trying to investigate a murder! How on earth he was going to be able to put on his official diary the mileage he'd recorded he had simply no idea. And the result of it all — would Crow say there's no fool like an old fool? He didn't think so . . . particularly if the information he had for the Chief Inspector was as relevant as Fanshaw suspected it to be.

He sighed, glancing at his watch and reached for his mail. He'd better run through it before he ate the meal that Mrs Palin, his housekeeper, would have left in the oven for him.

The first few envelopes revealed nothing of importance: notifications of promotions of office staff he did not know, an invitation to attend the opening of a school in his district, a statutory instrument on teachers' pay, a copy of *Trends in Education* and two professional journals on circulation from Inspectors' Despatch.

He left the largest envelope until last. It contained a yellow Minister's file and he groaned. That meant immediate action. The Secretary of State did not wait upon the digestion. Fanshaw opened the file and read the minutes it enclosed. The last minute sheet was from a Chief Inspector.

'HMI Mr R Fanshaw

You will see from the above minutes that considerable disquiet has been expressed by the Minister that the delicate situation regarding student activity at Burton Polytechnic would seem to have been exacerbated by actions of the administrative staff. There now seems every likelihood that a question will be raised in the House in connection with the attached letter below. The background to this is that a complaint has been made to the local MP Mr Collins, concerning this matter, and he intends raising it as an issue with the Minister in the House. We need to be fully apprised of the facts of the situation, but more important, I think you will agree, is the desirability of *no repetition* of the action taken by the rector, Peters. It would seem he has acquiesced or even encouraged industry in the sending of "spies" into the student meetings to obtain reports of the proceedings These reports presumably go on private student files and the students are incensed about this and the involvement of business interests. We are not concerned to enquire how the student making the complaint came into possession of the attached letter, nor would we normally be concerned in this matter at all. But the Office is hesitant about making a direct approach to Peters to suggest he desist until things 'cool down'. It is suggested that his District Inspector might meet him and make the position clear. It would be helpful if you could see the rector as quickly as possible on this matter. The tenor of the discussion I leave to your own appraisal of the local situation.'

The Chief Inspector's usual scrawl appeared below the minute, with the date, and attached to the minute sheet was the letter mentioned. It constituted the evidence of someone having been sitting in at student meetings and making reports. The letter was not original, but a photocopy. There could be little doubt about its authenticity.

STRICTLY CONFIDENTIAL
A Peters Esq., MA, PhD,
The Rector,
Burton Polytechnic.
Dear Rector,
At Sir Humphrey's request I attended a meeting of the Student Action Committee which brought together some fifty other students. The meeting was addressed by the student leader Sadruddin Khan. My personal conclusions are based upon an admittedly limited knowledge of the local situation but they are as follows:-

(1) Nothing that Sadruddin said could involve any question of a prosecution under the Aliens Restrictions Act, 1919.

(2) Sadruddin's speech revealed a very definite bias against the polytechnic administration but he revealed an equally violent reaction to employers in general and I consider that he is extremely Left Wing in his leanings. It is possible that a certain indoctrination of other students could ensue, since he is a persuasive speaker and seems to exert considerable influence during his speeches.

(3) My suggestion is that the earliest opportunity should be taken to expel this student, but only on obviously constitutional grounds. Examination failure is the obvious one.

The attached notes give greater detail of the content of Sadruddin's speech, and these are intended for your confidential files.

Sincerely,

There were no notes attached, though marks of pinholes could be seen in the paper. The signature was indecipherable.

Fanshaw sat back angrily. This was too much! He saw no reason why HMI should become involved in a political quarrel of this kind, and he certainly regarded it as not his job. The Chief Inspector should not have placed him in this position . . . but he was stuck with it now. And it would have to be dealt with immediately. He rang the college at once.

The girl on the switchboard at Burton Polytechnic put him through to the registrar.

'Is Dr Peters in the college?'

'I'm afraid not, Mr Fanshaw, he's not available this evening.'

'When is the next student meeting scheduled?'

'The Action Committee? I understand there is a meeting this evening. They seem to be very active this week and—'

'Is any college or business representative attending?'

The Academic Registrar was silent. Harshly, Fanshaw repeated the question and the anger in his voice provoked a nervous response.

'I'm sorry, Mr Fanshaw, I'm not sure what you mean, and it's all rather difficult—'

'Listen to me! I know damned well that Dr Peters has agreed to people being sent into these meetings. I know it, you know it, and the *students* know it! They've got hold of letters on your files—'

'But they can't have done that, they—'

'I'm telling you they have! And there's going to be trouble unless the spy you've sent in is pulled out!'

'Trouble?'

'Political trouble — and maybe the students themselves will take a hand.'

The Academic Registrar uttered several mild epithets and worried verbally at his dilemma but finally admitted to Fanshaw that a man had been sent in from the college to the meeting. A junior clerk this time, a man Fanshaw had seen from time to time. Fanshaw groaned. It was worse than he had feared. An office clerk!

'Can you get him out of there?'

'Well, I don't know, Mr Fanshaw, we're short-staffed just now and I don't see how I can send anyone else to—'

'Forget it. I'll be around to discuss this with the rector in the morning.' Fanshaw's tone was curt and he replaced the telephone abruptly. In an angry frame of mind he strode towards the hall cupboard and began to put on his coat. Mrs Palin's dinner would have to wait. That young clerk would have to be pulled out of that meeting before trouble really started. If the students got to him, and grabbed his notes, the Minister really would find the bullets flying in the House.

What a job for HMI to do, he thought disgustedly as he drove away from the bungalow. It was all a far cry from the academic life he had once known, before he faced the Civil Service Commissioners, almost twenty years ago.

* * *

The meeting was already in progress when he finally arrived. Like other student meetings of late, it was held at Deercliffe Hall and Fanshaw was surprised at the size of the turnout. There were about eighty people there, as far as he could guess, and it was quite obvious that feelings must be running high at the college.

No heads turned as he walked in at the back of the hall. Sadruddin was speaking on the platform, waving his hand to emphasize points he was making, but Fanshaw hardly listened. The Arab's voice was a sharp background to his own thoughts as he stared around him, looking for the clerk from the office. It was several minutes before he caught sight of him, and all the while Sadruddin continued.

' . . . we cannot allow the standards of the college to be seduced by the infiltration of Big Brother Business! The paths have already been pointed out to us in the last year or so, at the universities and the colleges; there is only one way in which we can get our voices heard; there is only one way in which we can obtain the evidence we need, to disturb even the Establishment. We must go in, we must seize, we must take upon ourselves the mantle of democratization and revolution! For what else is there if we do not move? Is there any chance of action by the academic staff? Are they jealous enough of their positions? I tell you, if we leave it to them, all we will hear is the dull thuds of academic knives in academic backs as they struggle in the corridors of pseudo-power for the largesse that industry and commerce bestow upon them, forgetting the price that they will have to pay for such munificence!'

The clerk was sitting at the end of a row, at the side of the hall. At least he had had that much sense, but there were students behind him, and his attempts to hide the fact that he was taking notes only made more obtrusive the nature of his activity. Even so, the students about him were so taken up with Sadruddin's vehement outbursts that they appeared not to have noticed what the clerk was doing. The sooner Fanshaw got him out of there the better. Provided it could be done quietly.

Fanshaw moved among the pillars at the back of the hall until he stood directly in the shadow of one, opposite the young clerk. For a few minutes he tried to capture his attention but it was to no avail. The clerk was too concerned with getting his notes completed and could not be distracted. Fanshaw fumed, getting hotter as he waited. One or two students at the back glanced curiously in his direction and he knew that if he didn't get the man out soon something would happen, and violently.

But Sadruddin was reaching the climax of his speech to the Action Committee. He was advocating total war against the administration, he was advocating violence, he was advocating anarchy, and all in the interests of academic purity and autonomy. It was an interesting, explosive and well-argued thesis that would find few dissenters in this hall, Fanshaw suspected. But he was not interested in following the argument through.

Sadruddin was ending his speech, soon the tumult would arise, without doubt, and in the middle of the noise Fanshaw should be able to attract the clerk's attention.

This was how it turned out. Sadruddin finished on an almost hysterical note and a great wave of sound bellowed through the hall. Students leapt to their feet, hands above their heads, clapping, and the clerk stood up too, stuffing papers in his pocket as Fanshaw moved lithely forward until he stood at the clerk's side. He gripped the young man's elbow. A startled face turned to him, and he saw recognition in the young man's eyes.

'Come on,' Fanshaw said abruptly. 'Out!' The clerk opened his mouth to say something but caught the urgency in Fanshaw's tone. Someone jostled Fanshaw as he turned and began to walk towards the side of the hall but he said nothing. He glanced up towards the platform and Sadruddin was leaving it, his face flushed. But he was not looking at his audience; he was staring directly at Robert Fanshaw.

The clerk was at Fanshaw's elbow. 'What's up, sir?'

'Let's get out of here, with those damned notes!'

Fanshaw turned towards the back of the hall, but suddenly a small group of students materialized near the doors. It was taking too much of a chance to walk past them; Fanshaw wanted no trouble, no confrontation. Already the noise was dying, Sadruddin had left the platform, and so, it seemed, had the other student leaders and the hall was beginning to buzz in some confusion. Fanshaw's pulse quickened and he glanced around the hall.

'The side entrance,' he said urgently, and preceded the young clerk. They walked away from the hall and out through the side door into the corridor beyond. Fanshaw hesitated, then made for the swing doors at the far end of the corridor.

'We should be able to get out this way.' Another short corridor, turning left, but no exit. Back inside and they found a second door, barred, but easily enough opened. It led out into a narrow alley, running at the side of the building.

'Right,' said Fanshaw. 'Get the hell out of here, and report to the registrar in the morning. If I were you, I'd scrap those notes before you see him. They'll cause more trouble than they're worth.'

'I don't understand, sir.'

'Reason not, just do as you're told! I'll see you at the college in the morning. Away with you!'

The young man backed off, shaking his head and then he shrugged and walked quickly away as Fanshaw turned to close the door behind them. The heavy bolts clanged inside as they dropped automatically into place and

Fanshaw breathed a long sigh. He glanced over his shoulder and saw that the clerk had already vanished from the alley. Fanshaw rubbed a hand over his jaw and straightened his tie in a gesture of nervous relief. He began to walk up the alley. He thought he caught a pale glimmer of light from the last doorway on the left, but it could have been his imagination. When he drew level with the doorway he realised it was another exit from the hall. He heard a sliding, scraping sound as he walked past and his first reaction was that it was caused by a stray cat. But then the exploding stars came, and the numbing pain.

And the rushing noise in his head.

Chapter 5

Wilson was waiting for Crow as he came into the station next morning. Crow took off his coat and frowned at the detective-sergeant.

'Don't tell me you've got a problem this early.'

'I don't know, sir. Maybe. There's possibly a connection, but I can't be sure.'

'Connection? What do you mean?'

'Mr Fanshaw telephoned last night, trying to get in touch with you. Wouldn't speak to anyone else.'

'Something to do with the Harland enquiry?'

'Probably. Could hardly be anything else, sir.'

'So?'

'Last night he was attacked, sir. In an alley, outside a hall in which a meeting of the Student Action Committee was held.'

Crow sat down slowly, staring at Wilson's stolid face. He picked up a pencil from the desk and toyed with it, caressing it with long bony fingers. In a soft voice, he said, 'You suggest the attack might be connected with his call to me.'

'Don't know, sir. Could be something to do with the students and their problems at the college. But—'

'But it's a coincidence. Yes . . . I'd better go to see Fanshaw—'

'He's unconscious, sir. Head injuries quite nasty. It'll be some hours, they reckon, before he'll be able to help us at all.'

Crow was suddenly angry. He had liked Fanshaw, and there was the possibility that the man had been playing detective and had suffered as a result. If that was the case, however, it meant that a connection between the Harland murder, Lambert, and Fanshaw's injuries would be difficult to establish, for Lambert was in prison. He could not possibly have been responsible for Fanshaw's situation. On the other hand Crow still had an open mind about young Lambert's involvement in murder.

'I think we'd better check this one out,' he said slowly.

'Gates is already going through Fanshaw's clothing . . . just in case, sir.'

'Good. We'll get out to his home and do a bit of rooting around. If Fanshaw has been playing detective and has turned up something of interest it may well be at his home.'

'Unless the man who attacked him got there first.'

It was a thought that had lain at the back of Crow's mind also, and he decided to go out to the bungalow with Wilson immediately. They stopped at the hospital to collect Fanshaw's keys and received the information that he was still unconscious, and would be too weak to see anyone for purposes of questioning for at least another twenty-four hours. They drove on to the bungalow at Arnleigh, across the Down.

There was no sign of any forced entry and everything inside was clean and tidy. While Wilson walked across the road to speak with the woman who cleaned for Fanshaw, Crow looked around the sitting-room, without really knowing what he was looking for. Fanshaw had telephoned, Fanshaw had been beaten, this was all he had, but he could not afford to ignore the possibility of a link with the Harland case.

Wilson returned to say that Mrs Palin had no information of any assistance to them and Crow nodded; he hadn't supposed she would be able to help them.

He prowled out of the sitting-room and into Fanshaw's office. It was a small room, one corner of which was taken up by a six-foot-high grey metal filing cabinet. Beside the cabinet was an old desk of Victorian construction, fluted and whorled at its edges with ornate carving, and in the other corner near the window stood a cupboard, also six feet high, also grey gunmetal in colour. Standard departmental issue, he had no doubt. He stood in the middle of the room touching the chair in front of the desk. The wall behind him was lined with books, a catholic collection ranging from the strictly educational to the mildly pornographic accountancy, law, politics, business practice, banking. Apuleius and Boccaccio, Henry Miller and Norman Mailer.

He turned his attention to the desk. It was adorned with a reading lamp of superior Japanese manufacture, a desk pen set and a vast array of papers, somewhat scattered. Crow sat down at the desk and proceeded to sort them into some semblance of order. First he removed the pile of pamphlets and placed them on the floor beside the desk and then he shuffled the papers into rough piles, as Wilson came in.

'I'm going to take a preliminary look through these papers myself. We'll also need to know what's in some of these drawers, if nothing obvious comes out of my search. Are Gates and Framwell still at Burton?'

'Dealing with the Peters files, sir.'

'Well, we'll just have to draft a couple more constables in. What have you got there?'

Wilson was stooping, picking something up from the floor. It was cream in colour, paper covered, and published by Her Majesty's Stationery Office.

'Official Diary.'

'Take a look inside.'

'Two weeks to the page. Appointments noted in pencil. He's got something down for yesterday afternoon — the Branch college. And someone's name down for last evening. I can't read his handwriting too well . . .'

'Let me see.' Crow took the book from Wilson and inspected the scrawl closely. After a moment he made it out. Perhaps he'd been expecting to see it. 'Peters. Dr Antony Peters.'

'If he had an appointment with Peters last night, it must have been before Fanshaw went to the Deercliffe Hall.'

'No. Peters cancelled that appointment. He didn't see Fanshaw last night.'

'If he had, perhaps Fanshaw wouldn't have gone to Deercliffe Hall.'

'But he didn't see him. I *suppose.*'

The unexpected thought hung in the air between them like a palpable thing, disturbing in its intensity.

'We still don't know what it is that Fanshaw had to tell us, sir,' Wilson said after a short silence. Crow nodded and turned back to the desk.

'Take the filing cupboard,' he said, and started sifting through the papers. For over an hour they worked without speaking. Most of the papers on the desk were educational in content; many bore departmental headings, and related to approval of advanced courses at colleges of further education; others concerned arrangements for meetings, advisory committees, requests to give talks, preparation of surveys. There were a few official files; they were marked CONFIDENTIAL in two cases but this did not inhibit Crow from reading them. The second file he read gave him what he wanted.

'This is why Fanshaw will have gone to Deercliffe Hall,' he said, and passed the file to Wilson. 'Student politics.'

'I don't see how this relates to the Harland killing, sir.'

'Nor do I, yet, if it does at all.'

Crow continued sifting through the papers, but there was nothing of consequence; he glanced up and saw that Wilson was rapidly reaching the same conclusion about the filing cupboard.

'Mostly stationery.'

Which left them nowhere. Frustration gripped Crow. There had been occasions when he had badly wanted to clear up a case, when he'd felt a personal desire to take a man into custody, but this was different. Fanshaw had been on the point of telling Crow something, and now he was lying in hospital, unconscious, with a battered head.

Rosemary Harland had died of a broken neck.

'Fanshaw had something to show me — surely he'd keep it here, in his office, among his working papers.'

It was wishful thinking but even as he admitted it to himself his glance fell upon the pile of pamphlets that he had placed upon the floor to one side of the desk. He picked them up, flicked through them and discovered that one of them was a Burton Polytechnic prospectus.

There was a piece of folded paper placed between the pages dealing with staffing arrangements at the college. Newspaper. Crow closed the book and unfolded the piece of newspaper. It was a cutting. There was a photograph. He stared at it.

Wilson took up a position at his left shoulder, looking at the photograph, but Crow was hardly aware of the movement. His mind was spinning, sheering away from the track it had been following all morning. He had become obsessed with Peters in many respects, obsessed with his dislike of the man and the possible motivations and past action of the rector of Burton Polytechnic. Perhaps this accounted for his failure to pay sufficient attention to other matters. Lambert was in custody, Peters didn't move far without his solicitor, but Robert Fanshaw had been attacked last night, outside a student meeting.

And there was a photograph, a newspaper cutting in Crow's possession. It showed a group of young people, standing outside Burton polytechnic. Two of the faces were familiar to Crow.

Without a word he stabbed his finger at one of the people in the print and looked enquiringly at Wilson. The Yorkshireman nodded with a solemn face.

'We traced her, late last night, sir. Didn't follow it up until I'd seen you. Then this thing came up and there was no time.'

'There's time now,' Crow said coldly.

* * *

Esktop Hill had at one time been regarded as the fashionable area in Sedleigh. When the town had grown with the advent of light industry and the opening of the engineering works to the south, property on Esktop Hill had been expensive and much sought after. But most of the houses were large, and draughty and in need of repair, and during the forties and early fifties there was a mass middle-class exodus from Esktop Hill to the more favourably designed, modern and 'executive-type' buildings on the north boundary of Sedleigh and the villages beyond, like Arnleigh and Fenleigh. The big houses had decayed, their Georgian and Victorian and Edwardian fronts had peeled, and occasional broken windows had appeared while the gardens became festooned with weeds and thick undergrowth. A new population had moved in. At the bottom of Esktop Hill two derelict houses had been occupied for a while by squatters; a Pakistani family and two West Indian families had rented accommodation half way up; but the top of the hill had retained certain genteel individuals who sighed about the declining standards of the area.

Then suddenly it changed. The late nineteen-fifties brought the property developers back and the rooms were ripped out, the kitchens and lavatories gutted and the houses at the top of the hill became rehabilitated. The middle-classes did not move back because the hill suddenly became too expensive for them, as property values rocketed. The Pakistani family moved without any trouble after a discreet payment was made to them; the West Indian families moved eventually, but only after an action had been brought by them against the owners for intimidation under the new Race Relations Act. By that time the Hill was firmly upper middle-class and a breath of relief sighed and eddied around the splendid gardens and fountains and high-ceilinged rooms when the area became 'white' again.

The legal battle over Hilltop House continued, however.

It was a scar upon the face of the hill, it was a disgrace, something ought to be done about it. But nothing could be done. The situation was quite simple: when land values had been low a group of University students had created a trust, under the direction of one astute law student, and had bought Hilltop House to be held in perpetuity as a student residence. At that time eight students had lived there, and the number had since dropped to six, all of whom were now student members of Burton Polytechnic, since the University had moved to more spacious surroundings fifteen miles away, taking the students with it. The boom in the fifties and sixties changed the face of the hill but did nothing to affect Hilltop House because the trust deed had been drawn up too well by the law student; in his inexperience he'd rendered it virtually unbreakable — at least, it could be broken, perhaps, but only at considerable expense. The remaining trustee lived in the United States, was a wealthy engineer, and remained distantly philanthropic about the whole thing. He wouldn't go to the bother of putting up

171

the rent and he wasn't sufficiently interested in the property to improve it. So it festered, a suppurating sore on the face of the hill, while the students cheerfully misused it and the accommodations officer was inclined to strike it off her list. But there were always students prepared to live there and the residents of the hill let the whole thing rankle inside them, airing their grievance in an emasculated way at futile Esktop Hill Residents Association meetings, once a month, Fridays, seven forty-five p.m.

When Wilson opened the car door for Crow to struggle out there was a cold, unsummer-like wind blowing straight up the hill, throwing into some confusion the wild rhododendrons in the long front garden, and lifting a fluttering curtain at one of the windows of the big, unpainted house with its frowning false shutters and great snarling mouth of a doorway. Crow made his way up the broken drive with Wilson.

'Did you get the names of the residents?'

'I'm afraid not. It's rather difficult — the population is a shifting one, and though the students at Burton have a list which is supposed to control the users of the house, I gather that in fact the premises are handed on from one group to another. It's a very loose sort of arrangement.'

'You could say the same thing about the door too,' Crow observed, pointing to it as it moved in the wind.

'They keep open house, sir,' Wilson added sententiously. 'We traced the girl, largely through luck. Mr Woods couldn't help us but later on saw his daughter, yesterday afternoon — she'd returned home briefly for some things and there was a blazing row. She wouldn't tell him where she was going but he followed her 'bus in his car and saw her go up the hill. He wasn't sure where she was going, but we sent a policewoman up to the house last night and sure enough, she was there.'

'Let's hope she's still there.'

They made their way past some broken milk bottles and a ginger cat and when they knocked at the door on the first floor Sally Woods opened it to them. She wore a man's sweater, dark green in colour, and a pair of baggy corduroy trousers, rolled up at her ankles. Her hair was in disarray and she obviously didn't give a damn. Neither did Crow. He pushed straight past her and walked into the room. He looked around him impassively, but the girl must have instinctively recognized the distaste he felt.

'Nobody asked you to come!'

He turned to look at the girl. She stood with her hands on her hips, glaring defiantly at him, and he shrugged.

'No. That's right — we weren't asked.'

'Well, what the hell do you want?'

'Just a few questions.'

'You asked enough last time!'

'They weren't the *right* questions, were they?'

He'd been watching her eyes, carefully, and perhaps his attention had become too obvious for she suddenly turned and threw herself with an angry bouncing on the settee.

It gave off the sound of tortured springs.

'Aw, go to hell,' she said.

Crow watched her carefully. He didn't think that she was anything but normal at the moment; there was no sign of euphoria, nor of acute depression nor nervous tension. She seemed angry at their presence, a little discomfited, but no more. All this meant little, nevertheless.

'I'm not asking for co-operation,' he said. 'I don't need it. I'll get the answers from you the easy way, or the hard way down at the station. Either way I'll get them. You choose.'

There was an iron in his tone that got through to her, convinced her that it would be best to listen and answer.

'What do you want to know?' Her glance and voice were matched in their surliness. 'I suppose it's still about Rosemary.'

'In a way. But last time, like I said, I asked the wrong questions. I asked about Rosemary. I should have asked about you.'

'What do you mean?'

'You said you phoned the Harlands early that night. How early?'

'Around six, I think.'

'You told them she was staying with you that night, and you told me she didn't in fact do so. That was true. But what time did *you* get home that night?'

'What are you getting at?'

'You did go out after you phoned, didn't you? I'd assumed that you stayed at home, when Rosemary was at the Polytechnic, but I should have asked you the question. You did go out, didn't you?'

'No.'

'It's easily checked. We can ask your parents.'

There was no reply. Crow waited but there was no reaction from the girl. He decided to try another tack.

'You were very friendly with Rosemary Harland, weren't you?'

'You know that.'

'Did she look much like you?'

'Not really.'

'Same colouring?'

'No.'

'But about the same build, roughly, wouldn't you say?'

'I suppose so. But I don't see—'

'And like many girls of your age I suppose you occasionally exchanged clothes, you know, minor items that took the others' fancy from time to time.'

'No, we didn't do that.'

'But you borrowed her raincoat didn't you?'

'Well, yes, I did on one occasion but . . .' Her voice died away and she stared at her hands. 'What do you ask that for?'

'Where did you go, the night you borrowed her coat?'

'I don't remember.'

'Try. It was raining, I suppose, and you borrowed the coat from her and you went somewhere. Dancing?'

'I can't remember.'

'Drinking? *Smoking?*'

The girl's hand quivered, then was still. Slowly she sat upright on the sagging settee.

'I've told you. I borrowed it once, when it was raining, as you say, but it was a long time ago and I can't remember anything about it. Except that it was raining.'

Crow put his hands inside his jacket pocket and drew out the folded newspaper cutting.

'Who were you with when you went out that night?'

'When I wore the coat? How the hell can I remember? If I don't recall the night itself what would make me recall—'

'Who were you out with the night Rosemary died?'

'I . . . I didn't say I was out.'

'It was with the same man, wasn't it? The man you went out with the night you wore her coat?'

'Questions, questions, what the hell are you getting at? What's this all about. What are you trying to get me to say?'

She was frightened and she was nervous and her hands were clasped tightly in her lap. The corduroy trousers swirled absurdly around her knees and the sweater sagged on her shoulders and she looked very lost, very young. Rosemary Harland had been young too.

'Rosemary is dead. She was murdered. And you haven't told me where you were that night.'

'These questions about the coat, I don't understand, you're mixing them up with what I was doing the night Rosemary was killed and I'm getting all confused.'

175

'Then let me put things more clearly. We found traces of drugs in Rosemary's coat. She could have been using drugs; I'd assumed she was. But now I doubt it. I'm more inclined to think *you* might have experimented with them. Their presence in the coat pocket might be explained by the fact that you'd borrowed it. What I want to know is — who were you with when you wore it?'

'I've told you I can't remember.'

'Was it the same man on both occasions?' A door slammed downstairs and Wilson stirred at the door. Crow thrust the newspaper cutting in front of the girl.

'That's you in the photograph, isn't it?'

'Yes, of course!'

'And that man standing there, you recognize him?'

'Of course I damned well recognize him! What on earth—'

'Is that the man you were with when you wore that coat? And were you with him the night Rosemary died?'

'Sir—'

Wilson was moving warningly from the doorway but he didn't finish the sentence because the door suddenly opened behind him and someone pushed his way in, backwards. Crow straightened and glared as the man turned; a broad face, reddish, curling hair, blue eyes widened in surprise.

'What the hell's going on here?'

He was carrying a bag of groceries in his leather-jacketed arms. As he stood there gaping a tin of tomatoes lost its precarious balance at the top of the bag and fell to the thin carpet, rolling towards Crow's feet. No one spoke. Peter Rhodes dumped the bag on the floor at his feet and stuck his hands on his hips. He stared at Sally Woods.

'What the hell are the fuzz doing here?' he demanded.

'They've been asking me questions.'

'Rhodes—'

'What questions?'

'Stupid questions. They want . . . they want to know where I was the night Rosemary was murdered.'

There wasn't a damned thing Crow could do about it. He'd been taken by surprise at Rhodes's entrance; he'd not expected to see him here and the surprise had momentarily robbed him of his drive, lost him the advantage. It gave Rhodes time to sum up the situation; it gave the girl time to tell Rhodes what it was all about. As the two young people stared at each other, and Crow saw the understanding pass between them, he knew he'd lost this one, at least.

The rest was anticlimax, and perhaps only to be expected. Peter Rhodes turned, glared belligerently at the two police officers and said:

'Well, you can forget all that crap. I can tell you where she was.'

His lip curled contemptuously.

'She was with me!'

* * *

The afternoon sun strode through the narrow window and leapt across the plastic-tiled flooring in a broad swathe, glinting on the metal bottle caps and sending brown sparkles dancing in the Coke bottles placed on the floor at the feet of the five men and one woman in the room. They sat in a ragged circle, indolently; their dress varied from the curious to the outrageous to the simply casual, but none was affected by the drowsiness that could have been brought about by the stuffy warm atmosphere in the room, for they were listening to Sadruddin. The windows were closed; they were too high to be reached without a window pole and the old schoolroom used by the Action Committee had long since lost such refinements — it was used by the Administration Department for management games during the early part of the term. The wind had risen outside rather than dropped, and it had lost its coolness as the sun broke through; now it was a warm, dry summer wind that stung the cheeks with dust and grit.

' . . . for us all to remember that after today we'll need to broaden the issues. We'll have to attack the links the Polytechnic has made with industry; we must show that we feel the big business structure intolerable, we must attack the concentration of industry, its lack of responsibility, its mendacious advertising, and its total wrecking of the academic environment.'

The room fell silent and Sadruddin's words seemed to hang there, enclosed by the whistle of the wind, contained by its gusts to this room alone. He lowered his dark eyes and glanced around at his companions on the committee.

'And that will be today and tomorrow and next month and next year. But there are some basic things to worry about. Now, are we all aware of the arrangements?'

The bespectacled youth on Sadruddin's left crossed one cord shoe over another.

'I think we all know how things go. We've each got our action groups assigned; we know how to swing it.'

'The essential thing is to ensure that you move in each instance from the rear. If there is a sufficient body of students in front of you we'll provide the impetus at the various flash points, so as to bring about the maximum effort. We should be able to take the Administration building within fifteen minutes, the business block within another five. The files will be housed somewhere in there — and we'll find them. And when we have them we can blow the whole rotten system apart. Storey, is the coverage all tied up?'

The bearded man addressed by Sadruddin smiled.

'The message is in, man, and the prophets of the masses are waiting. There'll be two television teams out. They were a bit chary after the last fiasco, but they bit, man, they bit!'

'So we're all set.' Sadruddin smiled. It was an easy, confident smile, directed first to the nubile girl on his right, not because he was particularly attracted to her, but because Sadruddin always paid women the compliment of noticing them, wherever they were. She was suitably affected, looking at him with adoring eyes. A chair scraped as one of the group bent forward to pick up a Coke bottle. The door opened behind them and their heads swung around, to stare at the freckled-faced man standing there in the doorway.

'Peter!' Sadruddin called out to him and raised his hand. 'You're late.'

'You might say I was delayed.' His tone was grim as he advanced into the room.

'Trouble?'

'Nothing I couldn't take care of.' He marched across and took a chair. 'Everything finished?'

Sadruddin glanced around, his teeth flashing whitely as he grinned.

'All tied up. The sit-in, at four-thirty, and then the frontal attack upon the portals of the Establishment. We'll have the Administration block and access to the files by five-fifteen.'

'Meeting's all but over then?'

'As you say. I'm sorry you missed it, but you know the score anyway. I—'

'I want a word with you. Privately.'

Sadruddin frowned. 'About the action?' He glanced around at the other committee members. 'What's happened?'

'Not about the action. I just want a private word with you. It's a personal thing. Me and you.'

Sadruddin was smiling but his dark eyes were watchful. He waved an arm to the others. 'Well, we'd finished anyway, and we've twenty minutes to the opening so why don't we walk through to the cloakroom and have our . . . er . . . little chat there. Okay, comrades? We'll see you shortly. Time to get things started anyway.'

Rhodes shoved his chair back with his foot as he rose and it fell with an angry clatter. He marched out of the room ahead of Sadruddin, who glanced around the committee with a raised eyebrow before following at a more leisurely pace.

Rhodes crossed the passageway and entered the narrow room where the pegs used for coat-racks still hung. Sadruddin sauntered along behind him. Rhodes closed the door after Sadruddin entered and leaned back against it, his hands behind him. He watched as Sadruddin gripped two of the pegs and swung on them, sliding his legs under the racks, grinning back over his shoulder. One of the pegs was loose and came away suddenly depositing Sadruddin on the floor. He laughed, an amused pleasant gurgling sound and scrambled up clutching the broken metal peg in his fist. The laughter died and he stood there staring at the peg, smiling slightly.

'Well, Peter?'

'I've just been talking to Sally.'

'Sally . . . ? Ah yes . . . Sally.'

Sadruddin twisted his lips in an apologetic way as he spoke and inclined his head to one side, looking at Rhodes with foxy eyes.

'She had a visit from the fuzz.'

'Did she indeed! That would not have been nice for her.'

'She told them nothing.'

'What was there for her to tell?'

'I don't know. I was hoping you'd be able to fill me in on the details.'

Sadruddin turned away and strolled to the wall, to lean casually against it. He toyed with the metal peg and smiled again at Rhodes.

'This all sounds very mysterious. I'm afraid I'm somewhat at sea as to what you're going on about.'

'Then perhaps I'd better fill in some background for you, first, before *you* tell *me* what it's all about! Sally left home two days ago and moved in at the Hill with me. Now you know damned well how it's been with me and Sally, you know damned well that we've been steady—'

'And-?'

Rhodes hesitated, and a slow stain spread over his freckled face. He swallowed hard, glaring at Sadruddin's sneering mouth.

'When I left to get some groceries this morning she was alone. She told me the fuzz had checked on her last night but I thought that was just her old man pushin' things. But when I got back this morning there were two coppers there — that bloody Inspector Crow and a sergeant, and they were questioning Sally.'

'What did they want to know?'

'She didn't really get the drift straight away. Crow was on about some coat of Rosemary Harland's and trying to find out whether Sally'd ever borrowed it from her. Sally was fool enough to say she had, but she wouldn't tell them when it was. Then they asked her where she'd been the night that Rosemary died.'

He paused, and Sadruddin's eyes flickered up to him. His voice was soft.

'What did she say?'

'She said nothing, at first. It was at that point that I burst in. She told me what they wanted. And I told them that she'd been with *me* that night!'

Sadruddin laughed, but it was an unpleasant sound, a contemptuous sound.

'The good old English chivalry! It will out in the most surprising places! Peter Rhodes, pricking forth to save the fair maid beleaguered by the giant terrible! All right, so you snatched her from the jaws of the inquisitors, so what? What's it got to do with me? You want applause?'

'You bastard!'

Sadruddin stiffened involuntarily, then relaxed again, but in his casual stance there was still an element of easy strength, a coiled spring.

'English is an inexact, imprecise language,' he said and his voice was edged with menace. 'There are occasions, nevertheless, when it can express meaning in definite terms. Be careful, Peter, for I'm no Englishman in my reactions!'

'You know damned well that Sally wasn't with me the night Rosemary died.'

'Do I?'

Rhodes stood up and away from the door, taking a step forward, crouching slightly. His eyes were hot and angry.

'Those bloody policemen kept at us for twenty minutes. After they'd gone Sally was in tears, and she was scared. I want to know why, Sadruddin.'

'How should I know?'

'Don't play the fool with me! I talked with her, wormed some of it out of her. That coat of Rosemary's—'

'Coat, coat, who cares about an old coat!'

'She knows well enough when it was she wore it. It was when she went to Boldini's.'

Sadruddin's eyebrows lifted and his eyes hardened. He smiled faintly, and let his breath out in a slow sigh.

'Ahh. I begin to understand . . .'

'You knew how it was with me and Sally,' Rhodes said angrily. 'What the hell do you think you were playing at? I was your friend—'

'Friend?' Sadruddin sneered again and tossed the peg lightly from one hand to another. 'What do you mean, *friend?* You were my shadow, Rhodes, you followed in my wake, you padded at my heels because you saw what I could do. You trailed along, hoping for the crumbs that dropped from my table but don't talk to me of friendship! I know damned well that if you had the slightest chance you'd have leapt up to take over from me. You see yourself as a leader not a follower, a Hitler not a Mussolini, and now you try to say you're my friend! You'd have driven a knife in my back as soon as look as me!'

'That wasn't the way I saw things. I know now I was wrong. I should have known it sooner; I should have realised it when Sally told me she'd been to Boldini's — with *you!* You lecherous bastard—'

'I warned you, Peter!'

'And I'm warning you! She's my girl, and you knew that; you can do as much damned whoring around as you like as long as you keep away from Sally, you knew that, but not only did you talk her around but she went to Boldini's with you!'

'Peter,' Sadruddin said in a cynically soothing tone. 'You must realise, women are all the same, they are all whores at heart!'

'You—'

'Careful!'

Rhodes had been poised to spring, his freckled face suffused with anger, his fists clenched, but Sadruddin's voice and stance checked him. The Arab was crouching away from the wall now with the metal peg held in front of him, gripped tightly, its jagged end projecting towards Rhodes's face.

'This can do a lot of damage,' Sadruddin whispered excitedly. 'Spread those freckles all over your face . . .'

They stood there, tensely, waiting for the other to move and Sadruddin was smiling his tiger smile, balanced on the balls of his feet, swaying slightly.

'Come on, Sir Galahad!' he said with quiet menace in his tones and then the smile faded and he straightened. The door handle rattled, the door opened and two men stood in the doorway. 'Well, well, well,' Sadruddin sighed. 'The fuzz!'

Inspector Crow stood in the doorway, his arms dangling loosely at his sides, his long head thrust forward. Wilson stood just behind him. Sadruddin gave a tight little smile.

'Come in, gentlemen, join the party.'

Crow glanced towards Rhodes who was backing away from the door.

'I thought if I followed you it would be simpler,' he said. 'Instead of chasing all around the college and the town to find Sadruddin, I guessed it'd be easier to let you lead us here. You've told him all about it, then.'

Rhodes opened his mouth but Sadruddin made a short chopping motion with his hand, interrupting him quickly.

'All about what, Inspector? We've just been having a discussion about the demonstration we're having this afternoon.'

The smile under the black moustache remained constant, as Crow stared at him. Sadruddin strolled across towards Rhodes and flung one arm across his shoulders, gave him a mocking hug. Rhodes stared at him, his eyes wide and uncertain. Crow stepped farther into the cloakroom.

'He's told you about our visit to the girl. That's why he came running straight here.'

'There's been a committee meeting—'

'He wanted to see you . . . just you. After he had it out with his girl.'

Sadruddin's arm was still around Rhodes's shoulders but the smile had hardened into a grimace.

'All right, you seem to know all the answers, why bother to ask any questions? Just tell me what it's all about.'

'I can't,' Crow replied coldly. 'Not all about it. But I can give you some guesses, most of which I can probably get proof of, once I start sweating it out of you. But it'll be easier for everyone if you just admit to it.'

'You *must* be joking!'

'We've been standing outside for a little while, listening to the argument. Boldini's. Is that the place where you got the drugs?'

Sadruddin's eyes opened innocently. 'What drugs?' he asked, but Crow noted the way Rhodes moved away from the encircling arm, and the convulsive grip Sadruddin employed to retain hold on his companion's shoulder.

'We found traces of drugs in Rosemary Harland's raincoat pocket. I thought at first it must have been the Harland girl who had used the drugs but couldn't find any link. Then a man told me last night that he had some evidence to show me. I found it, after someone had tried to kill him. It was a photograph. It showed four people outside Burton Polytechnic. I recognized two of them: one was a man called Sadruddin, the other was Sally Woods. Rosemary's friend. So things began to click into place. Maybe Sally had been running around with Sadruddin. Maybe she'd borrowed Rosemary's coat. Maybe the occasion when she borrowed it she, or her boyfriend—' Crow saw the quiver run through Peter Rhodes — 'had shoved a packet into that pocket. It left traces of the drugs there.'

'All wild surmise, like Cortez and the Pacific, Inspector.'

'Maybe. But if you did take Sally Woods to Boldini's and if you did sample drugs there and she was wearing that coat, well, other questions need to be asked. Such as where you were the night Rosemary died, and where you were last night. Such as why did you find it necessary to kill Rosemary, and how you learned that Fanshaw had discovered a connection between you, Sally and Rosemary.'

'Fanshaw? Who the hell's Fanshaw? And you must be crazy, trying to say I killed Rosemary Harland!'

'All right. Clear it up for me. Let's start with the night she died. Where were you?'

'What the hell! I can't remember — not just off-hand. And why should I have to?'

Crow shrugged and eased farther into the room, lurching slightly as Wilson touched his shoulder, following him.

'You have to, because I'm asking. Because a woman died, and a man was almost killed last night. The drugs—'

'You can't pin that on me! What have I got to do with that coat? You can't stick that one on me!'

'But *I* can!' Rhodes, white-faced, dragged himself violently away from Sadruddin's arm and backed away towards the wall as the Arab wheeled to face him, angrily. 'I can fix you, and I'm going to! You're right, Inspector, in most of what you say — after you left us at Hilltop I dragged it out of Sally. She's my girl, but she's been running around with this lecherous swine behind my back!'

'Rhodes!' Sadruddin's face was twisted and the coat peg was gripped tightly in his hand. 'Be careful what you say — these, they're the fuzz, man!'

'Go to hell! I dragged it out of Sally — she's been going out with Sadruddin and he's taken her to Boldini's a couple of times. It's a club down at East Street, not licensed, used just by students and weekend junkies, you know, the pill-heads who come in for "blues" and "bombers". But *everybody* gets blocked up there on a Saturday night. The second time Sally went there with Sadruddin there was a bit of a scare just before they left — rumours of a raid by the police. It came to nothing, but on the way out he shoved some loose packets into the pocket of her raincoat and sent her out alone. He met her later and took them back from her and that was that. She was wearing Rosemary Harland's coat. That's how the traces of drugs got there.'

'I'm going to cut you, Rhodes!'

'No. There'll be no cutting.' Crow's tones were level and professionally undisturbed. He stood watchfully, making no move in Sadruddin's direction as the Arab backed against the coat rack, his dark eyes flickering from

Rhodes to the policeman. 'You'll just tell us where you were the night Rosemary Harland died.'

Sadruddin opened his mouth, sneering, but Rhodes broke in quickly. 'He was with Sally. He'd called her up, said he wanted to see her, and like the fool she is, she went. I lied earlier, when I said I was with her. I was trying to protect her but in fact I was just protecting him. He was with Sally, mixed up with a group of skin-poppers, and he was blocked out of his mind, and she brought him to the Polytechnic—'

'Liar!'

'He stayed the night there—'

'Rhodes, I'll kill you!'

'You remember, Inspector, you remember yourself, the morning of the demo! You grabbed me out of the crowd, didn't you? If Sadruddin had been there *he'd* have been leading the action! But I was the one in the middle, wasn't I, and remember how we were milling around? We were waiting, wondering where the hell he was, but he was an hour late. Well, *that's* where he was! Still inside Burton, where he'd stayed all night.'

Soundlessly Sadruddin leapt. His surge carried him to the far wall and on top of Rhodes, as the student raised an arm to defend his face. The Arab was clinging to Rhodes, arms and legs, scratching like a cat and then the coat peg gleamed dully, grey-black, as it rose and fell and Rhodes screamed, dragging himself and Sadruddin sideways. They fell, crashing to the ground in the corner of the cloakroom and Crow and Wilson ran forward to drag the struggling pair apart. Sadruddin came up spitting and cursing in Arabic, his hair wild, loosened from its knot, falling crazily in his eyes and Crow and Wilson fought with him until the stocky Yorkshireman got a lock on Sadruddin's arms, to force him, still cursing violently, to his knees.

Rhodes was moaning, slumped in the corner with one hand to his face. Crow bent over him, breathing hard at the unwonted exertion. Blood welled from the cut on

Rhodes's face, seeped between his fingers and Crow straightened. He nodded curtly to Wilson.

'Hold him. I think I saw a phone at the office when we came in here.'

He strode out of the cloakroom. There were two men standing in the corridor staring at him, one with spectacles and green cord shoes, one with a beard and black eyes. They watched impassively as he walked past them and headed for the office. He opened the door and marched in, taking up the telephone without a word to the gum-chewing girl clerk paring her nails over her typewriter. Her false eyelashes went rigid and her eyes were round as she heard Crow's call.

He went back to the cloakroom. The two men had gone. The cloakroom was silent but for Rhodes's faint groaning and Wilson's heavy breathing, catarrhal in the confined space. Sadruddin, buckled over forward with his long black hair touching the ground and his head and shoulders bowed, looked almost as though he were praying but for the fact that Wilson stood splay-legged above him, fiercely gripping his wrists and elbows behind his back. Crow picked up the coat peg that Sadruddin had wielded and slipped it into his pocket. He spoke to Wilson and the grip was relaxed. With a jerk the sergeant dragged Sadruddin upright, and wearily the Arab rose, scrambling to his feet. Crow wasn't deceived. He had no doubt that Sadruddin was a long way from submissive yet.

'All right. Want to talk?'

Sadruddin's eyes glinted with malice. A light sheen of sweat covered his face, making it shine like polished leather.

'About what? I thought you had all the answers.'

'Most of them. We've got enough on you to book you anyway. Suspicion of drug pushing. Assault and battery. Suspicion of murder.'

'You must be crazy! Why the hell should I want to kill Rosemary Harland? And this other character — I don't even know him.' Anger hardened Crow's voice.

'You didn't have to know him, just know that he had something on you.'

Sadruddin raised his head. His lean face was etched with an anger tempered by the touch of fear, the skin tight-stretched along his jaw as he glared at the police inspector, and the man holding him.

'You stupid, thick apes! You can't see farther than your noses! You're just so bound up with prejudice that you're grabbing at me, making *me* the target! You looked around and you thought *drugs,* that means students, and you thought *students,* that means a wog, and the train led straight to me, didn't it, straight to me! That's how it worked, and that's how you headed for me, motivated by prejudice and something else, just as unhealthy, I've no doubt!'

Crow opened his mouth to reply, but uncharacteristically Wilson broke in, his voice thickened with anger.

'You bloody foreigners are all the same! You come rushing in here, into this country, for the freedom you can't get in your own land and you push drugs and you disrupt our colleges, and kick our coppers and you play hell with our laws and then scream prejudice as soon as anyone lifts a finger against you! If I had my way you'd have been horsewhipped and shipped back to where you came from long ago! Long before you ever had the chance to corrupt a kid like the Woods girl, or murder Rosemary Harland!'

Sadruddin cooled. He stood there and his head was high, his mouth twisted under the moustache. Contempt for the policeman was clear in his eyes. He half turned his head to grimace at Wilson.

'Well, Sergeant,' he said grimly, 'you really underlined it for me, man. And the Inspector — does he follow your book?' He winced as Wilson tightened his grip on the captive arm but Crow could see Wilson's face and knew that the anger in Wilson was again under control after that violent outburst. Crow breathed deeply, and straightened his long back.

'We'll carry on with this down at the station,' he said and turned to help Rhodes to his feet.

'You'll never make it, man,' came the voice from the doorway.

Chapter 6

The man with the beard stood casually at the door, his hands dangling in front of him. Wrapped around the knuckles of his left hand and caressed by the fingers of his right was a filthy bicycle-chain. Dirt and grease stained his hands and the front of his jeans. Just behind him stood three more men; one was the bespectacled youth. He had now removed his glasses and his eyes seemed large and red-rimmed, too brilliant and apparently swimming with tears. Crow received only a vague impression of the others concerned; his eyes were fixed on the man with the beard.

'Don't take on anything you can't handle, son.'

The coolness of his tone had no effect upon the bearded student; he scoffed openly and raised both hands until they were level with his chest, belligerently. 'There's nothin' here I can't handle, man, nothin' at all! Now jus' leave the boy alone and we'll go our ways, eh?'

Sadruddin gasped slightly as Wilson twisted at his wrist, thrusting him forward slightly. Crow's expression hardened as he stared at the group in the doorway.

'You people had better step out of the way. We're police officers and we're taking this man to the station for questioning.'

'No. That's where you're wrong. You fuzz, you'll be lucky to get out upright if you try that one!'

'We're taking him. We want this man at the station for questioning in relation to—'

Wilson gasped as Sadruddin lurched suddenly, swinging around and driving his free elbow into the sergeant's stomach. Sadruddin called out in pain as he did so for Wilson did not relinquish his grip in spite of the sudden assault, but the two of them went cannoning against the wall, and the bearded man leapt forward also, sweeping into Crow and sending him lurching off balance. Crow shouted, but Sadruddin was driving Wilson against the wall and screeching as the students ran into the cloakroom, pushing Crow aside and thrusting at the sergeant.

'They're trying to stop the demo — get him, he's breaking my arm!'

Spinning painfully against the racks, with coat pegs digging into his back, Crow saw Wilson raise a heavy foot, kicking out as the three students attacked him, tearing at his clothes, pulling his arms away from the struggling Arab. Crow grabbed at a shoulder and pulled and the student turned, his head thrusting almost automatically at Crow's unprotected face, but the inspector jerked back and the man's forehead came into contact with the side of his jaw only. The force of the blow was enough, nevertheless, to send Crow stepping backwards momentarily, half dazed, and then there was a brief shout as Sadruddin was pulled free of Wilson's grip. Like a maddened, roaring bull, the sergeant surged forward again, reaching out for the students with angry hands but a green cord shoe kicked him in the stomach and he folded, jack-knifing forward with his head down. Crow, recovering, staggered forward to intercept the students as they headed wildly for the door but Wilson was straightening again and impeding him. They collided, and the students poured out into the corridor, shouting in excited triumph.

'Get after them!' Crow was gasping for breath and cursing; he threw a quick glance in Rhodes's direction but the student was standing against the wall still clutching his face. His features were chalk-white against the red smear of blood. Crow lurched after Wilson, pounding out into the corridor. The main doors of the building were open and a scared girl stood with one hand to her mouth and the other raised as though for protection as the escaping students rushed past and out of the corridor.

The wind scurried builders' dust against Crow's eyes as he ran out into the yard: extensions were being carried out and the yard was littered with concrete rubble and planks, scaffolding clips, tubular scaffolding poles and loose broken bricks. He was in time to see Wilson stumbling over some rubble after the group of students and Crow caught him up as he reached the corner of the building. It stood on the perimeter of the campus and Sadruddin and the others were running wildly for the centre of the campus rather than away from it. A moment later he realised why. A car was pulling up not thirty yards from where he stood; it was the squad car Crow had sent for by phone.

'Get after them!' He was yelling to the wide-eyed driver and the officer with him, pointing after the fleeing students. 'We'll lose them in that blasted crowd!'

Across the campus sward was a milling group of students. At the periphery they were drifting aimlessly, wandering, some girls and men indulging in horseplay, one or two embracing as they walked. But nearer the looming teaching blocks, straggling across the car park, and bunching near the steps of the Administration building four hundred yards away the students were more numerous and more clearly motivated. They had massed together there, militantly, and there was some semblance of purposive action apparent. But heads were already turning at the advent of the running group, and the pursuing policemen. Straggling shouts arose, and Crow heard Sadruddin's name and he cursed. If Sadruddin reached those lines long before his pursuers he could easily be lost in the press.

Wilson's legs were shorter than Crow's but he was younger and the men kept pace, side by side, gasping. A few students put out their hands but then leapt back as with a roar and a whining klaxon the squad car surged past Crow and Wilson and lurched and bounced after the racing fugitives. Someone fell, the boy, with the glasses and the green cord shoes, but the running policemen ignored him as he rolled. They were after Sadruddin; the others could wait — there'd be time later.

Sadruddin was plunging into the outskirts of the crowd on the car park. Contrary to Crow's expectations and fears, he wasn't lost to sight. He would have wanted anonymity at this moment but his entry into the student groups was catalytic: the students moved inward, swelling like a wave, twisting and lifting as arms went up and Sadruddin's name was called in welcome. Wilson and Crow thrust their way into the fringes of the crowd and the bearded man was suddenly turning, facing them, uncoiling his chain. Another student lurched excitedly into him, throwing him off balance, and Crow felt a savage pleasure as he drove his bony knuckles into the man's stomach and ran past. The chain looped through the air and someone shouted a warning but the policemen were past and thrusting their way among the students.

Sadruddin was twisting and turning into the mass of students like a rabbit into corn stubble; he was lost to sight but waving arms and turning heads showed Crow the direction of the Arab's flight. Dissociated yells punctuated a growing murmur as Crow butted along, thrusting men and women out of the way, and Wilson plunged along just behind him. A wall of young men surged up ahead of them and broke again, crumbling at their forceful progress. But the message was filtering through.

'They're after Sadruddin! They're trying to break it up!'

As the calls were taken up the walls before them became stronger and angrier and refused to crumble; dark faces lowered at them and hands plucked at their sleeves. It was a girl, finally, who brought them to a halt and provided the trigger for the rest of the mob. Sadruddin had reached the steps of the Administration building and Crow was shouting when a girl in a suede coat and brown floppy hat suddenly threw herself at the inspector, clutched him around the neck and sank to the ground. It was unexpected and Crow fell forward on his face, with the girl underneath him, gripping his shoulders. Someone delightedly shouted 'Rape!' as Wilson's impetus carried him forward, stumbling over the struggling bodies on the ground but Crow twisted and shoved himself free from the encircling arms, one hand planted on the girl's breast as he thrust himself upward and broke her grip. He was on one knee and the girl was trying to kick at his groin when Wilson took him under one arm and helped him up. Crow stumbled away from the girl and Wilson gasped, 'The Administration building!' but they were unable to progress farther. A leering, chanting group was forming around them, mouths opening mindlessly, slogans whirling around their heads like bullroarers, arms linked, surging, wheeling, advancing, retreating like a savage mimicry of a Maypole dance. Crow rushed head down at the wall and tried to fight his way through but shoulders and chests butted at him, hands turned him and thrust him until he was colliding with Wilson.

He stood still suddenly and the stamping mob circled them. Wilson was panting furiously at his shoulder as he glared at the young men and women who grinned and sang and danced around him. For perhaps fifteen seconds he stood immobile and the light of triumph shone in the faces moving past him, a triumph buttressed by the euphoria, supported by a sense of power. And he broke it.

'I want that man for murder!'

There was a waver, and a shudder among those near him, a vacant uncertainty flickering into the faces that jeered at the policemen.

'Murder!'

He bellowed the word again and it went in like a knife, slicing the life out of the voices, killing the excitement, slashing the urgency and the triumph in their veins until the noise and the movement bled away quietly and slowly, until heads began to turn, back towards the Administration building.

Crow pushed his way forward roughly, caring nothing for anyone who might get in his way. Just as the intelligence had sped through the crowd earlier so the rumour now moved, speeding across the near group, drifting and eddying across the rest of the campus until the students came inwards towards Crow and the steps for which he strode, with Wilson still struggling behind.

'Sadruddin . . . murder . . . Sadruddin!' It swirled around their heads, dulling the shouting to a muted sound, the murmur of wind in a chimney, and then it began to rise to a quickening excitement as Crow and Wilson finally reached the steps.

There was no sign of Sadruddin. Three students stood at the top of the steps. Crow ran up to them and they tried to fade, lose their individuality, but he caught one by the arm. There was an uncomprehending, frightened look in the boy's eyes.

'Where is he?'

'I . . . I don't know.'

'You saw him! Where did he go?'

'He . . . I didn't realise . . . he went into the block.' The boy rallied suddenly as Crow's fingers bit into his arm. 'How was I to know? I wasn't to know, was I?'

Crow turned and ran towards the block and the boy's voice shouted after him. 'How the hell did I know?' Then Crow was past the glass doors and scared faces peered at him from the offices, girl typists and clerks staring wildly as he and the sergeant clattered into the hall.

'Sadruddin! Where did he go?'

'The girls stared at him, incapable of speech or comprehension. A sudden flurry at the door to the room where Rosemary Harland had worked drew Crow's attention. The rector emerged. His face was pale.

'Inspector Crow—'

'Sadruddin?'

'Ten minutes ago I ordered all doors to the block, excepting this one, to be locked.' The hardness in Peters's eyes matched the decisiveness of his tones. He strode forward, stiff-backed. 'I heard the shouting, saw what happened. He came into the block. He can't get out again, except this way.'

'You *certain?*'

'Certain!'

Crow swung around, gasping, to Wilson.

The sergeant's face was mottled red, and his eyes were half closed. 'Dial — squad cars at once. Everyone available. I want this . . . bloody place sealed off. Completely. Communications?' He was addressing Peters again as Wilson hurried away in the direction of Peters's office. The rector nodded firmly.

'We have an intercommunicating speaker in every room and hall in the block. You want an announcement made?'

Crow breathed deeply, trying to control his speech and the quick pounding of his heart. He nodded.

'Everyone in the building down here, to the hall. Report to you. Account for them, if possible. And the students. Disperse them.'

Crow didn't like Peters but he recognized the efficiency and lack of panic in the man. Whatever he was,

Peters wasn't tardy in his acceptance of orders and his summing up of a situation. Within thirty seconds, as Crow consulted the plan of the Administration block posted at the bottom of the stairs, he heard the booming, precise tones of the rector resounding through the hall and, presumably, repeating throughout the block.

'This is Principal Peters. Every person in the Administration and Business teaching blocks will immediately report to the main hall. I repeat: will *immediately* report. This is an emergency!'

There was a short pause and then the voice boomed out again. Peters repeated the command three times, there was a click, and then silence. It was broken by whispers, worried noises from girls coming into the hall from the offices. Feet clattered noisily on the stairs, men hurrying down.

'Get them out, outside the building!' The registrar turned sad, hurt eyes in Crow's direction; he didn't like being bawled at, he was a professional man, but he did as he was told and ushered the girls out like an indignant hen, fluttering protective wings and casting reproachful glances backwards.

'Four cars on the way, sir,' Wilson was reporting. He'd recovered his breath and his eyes were alert again. Crow nodded.

'Get that registrar to check off everyone who comes down into the hallway, two of his clerks can help him. Once they're checked get them out of this building. I want just us and Sadruddin here!'

Heavy boots clumped in the hallway. Two uniformed policemen from the squad car. 'Where the hell have you two been?' shouted Crow. The first one bobbed his head.

'The students, they bogged us down, sir. Couldn't get through.'

'And they'll bog down the other cars too if they're not dispersed. Get away, round the entrances. Check them, make sure they're closed. Then report back.'

Peters's voice was booming again, but this time its message was not so clear inside the hall. Crow realised it was an outside address system, demanding that the students disperse. It achieved a strange milling among the students, a circling motion like disturbed cattle in a herd. A few timid souls at the back drifted under the trees, to watch from a distance, and the steps themselves emptied of students but the car park and the greens themselves remained thronged, and overlaid with a buzzing excited sound. It grew louder as above it came the wail of distant sirens. Squad cars.

Peters came out of the office again, hastening towards Crow. His jaw was grim. 'Doesn't look as though they'll move.'

'More important things to do than move them. If they get hurt that's their affair.' He glanced around the hall. It was filling rapidly. 'How many staff are likely to be in the block?'

'Hard to say. Perhaps sixty, seventy.'

'Get them shunted out as soon as they're checked. Now then, you say the block is sealed?'

'I didn't want student trouble — I suspected they might try to take over the block when I saw them assembling. I'd warned the caretakers and ancillary staff to stand by: ten minutes ago, before Sadruddin entered, I had all entrances closed.'

'So this will be the only way out?'

'Unless he can fly.'

There was no humour in Peters's eyes. Crow was beginning to think he'd underestimated the man in one sense at least. Unprincipled and intelligent, this he'd accepted; he'd guessed Peters might go far to achieve his own ends, also, but this cool decisiveness was something he hadn't seen in the man. He could use it.

'Right. Wilson, as soon as those cars arrive, disperse them around the block. And get those students as far away as possible. Bloody hosepipes is what we want! Peters, show me this plan. I want to see where Sadruddin might have run. Remember, he knows the block.'

Peters nodded and walked across to the plan mounted in a glass-fronted display case near the stairs.

'He could have run a number of ways but in his position I'd have taken one of three directions. Each would lead to a possible escape route. First, the obvious one, straight down the corridor here and out through the exit at the far end.'

'If he'd gone that way—'

'He'd have had to double back almost at once, as soon as he realised the doors were closed to him. There's no other egress so he'd come right back to our arms. Alternatively, he could try hiding in one of these lecture rooms here.'

'No. He's no fool.'

'I agree. The second route is down through the lab section and out towards this exit here. The disadvantage of this is that he'd have had to pass an open entry leading into the labs and would probably have been seen by Stewart.'

'Stewart?'

'Chief technician. He's got an office just here.' Peters stabbed his finger on the glass. It left a warm cloud, staining the cool transparency. 'In Sadruddin's shoes I'd have taken the third route.'

'Where?'

'The Business block.'

'Why?'

'Two sets of lifts, students and staff; four lecture theatres and three demonstration rooms; a large number of classrooms on four floors and three exits.'

'But all closed?'

'All closed. He wouldn't have known that.'

'He knows it now.' Crow turned quickly to glance across the hall. 'Wilson! They all down yet?'

The sergeant consulted the clerks and the registrar for a few moments and then called across the hallway in reply.

'Just two people from the Business block.'

'Who are they?' Peters's question was directed to the registrar. The little man turned to his sheet, hastily compiled from the emerging numbers, but before he could reply someone walked across to Crow and Peters.

'I think it would be Mrs Lambert and the technician, Mr Sanders. They were setting up some tapes in the soundproof room. I sent a man to them — they wouldn't have heard your call. They were preparing some lectures for her,' he added almost apologetically. 'What's all this about, anyway?'

Crow stared into the sad, defeated eyes of Vernon West and saw the flicker of anxiety that lurked in their depths. Before he could speak, Peters said, 'It's Sadruddin. The police want him for Rosemary's murder.'

'Sadruddin!'

'He's in the Business block. We think.'

It was not West's concern. Crow opened his mouth to order him away and out of the hall but the man's head turned and he was looking towards the stairs leading to the Business block.

'If he's up there . . . ah, there she is!'

Crow caught the relief in his voice and followed his glance. A man and woman were hurrying down the stairs. The woman was Joan Lambert. West was moving quickly towards her, one hand outstretched. Crow heard her call out.

'What's the matter? What's happening?'

'The police,' West was replying in a voice edged with a curiously mingled tension and relief. 'They want to question Sadruddin.'

'Sadruddin? What for? I . . . I saw him, just a few minutes ago.'

Crow was shambling quickly across to the stairs.

'Saw him? Where?'

The girl stared at him, wide-eyed, her blonde hair glinting in the sunlight that lanced through the tall windows above the stairs. 'He was on the third floor. Hurrying. I called to him, but he couldn't have heard me.'

Crow whirled around to face the hallway and its group of people.

'All right,' he yelled in a voice that was harshened by stress and excitement. 'All of you, get out of here. Now!' He turned to Peters. 'And that means you too.'

'You sure I can be of no further assistance?' Peters asked drily.

'No.' After a moment, grudgingly, Crow added, 'Thanks.' Peters smiled thinly and walked out of the hallway behind the staff. Just in front of him West was talking quickly to Joan Lambert. Wilson closed the doors behind them and the noise was suddenly shut off. The hall was cool and silent and still; the murmur outside the great glass doors was the warm murmur of a summer day, the kind of day that Crow remembered from childhood and had never experienced in his adult life. Maturity had no time for the summer days of childhood. He turned to face the quiet stairs.

'Wilson!'

'Sir?'

Their voices echoed in the empty hall, danced and swung on the stairs, climbed up into the roof and plummeted down again. 'What do you think?'

'The cars are just arriving, Sir. A minute only. He won't get far in that time.'

A time to sweat fear from every pore, Crow thought grimly. He plodded slowly up the stairs, his eyes on the corridor above. At the top he paused. There was a view here across the campus. He could see the dark figures of the students on the grass, a stain swirling and spreading, forming and reforming in excited, questioning groups. White faces staring upwards. He could see the church spire of Sedleigh too, and the far Downs. Crow's lips tightened.

In the block above him Sadruddin hid. He wanted Sadruddin.

He wanted him.

Boots echoed in the hallway. Crow turned and looked down. Four policemen, another group just entering.

'All right, Wilson; station one on the main doors, one at the foot of the stairs, one here at the top. The rest, bring them up. We've got to search the block. You've got the squad cars at the exits?'

'Yes, sir,' replied Wilson, puffing his cheeks out as he came up the stairs. 'All covered.'

'Let's go,' Crow said dourly.

Their boots echoed down the corridor. Wilson had brought with him a map given to him by the registrar. Their work wasn't going to be particularly difficult in organization. A man on each lift. Two groups moving up the stairs floor by floor with intermediate searches of the individual floors. They'd get him. And if he broke through, they'd get him below.

Unless, as Peters had said, he could fly. They followed the plan. When they reached the Business block Crow ordered the split and stationed the men on the lifts. As they reached the first floor and began the search of the rooms Crow prowled the corridor, his head lowered, staring at the map in an attempt to fix his mind as Peters', attempt to decide what Sadruddin would have done, which way he'd have gone.

'Paternosters!'

'What's that, sir?' Wilson had materialized at his elbow.

'Paternosters,' repeated Crow, pointing them out on the map. 'Peters didn't mention them. Look, here they are, linking the third and fourth floors with the labs below.' He caught Wilson's grimace of incomprehension and added, 'They're sort of continuous lifts without doors — if you don't jump at the right time they can castrate you.'

'It would give him an escape route from the Business block back down into the Administration block, through the labs.'

'It would. But there's a man at the stairs below. He'd see him. Send someone back to warn him.'

Wilson dispatched a man downstairs. Crow frowned. So much for Peters's efficiency. He was just as human as the rest, under stress. He forgot things. Paternosters!

They reached the second floor. They searched it with an equal lack of success. The third floor took longer since it involved two lecture theatres and a large demonstration room equipped for film projection. When it was done Crow headed for the stairs. Only the fourth and fifth floors remained. He was half way up the stairs when he heard the whining sound.

He broke into a lurching, struggling run up the stairs but even as he did so he knew it was stupid. He stopped, turned, and came charging back down again.

'Two of you!' He roared at the startled constables. 'Get up there, check quickly. Those bloody paternosters!' He yelled at Wilson. 'Get the groups upstairs while I go down. I'll organize them below. My guess is he's headed for the labs!'

As he rushed down the stairs he was imbued with a violent exhilaration. It was compounded of two emotions: one was the sheer excitement of the chase, the manhunt, and it was an emotion almost atavistic in its quality. The second emotion was equally basic to his existence — he wanted Sadruddin because the man had used violence to police officers, because he had flouted law and authority, because he had shown contempt for all that Crow stood for.

And he might have killed Rosemary Harland.

Crow was already shouting to the men below as he came pounding along the corridor and the bridge from the Business block to the Administration building. The man at the top of the stairs showed a face slack with incomprehension and then the message got across and he disappeared. When Crow got to the top of the stairs he saw a huddle of people at the doors below, arguing, and two policemen already setting off down the corridor towards the laboratories.

Crow ran down the steps, breathing hard. 'What's going on?' he shouted but waited for no answer from the arguing group at the doors. He was already turning into the corridor and making his shambling way down after the two constables. They stopped at the far doors, hesitating. When he caught up with them they turned to face him.

'He could dodge us in the labs, if he's come down, sir.'

'He's come down all right, in a paternoster, I'll bank on it! But you're right . . . you, get back and pull in a couple more men from the stairs. We'll take him then, between us.'

It could be faulty reasoning, of course; it would strengthen this group but weaken the checks on the first floor. He couldn't help that. He turned and marched back behind the hurrying constable and heard some more shouting, from the hallway. They were still arguing there, just inside the doorway. Two policemen, and a woman. Joan Lambert.

When she caught sight of him she called his name.

'Inspector Crow — please, can I speak to you?'

He waved an angry arm.

'Get her out of here! What is she—'

'I can help you! I know it, I can help you!' Crow frowned and moved towards her in his ungainly fashion.

'What are you talking about?'

'Sadruddin. You want to get him out. Let me go to him, talk with him, I'm certain I can make him see reason.' Her eyes were alive, pleading with him and he thought of her husband still at the station while she begged to be allowed to see Sadruddin. He began to turn away, a knot of disgust twisting in his chest, but she caught at his arm.

'Please — if you go after him. . . I've seen him, he'll get violent. He . . . he might get hurt . . . or one of your men let me talk to him, this whole thing is ridiculous and I'm sure he'll have an answer, let me talk to him, he'll trust me if I tell him—'

She was semi-hysterical now and a constable took her by the arm as Crow nodded to him. Her voice rose as Crow turned away. 'Get her out of the building,' he said quietly to the constable but then his attention was drawn by a shout and the sound of pounding feet in the corridor.

'The labs! He came down the paternoster and we saw him, cornered him, but he's gone up again and a constable's gone chasing after him!'

The breathless policeman in the corridor was flushed in the face. Crow moved towards the stairs, exultingly. He was confident that within minutes they'd take Sadruddin.

* * *

When he reached the first floor he remembered that the guards there and on the stairs themselves had been brought down to search through the laboratories below. Crow looked back to the constable standing uncertainly at the foot of the stairs.

'Make sure those paternosters are sealed off below there — we don't want him making a dash out that way.'

He made his way up to the second floor and across the corridor to the third. A policeman stood on guard at the top of the stairs and as Crow reached him, breathing heavily now, he could hear voices from below, confused in the echoing ring of the stair well. The sounds suddenly swelled until they were no longer coming from the stairs but from the floor and the corridor above. A man, shouting.

'Come on!' Crow said quickly and hurried towards the next flight of stairs. The constable lumbered up behind him as he took the steps two at a time. Crow turned into the corridor on the next floor and it was empty but there was another shout from the far end of the corridor. The police inspector ran, his shoes skidding on the polished plastic tiling and as he turned the corner he saw them.

There was one shocked moment as they stared at each other.

Sadruddin stood there, his black, wild hair falling into his magnificently flaring eyes. He was standing with his legs braced and on the floor at his feet was a young, fresh-faced constable lying on his stomach, with one arm doubled up underneath him. He was groaning.

'Sadruddin!'

Crow's voice was cold and menacing. The police constable came to a stop behind him and the Arab moved swiftly. He dropped on one knee, swift as a cat, until his hand was wound into the prostrate policeman's hair and his knee was place firmly on the back of the man's neck.

'Stop!' he commanded, and his eyes were wild and staring, red-rimmed, his mouth slack with fear. But it was the fear that could turn into swift violence and Crow made no move.

'Don't be a fool, son,' Crow said quietly. Dark fingers jerked at the policeman's head.

'Come a step nearer and I'll break his neck like a twig!'

Crow and the policeman made no move. 'Let him alone, now, and come downstairs quietly. You'll only be making things worse for yourself by behaving in this fashion.'

'Worse? When you've already got yourself convinced that I'm a murderer? You've already appointed yourself judge — and sat in judgment on me. If you think I'll just cooperate, you're nuts. I'm not standing in as any fall guy for you. I'm getting out of here, Crow, and if you try to stop me I'll break this man's neck.'

He meant it. He was past reasoning, he was committed. He could think of one thing only, escape from the college, and he would go to any lengths to do it. He knelt there with his long hair falling about his face, and his mouth twisted as with his knee he applied a cruel pressure to the neck of the helpless man on the floor.

'Now draw off! Get away from this corridor! Get away, or he's dead!'

Crow hesitated, but he knew he really had no choice. There was the chance that if he rushed on Sadruddin the man could be overpowered quickly, but it would take only one thrust of the knee and one jerk of the wrist to snap the constable's neck. He thought of the woman who had pleaded with him below.

'Mrs Lambert said that—'

'*That stupid whore!*'

There was no point in further conversation about her; Sadruddin's feelings for the woman were obvious. But if he could be kept talking . . .

'You're being stupid yourself, Sadruddin. There's nothing proved against you yet, we just want to question you, and to behave in this fashion can only—'

'Question me, nothing! I'm not handing myself over! You're trying to pin the Harland thing on me, you're trying to make me a scapegoat for your own inefficiency and you'll make me pay for it because I'm an Arab, a foreigner, and—'

He stopped.

He and the victim of his attack were on a small square landing at the end of the corridor and directly in front of the paternosters. This was the route by which he had come up, and he must have been surprised by the constable who had followed him. He had quickly overcome the officer, and while he had been here with Crow the paternosters had not been in motion. Now, suddenly, they were whining upwards again and the noise thrust Sadruddin into hysteria.

'Get away from here!' he screamed at Crow. 'Get away, or he's dead!'

Hurriedly Crow gestured to the constable behind him and then himself turned away and moved back into the corridor. He began to walk away, looking back over his shoulder, but as soon as he heard the scurrying sound he turned again and ran back. The policeman lay groaning on the floor; there was no sign of Sadruddin. He'd entered the paternosters again.

'Look to this man,' Crow said quickly, and as the next open door of the paternoster came up he stepped in. There'd be other policemen below, also coming up, and they'd see the two constables, but Crow was out to maintain contact with Sadruddin.

The paternoster stopped on the fifth floor and Crow stepped out. He glanced to his left and saw the bridge running across to the Business block; the doors were closed, and he tested them. They were locked. Sadruddin was on this floor. He couldn't get down the stairs, or the paternoster now. His exits were sealed.

'Sadruddin!'

His voice splintered the eerie silence that had descended on the floor, but when the sound died away there was only the silence again. Crow walked slowly down the corridor and opened each door as he came to it. They were all classrooms, quiet, empty.

There was no sound.

He prowled forward and faintly in the background he heard the whirr of the paternosters in motion again. They'd be taking the injured man down to the ground floor, and sending support up for Crow. He moved on, carefully.

The last door but one led into a recording studio. It was a large room, equipped with modern television apparatus and backed by a soundproof booth. He opened the door of the booth but there was only a mass of electronic apparatus, including some videotape recorders as yet unpacked from their cases. Another door faced him.

It led into a language laboratory, stepped in serried rows of blankly shining glass-sided booths, all empty, starkly neat, and new. He walked quietly past them towards the door at the far end of the laboratory.

Slowly he put out his hand and opened the door. A room used by technicians, obviously stacked high with shelving that carried tapes for the recording apparatus and the language laboratory. And facing him was a trolley of solid construction, bearing a television set.

It was moving towards him.

Only at the last second did he see the muscled arm behind it and he couldn't get out of the way in time. The violent thrust had sent the trolley rushing towards him; the rubber wheels whispered across the cork tiling at a rush and the edge of the trolley caught Crow painfully across the shins. The force of the blow shook the television set off balance and the whole thing, set and trolley, turned over sideways, slowly, like a great tree falling, reluctant to bow its head to ground. As the set fell, thunderously, Crow lurched sideways, and caught a glimpse of Sadruddin, leaping from behind the shelved tapes.

Crow might even then have saved himself, but the blow and the collapsing trolley had made him stagger sideways; he came up against the raised dais of the laboratory and tripped, to fall against the console used by the teaching staff. Before he could recover his balance Sadruddin was out of the technicians' room and across the intervening space. He headed not for the door, but for Crow.

And this time there was murder in his eyes.

Before Crow could raise his arms the short length of cable was thrust against his throat, twisted around his neck and Crow's hands came up to grip the hard muscles of Sadruddin's arms. The muscles stiffened as the cable cut into Crow's neck, a surcingle that effectively cut off his breath as he struggled and tried to lurch up from the console past which Sadruddin bent him. He could see the man's dark face, twisted with fear and hate, and everything was drifting into a dream of pain and blood as he scrabbled ineffectively at the cable and the thrusting arms and he felt himself falling backwards as his legs weakened and the pounding in his ears increased. His tongue was thick in his mouth, thrusting between his teeth . . .

Then he was lurching forward, coughing violently and the air surged back into his lungs like a knife. Sadruddin was yelling and screaming and twisting but there were three blue-uniformed men there now and they handled him none too gently. Wilson was assisting Crow to his feet.

'You all right, sir?'

After a few minutes Crow's head cleared and the labouring of his lungs began to ease. He focused his eyes on Sadruddin and nodded wearily, caressing his throat. 'Let's get him down.'

'You shouldn't have come up alone, sir.'

Crow looked quizzically at Wilson.

'I'm inclined to believe you're right, Sergeant. Is it clear down below?'

'There's a crowd outside, sir, but everyone else is out of the building.'

'Let's go, then.'

They walked down the stairs, a silent, tight group, hurrying, with Sadruddin still twisting between two burly police constables, but his vigour and strength seemed to have failed him now and his head was hanging low, his long black hair falling forward. His spirit seemed to have deserted him.

They came down the stairs and into the hallway and there were a few policemen standing there. Crow told them to get the message around to the others that they could now leave their posts, since Sadruddin was captured. Peters was standing just inside the doors. Crow noted the expression on the rector's face; it was a mingled dislike, anxiety and shock. He said nothing, but stood aside as Crow led the way out into the sunshine.

It stopped the small group, stopped them dead. The sunshine was bright in Crow's eyes and the students were there in their hundreds and Crow had the student leader in custody. A murmur arose as they came out into the sunshine and it was an ugly swelling sound like a murderous tide on an empty beach. Sadruddin raised his head and Crow looked back at him; when he saw the fear in the Arab's eyes he knew that Sadruddin interpreted that sound as hostile, not supporting; he was seeing an inimical sea of white, savage faces turned up to the suspected killer of Rosemary Harland; perhaps he saw himself standing in an alien circus with the savage animals waiting to rend him if he moved away from the steps. So he stood, petrified, and there was a white ooze of saliva on his lips, a debouching stain of terror.

There was a sudden surge at the edge of the crowd and a woman screamed Sadruddin's name. Crow looked across and saw it was Joan Lambert, struggling with a policeman. Crow turned to wave his small group forward and the cortege moved. As it did so someone came out of the crowd, swaying slightly, leaning forward. A heavy man who came up the steps with legs of lead, a man whose pouched eyes were ravaged with pain, whose left hand plucked at his throat, whose right hand was extended stiffly like a ramrod. Crow was shouting suddenly, on the echoing steps.

'Get back, get back, damn you!'

It seemed not to reach the man on the concrete apron; it hung, an emasculated echoing murmur in front of the glass doors as Vernon West struggled forward towards Sadruddin.

Sadruddin seemed turned to stone, his jaw dropping loosely as he stared at the oncoming man. Then he seemed to straighten and he struggled violently in a sudden burst of energy, throwing off the restraining arms of his two captors to thrust forward against Crow. The inspector turned, grabbing at the student and they swayed, locked together, until the others grabbed him again. Then Sadruddin was on his knees, and the great surging sound from the students bayed up to the glass front of the Administration building. Crow shouted to Wilson to get Sadruddin to the car, but as he turned he saw the small knot of people rushing towards the man kneeling on the steps in front of Crow, kneeling and falling sideways.

It was Vernon West.

Sadruddin was being rushed past; Crow hesitated, then joined the small group clustered on the steps.

Vernon West lay on his back, on the concrete apron. He was twisting his head desperately, and his face was strained and stiff. Crow recalled the words of Dr Martin. Myocardial infarct. At least. Crow bent over West. The man's breathing was shallow.

'Did he say anything?'

The student on Crow's left shrugged. His face was white, his boyish eyes wide in his shocked face.

'Not really. Well, he said something, but I didn't quite catch it.'

'I did.'

This other student had patent-leather hair, thin lips and a cratered skin.

'I heard what he said. It was a girl's name.' He paused, as though weighing his words for their import. 'Valerie.'

* * *

He had seen himself as a hawk, soaring to the high cold peaks, or as a young lion, pacing slow and arrogantly among the quivering inhabitants of the red plains. He had seen himself as a man of destiny, a man who held power in his fist and whose words could sweep mobs to unreason and violence and anarchy. He had seen himself as an orator, and a leader, and he had been aware of the sexuality he exerted, gloried in it, used it, and despised those women who had succumbed so willingly and come back again and again to be bloodied and humiliated. He had cultivated an image, groomed the lean Arab face and the whipcord body into a casual, sexual grace, and his glossy black hair had been tied back smoothly to accentuate the clean lines of his face and the dark, flashing qualities of his eyes. Pale worn pastel shades for his jeans, faded shirts, leather jackets, they had all contributed to the image that was Sadruddin, the external manifestation of a dream, and an ambition, an urgent, desperate searching for identity and recognition and power.

Adversity had shattered it like a flint-starred windscreen, fragmenting the smooth hardness into a crazy unmotivated pattern, running everywhere, going nowhere, never arriving. The casual grace had gone, the lean arrogance had disappeared to be replaced by a cold, uncomprehending stillness. The mouth moved slackly, the eyes were hooded and shifting, incapable of meeting and holding another glance, and the narrow shoulders drooped under the weight of a prejudice that had pressed him into this subservience, this incarceration, this probing and questioning along the same lines, over the same track, again, and again and again.

He was broken and defeated by the injustice and unbelievability of it all and he was no longer the hawk, no longer the arrogant male lion. But it did Crow no good. For the fifth time he insisted.

'Again. Give it to me again.'

'I've told you. Over and over.'

'Again.'

It was symptomatic of the submissive fatality in the man that he complied once more, in the flat monotone that defeat had visited upon him. The black moustache draggled above his blue-shaded chin as he stared at his hands and repeated himself once more.

'I called Sally Woods. I wanted company. We went to Boldini's and it was eight-fifteen. I was already blocked, then, and I'd been given the push from my digs. But I had the keys in my pocket — the keys that we'd pinched from the caretakers weeks ago and had duplicated, the keys I used when I lifted that letter from the rector's files. The keys would have been used for the takeover of the Administration building. Sally took me to Burton. It was about nine. I don't remember a great deal about it but I think Rosemary Harland saw us, maybe met us, I don't know. We were together a little while and the next thing I remember it was morning and I was in a storeroom on the fourth floor and it was past time for the demonstration. I came down in the paternoster and there wasn't a soul around and I didn't know what was happening. I grabbed a girl typist in the hallway — I remember her face was all tied up as though she'd been crying and then she told me about Rosemary Harland being killed. I went to the main doors and there was a lot of yelling going on and then I saw you charging towards the doors. I stood there until you arrived and I was still shaking from the needle. I got out, then; called off the demo. That's all. I know nothing about the way she died. And this Fanshaw character . . . all right, I saw him in the hall the other night and I thought he might be a spy, and I told some of the committee to get him but I wasn't there. I didn't touch him. They went too far, but it was nothing to do with me.'

'As Rosemary's death was nothing to do with you?'

'I've told you!'

'You've left out a lot. Such as what happened after Sally Woods left you at nine-thirty.'

'I don't remember her leaving. I was out cold.'

'Not too cold to push Rosemary Harland down those stairs.'

'Cold. Dead. Gone. I couldn't have pushed a pinball.'

'You pushed Rosemary Harland. Dead.'

'No.'

Unsatisfactory. Useless. It was getting Crow nowhere. He had Sadruddin taken back to the cells and he pondered savagely upon the waywardness of women. Sally Woods had come to the station that morning with her lips tighter than a zip fastener. She was saying nothing, over and above the story he already had from Sadruddin. She had taken the Arab, high as he said, to Burton. Rosemary had helped get him up to the fourth floor. No one had seen them when they dumped him in the storeroom; lecturers and students had mostly gone. Sally had left at nine forty-five; Rosemary had said she still had some clearing up to do. As Sally had walked across the car park the only lights left burning had been on the ground floor. Then they'd gone out too and she'd assumed Rosemary had left.

But she hadn't, Crow thought angrily. She'd been murdered and dragged into the lift for no reason he could comprehend. Sadruddin wasn't talking, not beyond the little piece he'd already churned out over and over again. And even the Woods girl was saying no more than that; she'd refused to talk more about the coat and the drugs she'd picked up that night at Boldini's and Crow was angry.

Wilson came in and informed him that Lambert had been released on bail, against the filed charge of assault and dangerous driving.

'Mrs Lambert put up the bail?'

'Yes, sir.'

Crow shook his head, uncomprehendingly. 'Don't tell me they're affecting a reconciliation! '

'It may be the first step. But he just walked past her when he went out — she looked a bit upset and then went off in the other direction.'

Crow pursed his lips. As Wilson said, Joan Lambert had taken the first step, and he guessed that they might yet get together again. It was a marriage that had staggered along from the beginning, but both Joan and William Lambert needed the security that marriage provided — even if they then put it to risk by extra-marital activity.

Wilson waited and Crow looked up. 'While you were with Sadruddin,' Wilson said, 'there was a call from the hospital. Mr West wants to see you.'

'Vernon West?'

'The doctor said it was extremely urgent. He said it was important that you come, that West is failing, and that he wants to see you about the Harland investigation.'

Crow's thoughts swept back to the previous day and the student with the cratered skin, the one who had overheard West's last word. He stood up slowly. Sadruddin was in the cells, Sadruddin could keep. He walked slowly towards the door.

'Get a squad car laid on, and come with me.'

The drive down through Sedleigh to the hospital gave Crow time to think. Time to allow his mind to drift back over events and suspicions and situations. The dead girl, sprawled in the lift; Peters's angry, frightened face when he was faced by the shades of his past conduct; the noise the man had made when he lurched across the desk, spitting out the capsule; William Lambert's anguished eyes, denying complicity in Rosemary Harland's death; the pompous Joseph Woods and Peter Rhodes's jutting chin, arguing he had been with Sally the night Rosemary Harland had died. Sadruddin.

And now West. A new line, a new conclusion, a new suggestIon.

Vernon West.

The doctor was young, with excited eyes in a cool controlled face. He played with a pencil in the top pocket of his white coat as he came out to meet them, closing the door behind him.

'Inspector Crow?'

'Yes. This is Sergeant Wilson. I had a message.'

'That's right. Mr West has been in some agitation. He wants to speak to you.' The doctor paused. 'Have you ever read *The Count of Monte Cristo?*'

Crow eyed the doctor curiously.

'A long time ago.'

'There's a useful system described in that book which we'll have to use here. You see, Vernon West is paralysed.'

'Myocardial infarct.'

217

'That, initially, and then complete paralysis — or almost complete.' The doctor seemed surprised at Crow's appreciation of medical terminology. 'He can't speak, of course.'

'Then what's the point of my coming here?' Crow asked.

'The *Monte Cristo* thing. There's a man who was paralysed there. Mr West may have read the book. He soon caught on to it, anyway.'

'Tell me.'

'I saw Mr West after admission. This stroke he's had will kill him. He's going fast. But he's worried, anxious. His eyes followed me, almost pleading with me. I realised he wanted to tell me something. He did. We finally managed to communicate. It wasn't easy but we used a method of communication that was simple enough though prolonged in application. It depends upon asking the right questions, of course.'

'Right questions . . .?'

'You ask the question,' the young doctor said firmly, 'and he replies with his eyelids. He blinks, closes an eye. Once for negative, twice for a positive. As I said, it can be a long process.'

'What's it all about?'

'I think you should ask him yourself.' The doctor's tone was suddenly prim. 'In here, please.'

The room was stark, cream-painted walls dominating the iron bed and the single chair placed beside it. The man in the bed seemed smaller than Crow remembered, almost wizened. His jaw was sunken and it gave him an older appearance. Crow realised that they had removed his false teeth. He approached the bed, uncomfortably. West hadn't moved, but from the moment they had entered the room the man's eyes had followed them. They were a dog's eyes, a spaniel's eyes, sad and pleading and desperate. Crow glanced uncertainly at the doctor, who nodded. He turned to Vernon West.

'You wanted to see me.'

A blink, repeated.

'What about?'

A desperate stare. Crow looked in surprise at the doctor, then realised the problem. Ask the right questions, the doctor had said. 'You wanted to see me about the Harland case?'

A positive reaction from the pouched eyes.

'You've got information to give me?'

Yes.

'About Sadruddin?'

A violent and determined negative. Crow frowned.

'Sadruddin murdered Rosemary Harland.' A blink, firm and contemptuous in its negative intensity.

'Well, if he didn't who did?'

The stare was fixed, unwavering. Something cold crawled down Crow's spine, like a finger of ice, making him shiver. Vernon West's eyes were grey and cold too, unwavering in their determination, unblinking as they waited for the next question, the right question.

'You think you know who killed Rosemary Harland?'

Two long, slow blinks.

'Someone who knew her at the Polytechnic?'

Yes. Crow felt a stirring in his veins, the motive impulse of excitement.

'Student?'

No.

'Staff?'

Yes.

Crow stood tensely at the bedside, hesitating.

'Which of the staff was it?'

The eyes closed, in long, stubborn exasperation. Crow gritted his teeth, aware of the strained silence in the room, broken by the heavy breathing of Wilson standing just behind him. He tried again . . .

'It was the rector, Dr Peters?'

A blink. A second blink, a third, a fourth, a fifth and a desperate, frustrated continuation. If West could have moved he would have been shaking his head, in desperate vehemence. Then the lids lifted back and he was staring at Crow again and the eyes were ravaged, calling out to Crow with an old, years-old sadness. It was a sadness tinged with terror, drifting up from the past and the dust and the despair, like a prayer lost in the stars of deep space, crying up to a dark heaven, endlessly, for salvation, and peace and an end to it all. Salvation, and torment. The fires of a mediaeval hell within a man's eyes, as he asked for absolution.

Crow sat down slowly, staring fixedly at the eyes which held his, appealed to his, told him, opening up to him to expose the man inside, to expose the fear that screamed to come out before death took him by the throat and dragged him into eternity.

'You,' Crow said in a strangled voice. 'It was you.'

A glaze, a film, a clouding relief drifted like a penance over the grey eyes. A weak sigh escaped from Vernon West's stiff, open lips. Then the eyes closed.

Twice.

* * *

'Beautiful,' he said, 'beautiful, beautiful, beautiful.' His name was Scotland, he looked like a white slug, his manner was smooth as a golfer's swing, and he was a consultant psychiatrist at a London hospital. 'I'm glad I was called in because he displayed one of the most complete examples of schizophrenia that I've ever come across.'

'Displayed.'

'That's right. He died, late this afternoon. Just before I left as a matter of fact. Dear me, is that the time? I'll have to be away if I'm to get my train. Now where were we?'

'I just want to know why,' Crow said tonelessly. Dr Scotland removed his glasses and polished them with a white handkerchief.

'Well, you will know many of the circumstances of course, Inspector, but perhaps I should recap them, to put Mr West's conduct into perspective. It all began, as you probably realise, when he was divorced by his wife. I have every reason to believe that there was no real guilt attached to him — I think he simply found life intolerable with his wife and acceded to her request to furnish evidence for divorce. He was shattered when the court placed the custody of his daughter in his wife's hands, nevertheless, and access proved painful and difficult for him. Valerie West . . . a pretty child from her photographs.'

'Then he went to Australia.'

'That's right. He took a job at a university in Queensland but his heart was very much with Valerie still. He wrote to her at length, but it would seem her mother kept her replies to a minimum by the simple expedient of withholding many of West's communications. She wasn't just vindictive, of course; the fact was he'd married again, and Valerie was now known as Valerie White for simplicity's sake, and the mother found the whole thing a bit awkward to handle. Anyway, the girl got older, and at last she . . . er . . . fell in love.'

'Enter Dr Antony Peters,' Crow said quietly.

'Precisely. Valerie became engaged to Peters and then, according to West, Peters wanted to break it off. West didn't know this until later, naturally, but when he heard of his daughter's tragic death he threw up his job in Australia and came home. He'd understood that she died accidentally, but he was shocked to discover that the coroner's verdict was only a conventionally careful one — in fact, there was some doubt as to whether the car had stalled at all. He was no fool. He soon realised that his daughter had as good as committed suicide. She had deliberately stopped that car on the railway line to be crushed to death by the express. I understand the car was carried almost three-quarters of a mile . . .'

'And that was when West decided to get Peters.'

'Not exactly. You see, you must appreciate that Vernon West is a very complicated man — sorry, *was* — but fundamentally he was conventional, believing in the basic virtues, not addicted to violence in any way. But this traumatic experience he had gone through unbalanced him, placed him in a situation where he began to question values. All accentuated by the breakdown of his marriage and the loss of his daughter and finally the crushing blow of her death, probably self-inflicted as a result of her jilting by Peters. At some point he cracked, but not openly.

He became obsessed with the idea of getting back at Peters — for it was Peters's rejection of Valerie which had precipitated his daughter's suicide.'

Scotland paused and crossed one fat leg over another. He wore yellow socks.

'He tried to discredit him, by supplying various personal details to a journal—'

'I've seen the article. It didn't damage Peters much.'

'No. And he followed him around, of course, subordinated his own career to the pursuit of vengeance. He could easily have obtained a university post but chose to work in the colleges instead. He wanted to be near Peters. Finally he got really near to him, working in the same institution.'

'And that's when he decided to kill him.'

'One can't be sure, Inspector. Kill, perhaps; hurt, certainly. You see, he said that placing the capsule among Peters's other nostrums was an attempt to cause his enemy at least discomfort, a burned mouth and so on. I'm inclined to think he rationalized to me — tried to say he intended no killing, merely a mayhem, but I think his other self, his *alter ego* was then in control. He wanted to kill Peters all right.'

'But things didn't go as they were supposed to.'

'No, they didn't.'

The doctor was silent for a moment, smiling thoughtfully with a soft, full-lipped smile. Crow thought of

West and the answers he'd given to the police in the long tiring questioning, blink by blink. West had used his keys to get into the college that night when the lights went out and he'd entered Peters's office to lace the poisoned capsule in the box where Peters kept his anti-histamine capsules. West had long known of Peters's allergy and of the decongestants Peters kept in the desk; he had obtained the poison from the Chemistry Department, opened a capsule and placed the poison among the coloured anti-histamine grains. He'd found a driving glove in the drawer and worn it to prevent fingerprints appearing on the desk or box.

But then he'd been disturbed.

Rosemary had left her handbag in the general office and had come back to collect it after helping Sally to take Sadruddin to the storeroom upstairs and seeing her friend off the premises. She'd noticed a faint glow, torchlight, in the rector's office and she had opened the door. And there was West, replacing the box, startled, panicky and dark-shadowed.

She couldn't have recognized him but the sight of a dark figure, an intruder in the room, had terrified her. She had screamed, turned and run for the stairs.

'West maintained to the end,' the doctor said, 'that her death was accidental. He says he came out behind her and in the darkness she tripped at the top of the stairs, fell, struck her head against the rail, and broke her neck. I suppose we'll never know, now, not really, but you always regarded it as murder, didn't you?'

Crow nodded.

'The signs pointed to it. The removal of the body to the lift, the cleaning of the rail all we found there was a smear of blood and skin—'

'He was panicky, irrational, unable to think straight. He wanted to hide her, clean the evidence away.'

'Well, it confused us, made us think it was murder. There's still the possibility, of course, that he *did* push her.'

The doctor's little eyes flickered reflectively over Crow's face.

'It's unlikely. But you never suspected West?'

'Again, we were confused, put off by his heart attacks. He'd gone home and had a mild attack in the afternoon. He told us in the hospital later that the attack had incapacitated him, but in fact it gave him no more than a shock. Perhaps it provided the trigger — made him decide to act against Peters before it was too late. So that evening he went to the Polytechnic and Rosemary died . . . but the exertion and the excitement brought on another attack. He just managed to get home before he collapsed into bed and next morning he was at the hospital. With an alibi.'

'Yes . . . From my observation of him I don't think he could have been capable of killing the girl deliberately. His anger was directed at Peters, his vengeance motivated by the loss of the daughter he loved — but he had seen a girl die, another man's daughter, and he was at fault. The sight of her there on the stairs distressed him, frightened him, and all he could think of was to hide the body. He wrapped her cardigan around her head to prevent bloodstains appearing on the floor and he dragged her to the lift. Then he staggered home . . .'

Dr Scotland placed podgy hands over his broad soft stomach. It rumbled slightly and he allowed an apologetic smile to drift over his rubbery lips. 'I had to eat at the hospital,' he explained.

Crow rose and stood gloomily in front of the window.

'West tried to implicate Peters in the girl's death.'

'Ah, well, he was still strongly motivated towards removing Peters, and I suppose he thought the law might do it for him. He was in no condition to act again, he was a sick man. Rosemary Harland was on his conscience, and Peters was still there, untouched. He must have prayed that Peters would be arrested for her death. But it wasn't Peters who was suspected in the end, and there was the obvious distress of Mrs Lambert, whom he liked, at the arrest of the young Arab gentleman—'

'Gentleman!' Crow snorted and turned to face the doctor. 'You should have seen him attacking a fellow student called Rhodes! The lad was lucky to get away with minor facial injuries!'

'Well, these foreigners are hot-blooded, aren't they? Still, the point is when West saw Mrs Lambert struggling and crying out, and saw Sadruddin arrested for suspected murder he was so disturbed that he stepped forward to tell the truth—'

'It's a pity his conscience hadn't bothered him sooner.'

'Perhaps, like most of us, he needed the advance of death to commit himself irrevocably to the truth.'

The doctor reached for his coat, where it hung behind the door. Crow helped him put it on and said,

'I must confess that while I was buzzing around in blind alleys there was one man who had already discovered West's hatred of Peters.'

'Ah yes, this Fanshaw fellow. I gather he had traced West's history?'

'That's right. He was curious about West's attempt to implicate Peters and he started looking into West's background. The principal of his first college in England was able to tell Fanshaw about the death of West's daughter and the remarriage and change of name by her mother. Then the connection appeared; after all, it was only hidden by a surname. And Fanshaw guessed that West hated Peters — and yet was working for him.'

'I'm surprised Peters never caught the connection.'

'Perhaps he did know Valerie's original name, but why should he connect a girl from his past with the head of one of his faculties?'

'I understand that Mr Fanshaw is well on the way to recovery. However, I must be away, Inspector.' The doctor smiled benignly and extended a pudgy hand. As they shook hands his expression changed and Crow suddenly saw in the fat man's face a humanity and a compassion that belied the clinical delight he had seemed to take in recounting West's schizophrenia. 'Did you read West's eyes?' Scotland asked softly. 'They never changed in expression, you know; not even when he was dying. It was still there, right at the end. In his mind he could never die other than unshriven.'

After Dr Scotland had gone Crow sat silently in the chair behind his desk. There was a report in front of him from Wilson: four students had been arrested for the attack in the alley upon Robert Fanshaw. Sadruddin had given their names quickly enough.

Sadruddin.

There was more than enough evidence to mount a prosecution against the student leader. The lab had reported traces of drugs in his clothing and the Woods girl would be able to testify that he had provided her and others with narcotics. Rhodes was vindictive now, and was insisting that she testify — and he himself would be pressing charges of assault. There were other charges, assault upon the police, obstruction.

But not murder.

Crow had been wrong there. He had seen that photograph, linked it in his mind to the attack upon Fanshaw, and against the background of the Harland enquiry he had reached the conclusion that Sadruddin was the quarry. He remembered the way Wilson had reacted angrily, in an outburst of prejudice against the foreign student. Had Crow also been guilty of leaping to a conclusion too quickly because a student, and a foreigner to boot, was an easy scapegoat? Had he sat in judgment before taking the evidence?

He stood up, disturbed in his mind, and walked through to Wilson's office.

'I'll see Sadruddin now.'

Wilson rose and left the room, to bring the Arab student up to Crow's office. Crow waited uneasily: he did not relish seeing the young man again for he remembered him as he had been — lithe, arrogant, strong and glorying in his strength. But the events of the last few hours and days had broken him. And with Sadruddin's collapse the student rebellion would collapse also. With Sadruddin and Rhodes lost to the extremists, Peters's task at Burton would be rendered less difficult. It was ironic, in a sense, that Peters of all people, should derive some benefit from the whole affair.

There was a tap on the door and Wilson entered, with Sadruddin behind him.

'He'd already heard,' Wilson said quietly. 'Down in the cells.'

Crow felt almost a sense of relief as Sadruddin swaggered in. The man had recovered his composure. His skin seemed to have darkened, the firmness had come back to his features and his head had come up. His eyes were clear, hard and contemptuous. He strode in arrogantly, and placed his clenched fists on the edge of Crow's desk, leaning forward belligerently.

'I heard all right. And I'm going to fix you, copper. False arrest, assault, battery, false imprisonment, the lot! I'm going to have your skin, Crow!'

Crow stared coldly at the angry, confident face and sat down, drew the charge sheet relating to Sadruddin towards him. It was good to have a real adversary again, in this student.

'You can try that, young man,' he said, 'after *we've* thrown the book at *you!*'

And on this at least there would be no question of premature judgments.

THE END

Thank you for reading this book. If you enjoyed it please leave feedback on Amazon, and if there is anything we missed or you have a question about then please get in touch. The author and publishing team appreciate your feedback and time reading this book.

Our email is office@joffebooks.com

www.joffebooks.com

More Inspector John Crow books coming soon!
Join our mailing list to be the first to hear about them
www.joffebooks.com/contact/

Made in the USA
Middletown, DE
20 November 2020